PRA

That Sum...... ......g

"Shimmering with sun-soaked magic, *That Summer Feeling* has everything I love about a summer romance—swoons, humor, and that irrepressible hope that a great love is not only possible, but inevitable."
—Ashley Herring Blake,
USA Today bestselling author of *Make the Season Bright*

"A celebratory ray of sunshine. . . . I loved this world of big accomplishments, found family, and dizzyingly fierce love."
—Amy Spalding, author of *At Her Service*

"At times achingly sweet, and at others delightfully steamy, this friends-to-lovers journey had me hooked from the first page. Summer camp has never been this sexy."
—Erin La Rosa, author of *The Backtrack*

"*That Summer Feeling* is utterly transportive, dropping you into an endless summer of warmth, hijinks, and love. Garland and Stevie's journey together is equally as funny as romantic, as surprising as it is inevitable. This magical book had me wanting to sign up for summer camp the second I started reading."
—Carlyn Greenwald, author of *Director's Cut*

"If you're looking for a lighthearted, sapphic romance with an adult summer camp setting and a touch of the found-family trope, then *That Summer Feeling* will make you long for summer!"   —The Nerd Daily

"Bridget Morrissey's latest leans completely into the sleepaway camp angle, answering a question I bet a number of us have wondered: If I returned to this adolescent time of possibility as an adult, could it show me a new path in life?"   —Paste

"A pitch-perfect 'I divorced a man now what' novel that's equal parts a journey of self-discovery and a swoony gay love story."

—Electric Literature

Praise for
A Thousand Miles

"It's impossible not to fall for Dee and Ben while they fall for each other on the journey of a lifetime, told with heart-wrenching emotional insight, undeniable passion, and laugh-out-loud humor on every single page. *A Thousand Miles* is an instant favorite."

—Emily Wibberley and Austin Siegemund-Broka,
authors of *Book Boyfriend*

"An oh-so-sweet romantic comedy that tugs on all the right heart-strings. I adored it."   —Kate Spencer, author of *One Last Summer*

"Morrissey's dual-POV romance is full of sarcastic banter and lovable characters, but she also explores the delicate complexity of identity, loss, and reconciliation. It's a delightful, engaging gem of a read."

—BuzzFeed

"*A Thousand Miles* is a treasure trove of heartfelt warm fuzzies."

—Romance Junkies

Praise for
Love Scenes

"An endearing and entertaining read, *Love Scenes* is the romance all lovers of Hollywood need."   —Shondaland

"Real, raw, and immensely tender, *Love Scenes* is a book about second chances: in love, in work, in family. Bridget Morrissey writes with the kind of effortless warmth and complexity that elevates characters to real people you know and love, with quirks and flaws you understand."

—Emily Henry,
#1 *New York Times* bestselling author of *Funny Story*

"*Love Scenes* is pure joy from start to finish. With Hollywood antics, a simmering slow-burn romance, and a tremendous amount of humor and heart, this book makes even its most famous characters feel like friends. A love letter to the messy, wild, wonderful families who make us who we are."

—Rachel Lynn Solomon,
New York Times bestselling author of *Business or Pleasure*

"*Love Scenes* is an enemies-to-lovers story set against a Hollywood backdrop, but it's so much more than that. It's the messy love of a complicated blended family. It's the ugly parts of Hollywood, not just the glitz and glamour. It's a heroine fighting to be her own person despite what the gossip sites and a songwriting ex-boyfriend say. It's an earnest, swoonworthy hero doing his best to be a good man, despite his past. Bridget Morrissey has a voice that leaps off the page and invites you to join her for a page-turning good time. Good luck putting this one down!"

—Jen DeLuca,
USA Today bestselling author of *Haunted Ever After*

"A fascinating peek at the on-set lives of movie stars. Nuanced characterization and an endearing ensemble cast make this one a must-read!"
—Michelle Hazen, author of *Breathe the Sky*

"Morrissey is at her best when she allows Sloane's musings to shed light on the caprices of the entertainment industry. Even as Sloane's bond with Joseph develops with charming ease, her evolving relationships with a diverse array of relatives illuminate the many peculiarities inherent to understanding, accepting, and loving family. A compelling and unique riff on the potential of second chances in love."

—*Kirkus Reviews*

BRIDGET MORRISSEY

Anywhere You Go

BERKLEY ROMANCE

NEW YORK

BERKLEY ROMANCE
Published by Berkley
An imprint of Penguin Random House LLC
1745 Broadway, New York, NY 10019
penguinrandomhouse.com

Book design by Katy Riegel

Library of Congress Cataloging-in-Publication Data

Names: Morrissey, Bridget, author.
Title: Anywhere you go / Bridget Morrissey.
Description: First edition. | New York: Berkley Romance, 2025.
Identifiers: LCCN 2024040605 (print) | LCCN 2024040606 (ebook) |
ISBN 9780593817124 (trade paperback) | ISBN 9780593817131 (ebook)
Subjects: LCGFT: Romance fiction. | Novels.
Classification: LCC PS3613.O777925 A85 2025 (print) |
LCC PS3613.O777925 (ebook) | DDC 813/.6—dc23/eng/20240830
LC record available at https://lccn.loc.gov/2024040605
LC ebook record available at https://lccn.loc.gov/2024040606

First Edition: April 2025

Printed in the United States of America
1st Printing

The authorized representative in the EU for product safety and compliance is
Penguin Random House Ireland, Morrison Chambers, 32 Nassau Street,
Dublin D02 YH68, Ireland, https://eu-contact.penguin.ie.

Seels, this one is for you.

How could it not be?

Anywhere
You Go

July

1

Tatum

My favorite shift at Rita's Diner is noon to six, right between the lunch and dinner rushes. There's a sweet spot around three thirty. Only the regulars are here, plus a few random stragglers. Light streams in through the tall windows that run the length of the building, pouring golden magic onto every cracked vinyl booth and checkered floor tile. The outdated things in this place look lovely at this hour. And the lovely things look even better.

Like June Lightbell. She may as well be surrounded by a choir of angels at this time of day, sitting like she does with one leg crossed atop the other, her head propped up in her hand with an elbow on the table. The sun slices a delicate beam across her face, accentuating the sparkling highlighter on her cheeks.

She glances up to wave. I wave back, nonchalant, as if these small exchanges don't hold much weight. As if it didn't alter our dynamic at all when she asked me out and I turned her down. So what if the sight of her continues to make my stomach do a cartwheel? That will go away.

It's just taking a little longer than I expected.

My phone pings—an email to my special inbox.

"Tatum," my manager, Denise, says. "Devices away."

"One sec," I tell her, reading quickly. "I've got a new client asking for a one-day turnaround. Looks like they want a breakup text."

My loved ones used to joke that I could make a living off writing other people's difficult messages for them. Resignations, breakups, family fights, that kind of thing. It seemed like every other week I was helping someone draft a life-changing document. What would start as *What do you think I should say to my boss about deserving a raise?* would turn into me sending over my fourteenth revision in an email detailing my cousin's intrinsic value to the front-desk team at the hair salon. About a year ago, I decided it was time to expand my reach and set up an actual website.

I certainly don't *make a living*, because I don't charge anything, and these days, people love to tell me that AI has replaced my unique gift anyway. Good thing it's not about money. Drafting messages for other people gives me a sense of purpose. I can gift them the words they struggle to find. I get to feel good about helping someone else put their best foot forward in the world. And really, it's nice to solve someone else's problems. Mine are unsolvable. It would be like trying to remove the flour from a loaf of bread. The issues are all the way baked in.

My clients submit anonymously through my website, and their information is encrypted. Occasionally I have to follow up with questions about what kind of tone they're hoping for, or some details that will really make the message sing. Sometimes they reveal personal information in that process. Most of the time, I never find out who it is I'm pretending to be.

Every so often, someone is upset, and they email me to complain. It's usually about a breakup that's gone south, and it never has anything to do with my expertly crafted message. I can't control what happens after someone else presses send. That's life. We can say every single thing exactly right and still not get the result we imagined from it. That's the part that AI will never understand—the complexity of being human.

"June's looking at you," Denise says.

My eyes dart to June's table again. Her hair is always changing, and for the last two weeks it's been in a sleek black bob that comes in just above her chin. It looks perfect on her, but I could say the same of every style she's worn. The natural curls, the braids. All of it looks incredible. There's a coyness to this particular hairstyle. She's paired it with a long beige trench coat and black Mary Janes, and she looks very Parisian chic for someone who lives in Trove Hills, Illinois.

She *is* looking at me. Waving again. Except it's not a wave hello. She's waving me over.

"I brought you something," she says, pulling a tiny vial out of her bag. "I think I finally got your mix right. Bergamot, vetiver, and fig are the base." She pinches the tiny container between her long brown fingers, popping the lid off to smell what she's made. "With some patchouli and cedar as the middle notes. A little bit of black tea on top. There's a milk scent in there too, but it was hard to get it to show up with everything else. Let me know if it comes through for you."

June Lightbell has made me my own perfume.

She pushes the open vial toward me, wafting the scent up to my nostrils.

"Smells . . . earthy," I say, remembering her using that word once. Asking me if that's what I liked. I told her I did, because I didn't really know what it meant when it came to perfumes. In truth, this smells . . . strange. Like someone sprayed a tree-scented air freshener over mildew, then tried to cover that scent up with something sweeter.

"I wanted it to be like getting lost in the woods during a storm," she says, "then finding a tiny house to hide inside, where there's already a fire going and tea brewing on the stove."

God, her voice is *something*. It's coy, but it has these occasional low notes—a darkness that simmers beneath the surface of her gentle coolness. I'd love to have that voice right up against my ear, telling me I'm a good girl.

I shudder, hating my mind for how it wanders. June has come in to the diner a few times a week for over a year now. By this point she must agree with me that my artful rejection was the right move for us both.

She has a girlfriend now. Her name is Vanessa. Vanessa is incapable of letting a small moment embarrass her. Not when she got my name wrong for the third time in a single day, or when one of the cooks accidentally walked in on her in our bathroom because she forgot to lock the door.

June and Vanessa are a perfect match. They wear trendy clothes together and talk about astrology at a level I don't quite understand, obsessing over how someone's eighth house Venus would totally overwhelm a tenth house Sun, or something like that. They sometimes touch each other's hands as they eat, laughing in this hushed, private way that tells me their relationship is full of inside jokes no one else could possibly comprehend.

It's the way all of this is meant to be.

In fact, I find Vanessa's presence in June's life to be motivating. Around them both, I become the most heightened version of myself that exists—the sweet, quirky waitress who flits by to drop off their drinks, saying silly little things to pad out their cute life together. "Don't forget to put on your coat! Can't have you both catching a cold on me!" I tell them when it's chilly outside, or "This one's on the house" with a joking wink when I refill their waters.

It's my favorite part of this job. Every day, I get to make something special out of the mundane, sprinkling good cheer atop someone else's scrambled eggs and toast. I have the constant opportunity to fill other people's lives with charm, and because I do so, my life feels charming too. It's simple and sweet. Uncomplicated.

When Vanessa isn't here, my personality is a little more subdued, but it's still an enhancement of sorts. Safe in the world of Rita's wood-paneled walls and yellow vinyl booths, June doesn't complain when her burger is overcooked or her coffee tastes burnt. I've never once told her about the countless times my shift's already ended and I've been waiting for her to finish up so I can close out her check. She can ask me out here, and I can turn her down, and it doesn't change who we are to each other, because the bubble protects us both.

That's the magic of a good diner.

"It's so nice," I say to her, leaning down to waft the perfume's scent toward me again. Maybe it's an acquired taste, like olives.

Unfortunately, I've yet to acquire that taste.

"It felt like you," she says. "Mysterious, but comforting." Her voice is a feather that's run up my spine, giving me shivers. "Layered."

She was thinking about me at home. Smelling different things, putting them together, trying to make them equal something that feels like me to her. And apparently I feel like a house in the woods during a storm, mysterious and comforting. Right now I actually feel like an underbaked cake balanced on a precarious ledge, moments from crashing to the floor, but June doesn't need to know that.

She wraps her hand around my forearm. The shock of the touch makes me hold my breath. She has fine-line tattoos on her hands. Stars. A crescent moon. Roman numerals, etched down her fingers. She rubs the scent into my wrist, then pulls my wrist to her nose.

June believes I like perfume because one time, not long before she asked me out, I got curious about what fragrance she wears, and I very casually requested the name so I could maybe get some for myself. Instead of telling me outright, she *stuck her neck out to let me smell her* as she informed me she actually runs her own perfume business, so she wears a scent she makes for herself.

Now, for the first time ever, June Lightbell is smelling *me*.

Working at a diner means I reek of fried food most days. Or something even sexier, like ranch dressing. There is very little actual glamour in this place, though June's continued patronage has convinced me to make myself presentable, if only to honor the fact that she always looks so put together. Another layer to the daily performance.

Today my hair is in two messy buns. I have to wear it up at work, and this style holds my curls back the best while projecting the kind of friendly harmlessness I like to exude. I also did a full face of my favorite makeup this morning, attempting the high-risk, high-reward act of doing a winged eye and red lip. Now June is sniffing my skin, telling me this blend she concocted in her perfume palace reminded her of me, and I am quite pleased to have come out on the winning side of today's fight with my liquid liner.

"What do *you* think?" I dare to ask.

Disappointment scrunches up her nose, making a series of actual creases on the bridge. "It isn't right," she says as she lets go of me to reach for her journal and jot something down.

"I'm really honored you made it," I say, figuring that doubling down on my initial lie about enjoying the smell might be too obvious now that she's revealed her own displeasure. Besides, this much is true. I *am* honored. And maybe, deep down, a little confused by the gesture. But there's no point in bringing that up. "What do I owe you for it?"

To the table, she blushes. "Oh god, nothing. It's not the right formula. And I'd never charge you anyway. You always let me sit here for hours."

You wouldn't know she's a paying customer who goes out of her way to buy things every hour she's here, as if we might chase her out of our mostly empty establishment for not purchasing enough food.

"I can't take a fragrance from a *professional perfumer* without paying you for it," I reply. "This is your life's work!"

"Please," she says, laughing. "It's not that deep."

There's a twinkle in her eye that sends another little thrill down my spine. The exact kind of thrill I shouldn't be having around her.

Honestly, it *is* that deep. And that's why I can't let myself be charmed.

"How's Vanessa?" I toss out, hoping to squash the sensation. "I haven't seen her in a minute."

"Oh," June says, clearing her throat, all traces of her laughter erased. "She's good. She's been really busy lately."

"She works in tech, right?"

Only after I ask do I remember this is not something June or Vanessa has ever told me. It's something I learned from looking at Vanessa's social media.

"Gotta imagine that's a stressful job," I continue, pressing on anyway, convincing myself June doesn't remember this. "Can't let the robots take over."

June laughs, and seeing her lit up gives me another small thrill—the third in almost as many minutes—tingling all the way down to my toes this time.

Okay, fine. So I'm thrilled. What's the harm in making a pretty woman smile every so often?

I smell the perfume again. "While we're on the topic, I'd love to see a robot try to sneak a milk note into the top layer of a custom-made perfume. *Please.* They wouldn't know the first thing about how to balance that with the vetiver base, I can tell you that much."

June continues laughing, grinning all the way to her molars as she says, "They might think the answer is more cedar."

"Exactly." I point at her, letting her know we're on the same wavelength. "I know I'm doing my part. Just a bit ago, I turned to Denise and said, 'Have you ever noticed that most robots don't know how much cedar to put into a perfume?'"

June leans forward, chin resting in her hand again. "What did Denise say?"

"She pulled a notebook out of her pocket and said, 'Speak more on this, Tatum. I want to be prepared.'"

June lets go completely, her laughter full and genuine.

The thrill envelops me. I become pure lightness and joy.

Which means it's officially time to stop. It's overtaken my whole body. That is *dangerous* territory. I've gotten way too close to the edge. It's time to walk it back. That's the only way to get close to what I really want without letting it hurt me.

"I better get back to work," I say, looking off toward the kitchen as if I have something to do. In reality, I'll spend this downtime filling up sugar ramekins or reorganizing our tea packets by color. "Thank you for the perfume. I can't wait to use it like a captcha test, making all my customers smell it to prove they're not a robot. I've got my suspicions about Mr. Tompkins."

"I'll make you a better one soon," June assures me.

"That's not necessary," I say for good measure.

"Yes, it is," she tells me, determined.

"All right then. I won't fight you," I say, putting up my hands. "I'm looking forward to it."

It's true. I am always looking forward to another perfect day with June in this diner, where everything is beautiful and nothing is serious.

Just the way I like things.

2

Eleanor

A psychic once told me that in a past life, I was a squirrel who died in the middle of the road. I laughed it off then. Sometimes I still do. But on nights like this, when it's just past one in the morning, and the only thing keeping me company is the ever-present NYC traffic eighteen floors below, I see that squirrel. And it's not so funny anymore.

I shouldn't text him.

I won't.

My fingers begin drafting a message to get it out of my system. I won't press send. A late-night *You up?* text is for the lonely. That isn't who I am.

I, Eleanor Elizabeth Chapman, would rather be by myself forever than suffer through the agony of having a real relationship with someone wrong for me. My standards are so high it's impossible for anyone to meet them. There's no use in even trying anymore.

Yet here I am, all thoughtful calculation, typing out, Any chance you're around right now?

He knows I'm never off the clock. Some of my best work happens between the hours of one and three in the morning. This is when my thoughts are the clearest. If I don't sit down and do something productive, I will think of that damn squirrel. Plus we text enough outside of office hours that maybe I do need to reach him on something urgent. If I send this, it could be about business.

Tomorrow morning—this morning, technically—the Broadway PR firm I work for has set up a last-ditch press event for our biggest flop in recent memory, *Hannity Banks and the Great Escape*. It's an original musical that has about a dozen terrible reviews from all the major outlets and ticket sales that continue to plummet, and Anthony is a lead producer on it. The show's star will be singing her money number during the eight a.m. hour of one of the morning shows. Most of our team will be showing up to the venue at five a.m. to do a sound check ahead of the live taping. We need all hands on deck to make sure it goes well, somehow charming thousands of theater enthusiasts in the flyover states into booking *immediate* tickets to New York to see this marvelous spectacle as soon as possible. There are many scenarios that could merit me reaching out to him a few hours ahead of time.

When my thumb presses send, it's easy to convince myself I don't mean to deliver the text. That's what my half-empty glass of wine tells me. *It was an accident. You're not in your right mind, Eleanor.*

The wine and I both know I'm only buzzed. We're conspiring to believe otherwise.

So I texted him. What of it? If it's not me sending this kind of message, it's him. We hook up when we're bored. It's a mutually appealing situation. Just because I'm not going to date him doesn't mean we can't have fun together.

When a full hour passes without a response, and the conversation between the wine and me becomes much more sincere, I do what I tell myself I shouldn't—I pull up his social media. Like me, he posts about once a year. If tonight isn't the time for his annual update, maybe it's the moment for mine.

Three old take-out boxes fall off the edge of my dining table as I jerk upright. There is indeed a new picture on his page—one of those joint posts between two users. The first image is of a hand. A *left* hand. Displaying a diamond ring.

The caption reads, After four years together, he popped the question tonight in front of our closest friends and family. I love you so much, Anthony Michael Teller. I can't wait to be your wife.

Wife.

Girlfriend.

Four years.

I haven't even known him more than one.

"Fuck," I say to my two cats dozing on my couch. It feels important to vocalize my disbelief, in case another psychic sees this moment while reviewing the past lives of my soul's next iteration. I want them to comprehend the hot burn of shame engulfing me. These tears that fill my waterline are ones of pure disgust.

She's posted the requisite follow-up shots. Anthony on one knee. Kelsey—her name is Kelsey—with her hand over her mouth. If I squinted, I could mistake her for me. We are both above-average-height white women with blond hair. She's tanner and blonder than me, but she's in an outfit I would wear—white tank and dark jeans with an oversized cream blazer on top. Expensive bracelet on her left wrist. If I ever took a vacation somewhere tropical, let my hair grow past my shoulders and the sun kiss my skin, this might be who I could become—someone you'd propose to at a rooftop bar with your loved ones around to celebrate the everlasting beauty of your love.

I had no idea Anthony had a girlfriend. She has never tagged him in a post before. I would know, because I vetted his social media the first night we met, and I check up every few weeks to confirm. She hasn't attended any of the countless press events for *Hannity Banks*. I even asked Anthony once if he was single. He told me yes.

"Oh my god," I say aloud.

This feels like being pantsed in front of a crowd to reveal holes in my underwear and a tattoo across one thigh that says *naive* and one on the other that says *expendable*. Kelsey doesn't deserve what Anthony has done to her. What *I've* done without knowing. The wine starts talking again. *Send her a message. Tell her the truth.*

"Not yet," I say out loud. I have to be sure the wine hears me.

Hands shaking, I grab my work laptop, never more than a few feet out of my reach. CONGRATULATIONS, ANTHONY! I write in the subject line of a new email.

> Hey, team,
>
> I know it's late, but I want to be the first person to send my warmest regards to our lead producer, Anthony, and his beloved Kelsey on their recent engagement. We are so thrilled for you here at Garber and Link. You two make us believe in real love.
>
> Cheers to the happy couple!
> Eleanor Chapman (she/her)
> Press Agent / *Garber and Link*

I send it out, cc'ing my entire firm, as well as every other collaborator on the musical. Then I chug my wine, write a direct message to Kelsey before I can think better of it, and finish off my night by looking up the symbolism of squirrels.

3

Tatum

The older my parents get, the earlier they wake up. They've been telling me this for a while, and it's not that I didn't believe them, it's just that I never expected to run into their kitchen at 4:16 in the morning and find my mom midway through a crossword puzzle while my dad cleans up the breakfast they've already finished eating together.

I live in their guest house. Guest *cottage* as we call it, because it's two stories tall, made of dark stone and covered in ivy, surrounded by flowers in every shade imaginable. It's "positively darling," as my sister, Laney, once put it, using a British accent, because the cottage looks like it should exist in the English countryside, not the oversized backyard of a small-town Illinois bungalow.

It's lovely and idyllic and far enough behind the main house to give me a sense of independence, but close enough that when I hear a loud bang in the middle of the night, I can sprint over to my parents' place in less than a minute. I imagined having to dramatically shake the two of them awake. Instead my mom is already dressed in her daytime attire trying to remember how to spell *ostentatious* while my dad tells me he wishes he knew I was coming, because he would've made more eggs.

"I don't think I can do eggs this early in the morning," I say, still panting from the run down the garden path that connects our houses, hands shaking as I inserted my key into their back door's lock.

Dad looks at the clock. "I like to think they taste the same as they do when the sun is up. What's going on?"

Explaining the noise feels silly considering how relaxed they are in comparison to my frantic, half-awake hysteria. The words hardly leave my mouth before my dad laughs.

"That was just me," he says jovially. "I was getting my bags boards out of the garage, and I knocked over some boxes."

"We wake up very early," my mom says in her usual even-keeled voice, the exact same way she's told me this a hundred times before. Now I know how much she means it. She peers up through her readers to gaze at my dad, letting the look linger long enough for my dad to feel the intensity of it. "'Ostentatious' is about five letters too long, Andy."

There is no use in complaining about my dad choosing to get out his bags game in what I still firmly believe qualifies as the middle of the night, because my parents let me live in their cottage rent-free. Ninety-nine percent of the time, it's a perfectly good situation.

The cottage itself is a sticking point between them. Me living in it works out for all involved. It was built to be an oasis for my mom after my dad "let her down," as the story goes. When we were kids, that's what she told us, never saying any more on the subject. "Your dad really let me down."

What she meant is my dad cheated on her, and she didn't find out until years after it happened. They chose to work through it instead of splitting up, but that severance of trust between them has never totally healed right. The lingering hurt has manifested in countless strange ways, one of which is over-the-top gestures like having an entire second house built in our huge backyard. Mom's never used the cottage, even though it's the charming, cozy escape she said she always wanted. So *I* use it, because that's what I'm best at—finding solutions to other people's pain.

Plus the cottage gets great light. I can sit on the couch and read an entire book in one afternoon, and it feels purposeful and right. It's the kind of place where life is meant to be gentle. Slow.

Except now there's a situation even I can't make better. Dad recently informed my siblings and me he has another child from that long-ago affair—a son in his thirties whom Dad only recently learned about. It's the kind of thing I cannot fix. No well-worded note or carefully considered gesture can undo the existence of *a secret child*. I don't even know what to do with myself about it. No matter how many catnaps I take in the cottage living room, or puzzles I solve at the dining room table, nothing tricks my brain into believing this isn't a massive, life-altering deal.

If there's any positive, it's that it only serves to prove that my longest-held belief is still as true as ever—love causes too much hurt to ever be worthwhile. It's best to avoid it at all costs.

"Sorry for waking you up," Dad says as he comes around the kitchen island to give me a hug.

"Go ahead and ask him why he didn't get the boards out yesterday," Mom prompts.

This is one of her favorite tactics, telling me to ask a question that's actually a lead-up to some dig she wants to take at Dad. Maybe she feels better about it because she's doing it indirectly? It's not for me to understand.

In my younger years, I took the bait every time, believing I could mediate the situation and bring some sort of genuine resolution to them both. But the problem is never about the bags boards, the misplaced keys, or whatever other minor inconvenience that gets mentioned. The problem is actually so deep they'll do anything *not* to discuss it, fussing over countless tiny annoyances to make sure we stay as far away as possible from the real thing.

"Are you sure you don't want to give early-morning eggs a shot?" Dad asks, giving me a graceful out this time. "I promise to add extra cheddar cheese to them for you. And then maybe you can show me how to link my phone up to my car again? I can't get it to work anymore."

My dad is such a sincere guy. Sometimes painfully so. That's what makes it hard to understand the mess he made. His entire brand is adoring his family with his whole heart. I've already spent a lot of my life trying to reconcile that with why he cheated in the first place. Now there is a living, breathing person born from that situation, and it all makes even less sense than it did at the start.

"It should've just stayed paired through your Bluetooth," I say. "We can look at it later and see what happened, though. I'm sure it'll be very simple to fix."

"Thanks, sweetheart," he says. "I'm not sure what I did."

"You did *something*," Mom says.

My mom holds herself the same way during a fight as she does during a celebration—eerily composed, with scrutinizing eyes that call you on all your bullshit the way her words never will. She forgave Dad on paper years ago, but it's never felt like she forgave him in her heart, especially now that all of us know the full truth about the child. When she tells him the crossword puzzle word doesn't fit, there's an air of distrust to it. *Why would you ever think that word would be a good idea?*

It's the kind of subtext that takes years to notice. I've had almost an entire lifetime of practice, so well-versed in their passive fights that I worry I don't know how to speak any other language myself.

"Okay, I'll have some eggs," I say to my dad, hoping to move all of us in a different direction for the time being.

Mom starts sniffing the air. "Something smells strange," she announces, looking right at me.

Her scrutiny prompts me to realize I am, in fact, the source. "I put some perfume on before I went to bed. I was trying to get myself to like it."

"I wasn't gonna mention it, but you do smell a bit like my car did after I left the windows down during a rainstorm a few years ago," Dad tells me.

I wave them both off, settling into my seat at the table. "That's enough. It's not *that* bad. And it was a gift from June, one of our regulars at the diner. I didn't want to be rude and not use it."

Dad glances back from the stove as Mom peers at him over her readers. "Oh, we know June," she says.

The exchange they share is one of their rare moments of complete unity, a wordless conversation occurring solely through their eyes.

"How's she doing?" Mom asks me now, a notable lightness added to her tone.

"She's great."

My defensiveness will only make this situation worse, but I can't seem to shake it. To my knowledge, I have never mentioned June in their company. Not in a way that would warrant this kind of energy from them. I'm always telling stories about the regulars. Obviously June is my favorite, but I've been very careful to make that sound like a title she'd win with any waitress, not just me. My parents would know Mr. Tompkins too, and his habit of stealing our sugar packets. Or the sweet young family that travels twenty miles just to see me on Sunday nights, because they know I'll always give them an extra scoop of ice cream on their sundaes.

Dad cracks an egg on the counter. "We were just wondering."

Again, the unity. The second use of *we*. How beautiful that their fractured love for each other can only be overcome when meddling in my personal life. It must be so exciting to have found this shared path.

"Carson told you about her," I say. This reeks of my older sibling's handywork.

"They mentioned she'd asked you out—" Mom says.

"*Months* ago," I say.

"And you said no . . ." Mom continues, ignoring my interjection. She makes sure to let every sentence linger, for reasons she wants me to figure out on my own. "But now you're wearing a perfume she made you . . ."

This feels like a setup, even though I'm the one who put myself here. They couldn't have known the perfume was made by June, or that I'd be here this early in the morning. Still, they've clearly been waiting for this opportunity, and here I am, caught in their mysterious parental bait trap.

"I thought I'd aged out of these kinds of inquiries into my personal life," I say. "Or will that happen next year, when I turn thirty?"

"You never age out of that," Dad informs me. "It only gets worse. Sorry, kid."

"We're just wondering why you've turned her down," Mom explains. "Carson showed us a picture of her. She's lovely."

I didn't know it was possible to be this mortified before sunrise, but my parents are making an honest go at it. "She has a girlfriend."

"Has she made *her* a perfume?" Mom asks.

"She's made her several," I say. Sensing my lie has no grit to it, I search for the upper hand. "And they all smell better than mine." This is not the most compelling argument for me to make, but I'm doing my best on four hours of sleep.

Dad finishes whisking the eggs and pours them into his pan. "So she made you a bad perfume on purpose to prove she likes you less than she likes her girlfriend?" He's not asking to be malicious. That's not his style. He's genuinely curious. But it's all so embarrassing. I'm backed into a corner.

"Can we please discuss something else?" I plead.

"Of course," he says. "We just want to see you happy."

"I *am* happy," I say, managing to find the exact voice of a person who is definitely *not* happy. Which isn't true. It's just an unfortunate side effect of my frustration. "I really am," I add, doubling down to prove the point to my parents *and* myself.

When I look at my life, I do like it. There is nothing hard about it, or complicated. At least not beyond the complication at the core of it all—the conflicts I didn't cause, like the affair. The things I can't fix.

There is a lot of good. I get to write for other people. I get to make them smile. At night, there are books to greet me and a big comfy couch for me to lounge on. In the end, I am my own best company. No one else can hurt me when I don't let them get close enough to try.

"If you say so . . ." Mom uses her lingering effect as a final blow. "We've just noticed that lately you seem a little . . ."

"Disconnected," my dad offers.

Now my hackles are really raised. What do they want me to say? *Yeah, I am a little disconnected. My parents have been slightly unhappy my entire life, and now there's a whole secret child I've just learned about, and it's a permanent reminder of the unspoken tension that's existed in our family for years—a tension that's permeated every area of my life.*

I swallow back my urge to push this. No good will come from challenging them. They've stuck together despite it all. They would never understand why I'd object to that, because they think if they're okay with their decisions, then everyone else should be too. They wouldn't want to know that how they've chosen to love each other has affected the way I move through the world. That their inability to ever really talk about what happened has made me fear conflict in such a deep, all-consuming way, I'll do absolutely anything to avoid it.

All we'd do is politely argue about why I'm wrong for feeling that way until I give up on trying to explain myself at all.

"I feel completely connected," I say instead. "Very, very Zen."

Dad chuckles. Mom just stares.

I move the conversation to our safe topics—reality TV and the weather. All the while my thoughts hover over their curiosity, picking at the edges of it. What does it matter to them if I date June or not? I'm the one holding all of our lives together by being exactly who I am.

They are the last people in the world who should want that to change.

4

Eleanor

My phone rings under my cheek. My boss is calling—Mark Garber, the leading half of Garber and Link. This is not an unusual occurrence. Not even at 5:45 in the morning. He told me last night they didn't need me for the sound check this morning, so I'm not due to be in Midtown for another hour and a half. Still, there is a strange undercurrent to my disorientation. For some unknown reason, I am ashamed of myself.

"Hello," I say. It comes out strangled and quiet.

"What are you doing?" Mark asks, as alert as anyone could be at this hour.

"I'm about to get in the shower. Why?" This is not untrue, though it leaves out the empty wineglass in front of me and the lingering imprint of an iPhone on my cheek. Details Mark doesn't need to know. We're always all business with each other. He doesn't ask about my home life. I don't ask about his. I see photos of his husband on his desk and the twice-a-year posts about their vacation to somewhere tropical, and I fill in the blanks from there.

He sees pictures of my two cats and the occasional video of

me clinking wineglasses with some of our clients. That's all my life is—my cats and my work. Not in the sad way the media likes to paint ambitious women. Just a realistic one. This is who I want to be. There is nothing else I would rather be doing.

"You really don't have any idea why I'm calling you?" he asks.

It's unusual for him to be this meandering. One of his best attributes is his ability to cut to the heart of the matter. Mark isn't nearly as bullshitty as most of the other people in this business. That matters a great deal to me. It's nice to work for someone who tells it like it is. Whenever he compliments my hard work, he isn't blowing smoke. That's what makes the blunt edge to his current tone so strange. I recognize this voice from when other people in our office screw up. It's never been directed at me.

"I just woke up," I tell him.

"You sent an email to the entire production team at two in the morning to congratulate Anthony Teller on his engagement."

Everything slots into its place. The shame. Embarrassment. Regret. Nausea. It all has a name, and that name is Kelsey, Anthony's fiancée, whom I learned about four hours ago.

Instead of responding to Mark, I let the silence between us swell until he's forced to continue speaking. "I wouldn't have found it very strange, even with the time stamp, until Anthony called me a little bit ago. Hell of a way to start the day."

My pride bucks up against his disappointment. Yes, I sent that email late at night, but I didn't say anything inappropriate in it. It was a very kind message, all things considered.

"Was he not grateful for my well-wishes?" I ask.

"Considering you messaged his fiancée right after to let her know he's been sleeping with you for the past year, I'd say no, he wasn't very grateful," Mark tells me. "I wish I could consider this none of my business, but you made it my business by sending a company email on the subject."

"Messaging Kelsey was the right thing to do. I would want to know if I were her."

"I'm not interested in arguing about the moral correctness of your personal actions, Eleanor," Mark says. "I am, however, interested in what you do with company resources. And you misused them in a highly inappropriate way. Anthony is one of our biggest clients. You know I can't—" He falters.

Mark never falters. It's his whole thing. I've watched him stomach countless Broadway scandals and setbacks without so much as taking a deep breath before diving into action.

"I can't let you keep working for us," he finally spits out.

"What?" I say, suddenly *very* awake.

The take-out boxes that crashed to the ground last night are now crushed under my feet as I head toward the door, convinced that if Mark could see me, he'd change his mind. He can't fire me. I am his most reliable employee. His words, not mine.

"Nothing has to be strange between Anthony and me." I'm careful to sound calm, proving my ability to remain composed in a crisis. "I would never bring it up to him."

"Eleanor," Mark says again. His continued use of my name hits like a hammer to my ego, shattering my long-held belief that I am capable of keeping my personal mess out of my professional life.

"Remove me from the musical," I bargain. "Put me on the *Hedda Gabler* revival instead. They could use me on that team."

"*Eleanor*," Mark says, solemn. "I don't like this any more than you do. But Anthony is threatening to drop us if we don't remove you. He will never work with us again. My hands are tied."

This job takes up most of my waking hours. After a full day in the office, I either work a show or go see a show. Then I attend an after party. Then I go out with key team members or clients. Then I come home to draft emails for the following morning. It fills my hours with purpose. I *need* that purpose.

"If you have any questions about money, I can put you in contact with finances when office hours begin," he says. "I just wanted you to hear this from me. I hope you understand, Eleanor."

"I do." Look at me, still composed. Never letting anyone see me struggle. A professional right up to the bitter end. When I died as a squirrel, I bet I did it smiling.

"Thank you for everything you've done for our company," Mark continues. "I don't take it for granted. While these circumstances aren't ideal, I hope you take this time to go off and do something nice for yourself. You deserve it." His voice gets quiet. "And please don't be a stranger."

I end the call with a laugh that morphs into a sob. I've always been a stranger to him. That's the whole point. We only know each other professionally, where I have never been less than excellent, except for last night. One moment in the course of many, one choice—the right one, at that—and it's changed my entire life for the worse.

"You're okay, Eleanor," I tell myself, rocking back and forth to stop my tears. "You're okay."

It would be great to have a hug. Or anyone other than me to rely on right now. But there is no one who can hold me through this but myself. And so I will. Someway, somehow, I will get through this. Just like I've gotten through every other terrible, unexpected devastation life has thrown my way.

What "nice thing" could I do for myself here? There are reminders of my job everywhere I turn. If it's not our show ads on the walls of subway stations or sitting atop taxis, it's the actors walking the streets. Crew members taking the same train as me. Producers stopping into all the restaurants I frequent. If I'm not Eleanor Chapman the perpetually overworked press agent from Garber and Link, who am I?

A thirty-four-year-old orphan with two cats, living in a huge, messy apartment funded by the gigantic sum of money I got from my parents' tragic death. What a fucking person to be. The best thing I could do for myself would be to get the hell out of New York as fast as possible.

At first it sounds ridiculous. The kind of thing you say just to say it, presenting the most implausible scenario as a salt-in-the-wound insult. I roll my eyes at myself in the middle of my sobs.

The longer I cry, the more the idea lingers.

Syrup, my impossibly sweet long-haired tabby cat, traces figure eights between my legs, confused by my continued show of emotions.

"I know," I say to him, reaching down to scratch his head. My tears drip onto his brown fur. "You're here."

Salt, my slinky white domestic short-haired prima donna, lifts her head up from her window perch, otherwise unmoved by my waterworks. "You're here too," I assure her. "I didn't forget."

My apartment is littered with take-out boxes. Packages delivered but unopened. Stacks of books I've told myself I'll someday read when I take that theoretical vacation I've never bothered to actually go on. The piles of laundry I swear I'll get to when I have a true day off.

It's such a big space that it feels wrong to get rid of any of it. My cats love the boxes and the clutter, and I love my cats. More than that, I love the company. This place has so much more room than I could ever need, and the boxes fill up corners that would otherwise sit empty.

It's a lot like me. Without my work to clutter up my brain space, an unending fog of dread starts to settle over me, clouding my judgment. That's when I do ridiculous, impulsive things, like go to a psychic who proceeds to tell me about my past-life squirrel death. Proof that I should not be allowed any idle time.

Scrolling through my phone, I pick my favorite picture of Syrup and Salt. It's the one where they're cuddled together so tightly they look like a cinnamon bun. I open up my social media and prepare to upload my annual post.

Anyone know of an interesting vacation spot? I type for the caption. Anywhere other than NYC is good. Looking for somewhere I can go ASAP. I just need someone to watch my cats while I'm gone. Paid opportunity.

One thing is for sure—there won't be reminders of Broadway on a beach in Jamaica or in the rolling hills of the Irish countryside. Anywhere, really.

Anywhere but here.

5

Tatum

I've been doing some soul searching, and I think it's best we go our separate ways. I'm not properly committing to this relationship, and you really don't deserve that. Thank you so much for the time we've spent together. I wish you nothing but the best.

I read through what I've written again. The bones are good, but this message needs to strike the right balance between definitive and kind. That's my art form. Delivering a gut punch with a bow on top. The client wanted me to make this one delicate. I chew on my fingernail, thinking about how to communicate that. Maybe a little more self-deprecating?

Don't worry, I'm definitely the problem here, as usual.

Or go full niceness overload?

It's hard to say this to someone who has been nothing but wonderful to me.

"Whatcha writing?" One of our line cooks, Maurice, asks me, even though he's already reading over my shoulder. Peanut, the other line cook, peers at my screen too.

I startle, having no idea how long they've been standing there.

They don't know about my side gig. Maurice and Peanut are some of my favorite people on planet Earth, but they wouldn't understand the innate fragility of such a task. There's a real discretion to it—writing people's intimate messages for them. Maurice and Peanut happen to be the most direct, emotionally brazen people I know. They might be the only people in the world who are capable of drawing an actual argument out of me. We fight like lovers over French fries. We go to war over burger toppings. If they knew I ghostwrote other people's breakups, they would embarrass the shit out of those people somehow. And me. They'd drag me for enabling it.

"Nothing." I shove my phone into my pocket.

"You're breaking up with someone? I thought you were single forever," Peanut says.

Once Peanut learned I don't date men, therefore I didn't want to date *him*, he has made it his personal mission to vet every single woman I have ever so much as breathed toward. Somehow he's never heard about the time that June asked me out, which I consider to be a gift. He'd probably spend every shift convincing me to change my answer. Maybe he'd have been at my parents' this morning, joining their impromptu intervention on my supposed lack of happiness.

"Who is Tatum breaking up with today?" My older sibling Carson stands in front of the cash register, grinning. The mess of brown waves on their head looks a little damp. Could be from a recent shower, or could be from setting off the sprinklers inside another local establishment, then fleeing the scene. You never know with them.

I throw my hands in the air, cursing my ability to get so lost in a task that I shut out the rest of the world. "Should I just connect my phone to the TV and screen share my activities? Pass out a survey for everyone to answer at the end, just to be sure I'm getting all the proper feedback?"

"Yes. I need to see whose heart you're shattering. It's been a while." They lower their voice. "Is it who I think?"

Carson knows about my ghostwriting gig. And they obviously know about June. They *also* know I don't want the cooks to know any of this, which is exactly why they're taking this moment to fuck with me.

"Nobody's but my own," I say with a hardened squint.

The problem with Carson's unbreakable commitment to being a shit stirrer is that there is no way to disable them. If they are in the mood for chaos, chaos it is. I expect to be put on trial in front of the afternoon crew at Rita's, with Carson as lead prosecutor, offering up my short but memorable roster of ex-girlfriends, emphasizing the fact that I've broken up with every single one of them before *I love you*s could be exchanged.

I'm already drafting up my defense, preparing to explain that in each scenario, it was a kindness. I saved everyone involved from a worse heartbreak by cutting the relationship off before things could sour.

If Carson does the unimaginable and brings up June's name—with June herself in the diner—I will have to go for the gut and remind Carson that they can't keep a relationship going either.

Family trauma. Isn't it lovely?

Instead Carson dips their head down, letting a single brown curl flop onto their forehead. "On a serious note, do you have a minute to talk?" they ask me. "About the email."

Having no idea what email they're referring to, I say, "I'm at work," in my best Captain Obvious voice, even though there is no one else in the diner except for the one and only June, who has on headphones and bobs along to a beat none of us can hear. Hopefully her music is drowning out this very conversation.

"Dad sent us an email," Carson says instead, intuiting my ignorance on the subject.

"Is this about syncing his phone up with the car? I already fixed that for him this morning. And I don't have anything in my inbox." Because of my ghostwriting gig, I have email notifications on. I miss nothing. "Unless . . ." I say, already knowing where this is going.

Sure enough, my dad sent the email to the AOL account I set up when I was eight and never deactivated. No matter how many times I tell him that BeachyChick204 is not the place to reach me as a twenty-nine-year-old, and that I chose it after one childhood family vacation to the Disney resort in the Bahamas and no longer feel defined by the title—I just keep it around for whenever I have to give my email to a random website—he can't seem to stop using this address.

The subject of the email is, cryptically, Our Family.

"What's this about?" I ask. "Dad didn't say anything to me about an email earlier."

Carson shakes their head. "You need to read it for yourself."

I sigh, opening it up.

Hello to my three precious children,

As you know, I have been married to your mother for thirty-seven wonderful years. It hurts to remind you that I have not been faithful the whole way through. I know that it's been hard on all of us, dealing with the consequences of my poor decisions. Please allow me to apologize for any pain I may have caused any of you.

When I look up at Carson, they are suppressing a laugh of some kind. Nervous or genuine, I'm not sure.

"Seriously, what the hell is this?" I ask.

"Keep going," they urge.

> Your mother and I have worked together in couples counseling for many years. I am grateful to her every day that she gave me another chance to rectify the terrible mistake I once made.
>
> Recently, I told you all you have a half brother. Now I would like for you to actually meet him. We will be holding a family reunion of sorts. A family union, really, opening our arms to the newest "old" member of the Ward clan. The only way for us to heal is to accept him into our hearts. He is one of us, after all.
>
> It will be a week of activities around Trove Hills. All of it is already planned. I did my best to accommodate everyone's schedules. If you can't make it to every event, I would really appreciate it if you'd make as many as possible. There are lots of opportunities for all of us to bond. The schedule is attached.
>
> > With every ounce of love in my heart,
> > Your father

My dad doesn't have the spirit of a prankster. In fact, he is earnest to a sometimes painful degree. It's one of his most defining attributes, and why he's so good at his job as a family doctor. He is a sensitive soul who does not believe in pulling one over on you. Still, this has to be a joke. Or a scam. Anything other than a weeklong family reunion with our surprise half brother planned via an email sent to BeachyChick204.

"Am I hallucinating?" I ask Carson, who laughs so loudly it startles the cooks.

"What? You weren't expecting an email about meeting our secret brother sent with *every ounce of love in Dad's heart*?" they ask. "Personally, I was hoping Dad would announce this through a ten-part video series he could cross-post on all available platforms. I think we could go viral."

Flustered, fuming, and everything in between, I open my work email again and look at the breakup text I'm working on, erasing everything I've already written.

Hey,
 We need to break up. This isn't working between us.
 Good luck with whatever comes next for you.

I send it out to my client, then throw my phone into the cabinet under the cash register. Why bother with delicate tactics when the heart of the message isn't delicate at all? Why do I spend so much time being careful on behalf of other people's feelings when no one is careful with mine? The relationship is over. That's all the other person needs to know.

Head spinning, I comb through the storm of my thoughts until I can decide on my next question for Carson. "Has Laney read this email?" Laney is our twenty-five-year-old little sister who lives in Nashville.

"She's already booked her flight. She can't get in until Sunday. I'm picking her up from the airport," Carson says. "I told her not to say anything to you until you read it yourself."

This sharpens my anger into something specific enough to grab on to—Laney having to fly into town for this supremely weird situation. My siblings planning their travel situation before I've even learned of this event at all.

"Dad can't just drop something huge like this and then not give people the space to think about it. I would know! This is what I do!" My head starts to ache. "We have to spend a whole week with this guy? Dad didn't offer us any space to consider this or an option to take some time. And to *apologize for the pain he's caused*?"

My shift started twenty minutes ago and I'm already dreading the end of it. Leaving here means going home, and home is the guest cottage. Most nights I stop in the main house before entering mine, picking at the dinner leftovers that my mom hates to have crowd up her fridge. Sometimes we play a board game together or watch an episode of whatever random reality show my parents have gotten into lately.

I tell myself I do this so they aren't stuck with only each other. Really, I do it for myself too. We've all agreed to this strange little life together. As disjointed as it might be if you look too closely at it, in everyday practice, it's neat. Contained. Charming, even.

When my parents have fallen asleep, dozing off on the couch mid-sentence most times, I walk myself through their backyard, passing all the beautiful, elaborate flowers that Mom tends to as an excuse to stay outside, following the cobblestone path Dad built for her with his own two hands, and I enter the space I've lived in since I graduated from college. I usually read a book, comforted by the presence of a story—the knowledge that through fiction, someone else is rocking me to sleep after all, keeping me company in the dark quiet of the cottage—and my head hits the pillow softly, contentedly.

Now my dad is attempting to fix the thing I thought we were all collectively ignoring for the rest of time, and somehow, it hurts worse to have him do that. Because if he wants to fix it now, it means he's known all along that it's been broken. For all these years, he's ignored what's always been so obvious to me. Maybe for someone else, it would be a *better late than never* situation, getting his apology and his plan to have us "heal."

For me, it's *Why now, after all this time?*

"Let's just get through the week," Carson says. "And be nice to our brother. Whoever he is."

"Why should I be nice to someone I don't even know?" I ask. "Why do *you* want to do that? You're not even nice to me most of the time, and you've known me my entire life!"

This gets a half grin out of Carson. "It's *much* easier to be nice to a stranger."

This is classic Carson, always acting unaffected, pretending this whole situation is casual. Sometimes, it's a quality in them that I admire, the way they can brush off the biggest of deals. Today, it's an irritation. I need them down in the trenches with me. I can't be alone in my struggle.

"C'mon," I say pleadingly. They give me a semi-sympathetic look, which is the closest I'll get to any kind of emotion from them, so I switch gears. "What does Laney think?"

"She's excited," Carson tells me. "She wants to know what our brother is like. His name is Ben, by the way. She couldn't find out a lot about him online, but she found his wife really easily. Do you want me to show you?"

"No," I say resolutely, shoving down my natural curiosity in the name of maintaining my fixed position as *person who is staunchly opposed to this event*. In our sibling dynamic of three, it's the best way to secure an ally. If I can't get Carson to believe my stance is correct, I will have to try to convince Laney. As the youngest of the three of us, she's always a harder sell, forever determined to be independent. Hence her living in Nashville.

Except now we are four.

Now this whole scenario is different.

I really am alone in this. At least until I can text my group chat of fully biased friends who no longer live here. They will take my side no matter what I tell them. That will help me in an hour or so, when I've calmed down enough to redirect my energy toward explaining this whole mess. It would help even more if my sibling, another person directly involved in this situation, agreed with me right now.

Denise appears, handing me a plate of onion rings. "Take this out to table seven."

It's June's order of the hour.

I exhale, relaxed a bit by the prospect of interacting with her. Even when nothing else makes sense, I know our careful, considerate rapport will.

Except when I reach June's table, she's looking down at her phone. And to my infinite shock, she's *crying*.

"Is everything okay?" I ask.

"Vanessa just broke up with me," she says, showing me her phone.

As my eyes scan the text pulled up on her screen, my heart begins to sink, an anchor of despair that starts in my throat and drops into my toes, rooting me in my own misery.

For as much as I want to believe that someone in Trove Hills wrote a word-for-word re-creation of what I sent off to a client not five minutes ago, I know it isn't true.

"I wrote that," I blurt out. A weaker person would lie. Most days that's how weak I would be. Not today. Today I'm strong—trained under the wise tutelage of the line cooks. Today I have nothing more to lose.

June looks up at me. Her eyes—sweet, infinite brown, crystallizing in the midday light—stare into mine. She doesn't ask a question out loud, because she must know her face has asked it for her. *What do you mean?*

"People reach out to me online to write things for them. And your girlfriend—" I clear my throat. "Your ex-girlfriend, I guess. Vanessa." I force myself to say her name, accepting the full reality of what I've done. "She asked me to break up with you for her. She messaged me yesterday. I was spending all this time trying to get it right. Finally I was like, there's no way to get this right. Bad news is bad news, and we can't protect each other from it. So I sent out this really blunt message. And *you're* the recipient. I'm so sorry."

On that fateful day a few months ago when June asked me on a date, I said, *I don't think that's a good idea*. Because for as much as I'd thought about it, there wasn't a single scenario in my head that didn't result in either June and me breaking up, or something even worse, like quietly resenting each other in our hearts while believing we needed to stick it out, because we'd risked the diner bubble for this.

I told her then that I don't really believe in dating, because it was mostly true, and it also seemed like the fastest way to communicate that my rejection had everything to do with me and nothing to do with her. Well, it actually had everything to do with her and me together. But that seemed too complicated to express.

I thought then that I might not ever see her again. Surely she wouldn't want to come back to the diner after I'd turned her down. I consoled myself with the knowledge that it was a mild letdown instead of catastrophic breakup. That would have to be enough.

But June kept showing up. She went out of her way to treat me the same way she had before she'd asked me out. So I did the same in return. It wasn't even hard. I had no trouble treating her with my special Waitress Tatum care, mixing together all her favorite dipping sauces. Checking on her whenever she started to scowl at her computer screen, stressed about some element of her perfume business. Making her laugh as often as I could.

Now, impossibly, I've managed to find a way to break up with her anyway.

June starts looking past me—through me, really—grasping for an answer somewhere within the walls of Rita's Diner. Seeing the way this has rocked her, knowing it's rocked me much the same, I feel true guilt over my side gig for the very first time.

The ghostwriting thing has always been anonymous. That's part of the point. Maybe I'm the reason someone cried. Maybe I've blown up someone else's life. But the recipient doesn't know it came from me. I'm not the one who has to clean up the pieces. They got a message they needed to hear either way, and I got a sense of purpose out of it. I found the words someone else could not. I fixed for them what I've never been able to fix for myself. It's always supposed to be a win-win arrangement. I'm not supposed to know what happens after.

But I *do* know June. I know every slope of her face. I know her shoe collection and her rotation of handbags. She does a small black clutch whenever she's in her lace-up boots. She has a large green crossbody she pairs with her white Adidas sneakers that have the green stripes on the side. And she brings a pink backpack for days like today, when she's turned the back booth into her office. She gets a red imprint from her palm on her cheek because she spends so much time with her head in her hand, thinking.

Whenever she picks music for the jukebox, it's always Whitney Houston or the Bee Gees. There is no in-between. These are all surface things I guess, but they make up a lot of someone's life. June is an important piece in the fabric of my day, and I've just unraveled hers completely.

"I'm sorry. I'm just trying to understand this. How could you possibly know enough about my relationship to be the one to break up with me?" she asks. "And why would you want to? Who would ever hire someone for that? Why would Vanessa not just do it herself? Did she know it was you who'd be writing it? She couldn't type out like ten words all on her own? This all seems . . . too much. It's too much."

These are the right questions to ask. And she's not even asking them with malice. It's stemming from a place of confusion and hurt. I know it well, because it's the exact same place I'm in when it comes to this family reunion.

"It's always been kind of cathartic," I tell her honestly. "Vanessa might have known it was me."

For a brief moment I'm also hung up on the how of it all, wondering if Vanessa looked me up online the same way I've looked her up. My ghostwriting page is linked to some of my socials, but it's very low-key. Not something I hide, but not something I'm loud about either.

"But I didn't know it was her," I continue, wanting to be sure this point gets emphasized. "People submit anonymously through my website. My page gets traction every few months when strangers make videos about what I do. Through that I tend to get a whole new wave of submissions, a lot of which are spam or jokes, honestly. But I treat them with as much truth as possible, just in case. Most often, people find me because they know me. Someone in my family or friends has told them about what I do. They'll mention that in their submission, but I try not to look into it too much. I don't want to know exactly who they are. I've never had to meet a person face-to-face."

June takes me in again, examining my reddening face in the same way I've examined hers. In this appraisal, she seems to make a decision, nodding as if she's learned something about me that I can never rewrite, no matter how much I want her to believe I'm not a bad person.

"Why did she want to break up with me?" she asks, wiping fast-falling tears from her cheeks.

Not only have I never met one of my anonymous clients in person—that I know of for sure—I certainly haven't shared an initial request with a message recipient.

"She said you're too fragile," I tell her, wincing as I say it.

If this is how I lose her presence in my life, at least this will end with me telling the full truth. She deserves that much. And I'll have my perfume to remember her by, even if it doesn't capture the apparent complexity of me, the not-so-middle sibling who has a not-so-perfect-anymore life. Maybe moldy towel is exactly what I should be smelling like considering the circumstances.

June hides her face behind her hands. She's now crying so hard she's embarrassed by it. My impulse to care for her becomes too great to ignore. I slide into the booth across from her and reach out to grab her hands, which is not appropriate in normal circumstances, but this is far from normal.

"Please don't cry because of me," I say.

"It's not you," she sniffles out. "Not really. I don't understand, but that's not even my biggest problem right now."

This is another unexpected turn of events. Add it to the list. My hands are still on June's hands, coaxing them down to the table.

"What is it?" I ask.

"New York. She was supposed . . . to . . . come . . . with . . . me." She's upset all over again, choking on her own words.

I rub my thumbs atop her palms in soothing circles. "This is a good thing, then, isn't it? It's a nightmare traveling with someone you're dating anyway."

I say this like it's something I've experienced. The truth is, I have never gone on a trip with a girlfriend. I broke up with Sadie right before she was going to ask me to come home with her for Christmas. Wren and I made it through the end of spring together, and I knew we had to call it quits when the weather turned to sweltering muggy sunshine and she started mentioning how much she wanted us to get out of Illinois for a bit.

When things are going well, trips are places where people propose. Where couples exchange *I love you*s.

But trips can also highlight all the bad things. You learn your partner has really bad time management, or that neither of you has the same travel interests. Trips change everything, and I like to keep things the way they are. I'm comforted by familiarity. I understand it. Even my own pain. I know how to navigate it without causing any trouble for anyone else.

Or I did, up until five minutes ago.

June dares to look at me again. The immediacy of the glance, heavily charged, makes me pull my hands from hers. It's suddenly so personal—too personal for Rita's—and the distance helps me breathe better.

"I don't like to be alone," she tells me.

Forget the space between our hands. This is just as personal. Maybe even more so.

"Who does?" I try to joke, but our nerves are too raw.

June forces a courteous smile, directing it to the table. "I like it less than anyone you've ever met, I promise you that. I can't go on this trip alone."

"So cancel it," I suggest. "Besides, we'd hate to not see you at the diner." Who knows why I hide behind the royal *we* when I really mean me. *I'd* hate to not see her.

"It's not refundable," she tells me. "And I have to go, if I ever want my business to grow."

Denise calls for me to come back behind the counter, pointing to Carson, who has taken to stacking all the coffee creamers into a pyramid. Seeing my sibling gives me an idea.

A wild, impulsive, completely reckless idea.

"I'll go with you," I say, chasing the impulse before I can give myself a chance to overthink it.

June looks deep into my eyes again. Third time in one day. Three times more than she's ever looked at me like *this*.

"You don't even know what we're doing," she says.

"What are we doing?" I challenge, fighting to keep my voice from shaking. *What am* I *doing* is more like it.

"We're meeting with investors who might want to buy into my perfume business."

She continues to say *we*. She might be into the idea of traveling with me. How that's possible after my surrogate breakup with her, I don't know, but every single thing I understand about my life has been upended, so this is my new normal.

"We can do that," I tell her. If this is what it takes to fix what I've done, it's what I'll do. And this will take me away from Trove Hills and my new brother and this family reunion I want no part of.

The dynamic between June and me has already been altered by the ghostwritten breakup. Maybe this trip can undo whatever has changed between us today. Maybe in this one highly specific scenario, it will bring us back to our safely neutral territory instead of damaging us in some irreparable way.

"We leave tomorrow," she says.

"I know you won't believe me, but that timing literally could not be better. How long will we be gone?"

"Eight days," she says, sniffling.

"June Lightbell." I never use her full name, but it's important in this moment, because we aren't talking about her love of dipping sauces or her favorite Whitney song. We're talking about our real lives—our complicated worlds outside the bubble of Rita's. "I can't tell you how perfect this is, all things considered."

"Tatum Ward," she says back. "There's another problem. I don't have anywhere for us to stay. My girlfriend planned all of it. My *ex*-girlfriend," she corrects, wiping another tear away. "Fuck," she mutters, the intensity of her crying increasing again.

That *is* a problem. Trove Hills isn't super far from Chicago miles-wise, but the feel of this town may as well be light-years away from big-city life. I don't know how to navigate a place of skyscrapers and trains as it is, but I certainly can't plan several days of staying there on short notice.

"Do you know anyone who lives there?" I ask, running through my roster of former classmates and casual friends, trying to remember if any of them are in New York and would want to put us up for over a week.

"Wait, yes," June says, some hope returning to her eyes. "I have this woman who buys all my perfumes. I've known her for years. She lives in New York. And she just posted about needing someone to come watch her cats as soon as possible . . ."

"Reach out to her," I say. "We can watch her cats. We can do whatever she needs. Does she want somewhere to stay? She can come spend the week in the premiere Trove Hills guest cottage if she wants. I'll send her my blood type and Social Security number to get this place. Anything."

June grants me a small smile. "Are you really sure you want to do this?"

"Of course," I say, my resolve strengthening. "This is what friends do for each other."

"Friends," June repeats.

The uncertainty in the way she's said it throws me for a loop. June and I *are* friends, aren't we? Sure, we only see each other here, but we'd still qualify, wouldn't we?

"Friends," I say back, pretending to be certain. We can't *both* have doubts.

Whether this is the best idea I've ever had or the worst, June Lightbell and I will be going to New York tomorrow. Together.

As friends.

6

Eleanor

June Lightbell, the creator of my favorite bespoke perfume, replies to my story, telling me she can watch my cats if I let her stay in my apartment. She is the best perfumer in the business, reliable, with a high standard for excellence. That would not normally be enough of a reason to agree to something like this, but these are far from normal circumstances, so I say yes, with one catch—I don't have anywhere else to go yet. She informs me I can stay in her town if I want, sending me pictures of a sweet cottage, along with some other pictures of the town. It's all a bit old-timey. Kitschy, even.

Why would I go here? I ask myself.

But then I ask, *Why not?*

Which is exactly how I agree to go to some place called Trove Hills.

I pack a bag, book a flight, kiss my kitties on the head, and get on a plane. Upon landing in Chicago, I take an Uber, leaving the city and heading through the suburbs until I reach this tiny utopian town complete with a rail line running alongside the main road and an ice-cream shop built in the shape of a waffle cone.

I log out of my work email and turn off my phone, erasing the notifications that have been rolling in from coworkers and peers, asking me where I am and what's happened. As if they actually care about me.

They don't. They care about the story.

Walking down the long driveway of a random house, I follow June's directions until I reach the cottage from the pictures. I take a key out from underneath a garden gnome, unlock the front door, and find myself inside this warm hug of a home.

My steps instantly become lighter, not wanting to disturb this cottage full of life. The floors are real wood, creaky and knotted. Every piece of furniture looks like it was carefully selected for its feeling over its function, meant to lounge upon as long as possible. It's warm and inviting and almost unbearably idyllic.

A gallery wall of photos hangs along the staircase—shots of various people laughing, dancing, getting married, graduating from school, blowing out birthday candles, holding new babies. They must be a part of the same family, but there are so many different faces it seems impossible somehow, like this many people can't all belong to one another. It's overwhelming to someone like me, who doesn't have a single aunt or uncle. No living grandparents. Nothing.

This family watches over me as I move through this unfamiliar place. In their knowing stares, I feel a pressure that isn't mine. The weight of generations kept alive through mementos and memorabilia. History. Legacy.

In the kitchen, a bottle of red wine waits on the counter alongside a note from Tatum, the friend of June's who has put me up.

Eleanor,
What's mine is yours. Use whatever you want. And don't mind my parents in the main house. They're gonna be busy most of the time you're here, so it shouldn't be a problem.

Beware of my siblings, though. There's Carson, my older sibling. You'll know instantly if you've met them, because they are pure trouble. Then there is Laney, my younger sister. If you hear someone singing like a Disney princess at seven in the morning, that's her.

Thank you for agreeing to do this. I hope Trove Hills greets you with open arms. While you're here, be sure to stop by Rita's Diner and a get a slice of the banana cream pie. It's the best thing on the menu. Tell them Tatum sent you. It'll be on the house.

This warmth brings tears to my eyes again. It's a different kind of crying than yesterday's sobs of despair. It's jealousy maybe. Or tenderness. Both?

I know people live differently than I do. That's how life works. Being confronted with it is something else. There is no note on the counter of my place to greet June and Tatum, detailing the charming quirks of my home. There are no pictures of the generations of Chapmans who came before me. There aren't any pictures at all. The quirks of my condo are the potential for seeing rats on the sidewalk and the pounding from what I've guessed to be my upstairs neighbor's biweekly tap routine.

I open the bottle of wine and pour myself a glass.

With my phone turned off, this is the first time in my adulthood I have ever been unreachable. I have no friends to text about this random plan. There isn't a person alive who actually knows me who has any idea where I am, except for my doorman, who needed the information of the guests who will be staying in my place.

And June, who I've texted to let know I've arrived safely.

It should be relaxing. I'm *free*.

In some ways, it does put me at ease. But it's also terrifying, like sitting in a boat with no land in sight, the water so still it becomes ominous in its peace. Now that I don't have a job to do, a purpose to fulfill, I could disappear, and no one would even notice. They certainly wouldn't miss me.

At least I have the wine.

A WHILE LATER, AFTER I'VE TAKEN A SHOWER, I TUCK myself into the couch and read one of the romance novels on the bookshelves. For as much as I like the concept, reading is another activity I don't indulge in much. There isn't any glamour in imagining a world that's not my own, because when I leave the comfort of fiction behind, the truth hits me twice as hard. There have never been any happily ever afters in my real world.

Somehow, this cottage makes me want to lean in anyway. Sitting here, feet tucked under me, warm in my robe, devouring a story about falling in love, I could almost . . . well, I could almost get to longing for the kind of shit they write about in books like this.

The front door rattles, startling me out of the fantasy.

Maybe it's Tatum's parents? She told me they wouldn't be a problem, though. Which means it might be a burglar. Am I about to fight off an intruder my first night in this place?

Sighing, I stand up, working my hands into fists.

"Tatum! Since when do you lock your door this early? And where the hell did you put my key? I need to shower, and I can't go into Mom and Dad's house right now!"

Not an intruder. A sibling.

"Fine! I'm crawling in! But I'm not paying for anything that breaks along the way!"

With surprising grace, a person squeezes in through the window I'd opened earlier to let in a breeze. They land on the wood floor, grinning like a cat that's just caught a mouse.

They are also covered in glitter.

"You must be Carson," I guess.

They startle, their slinky grin replaced with confusion. Springing up, they fist their hands the same way I did a few moments ago.

"I wouldn't fight me. I'm a black belt in judo," I tell them.

"Is this how you stop me from stopping you from continuing to commit a crime?" they ask.

"I'm barefoot in a silk robe reading a paperback on the couch while drinking a glass of Malbec," I say. "You barrel-rolled through an open window covered in glitter. How am *I* the one committing a crime?"

"How do you know who I am?" Carson asks.

I fake a huff of exhaustion. "Tatum warned me you'd be like this." She really told me Carson would be trouble. That must be why I find myself wanting to be the one who makes it instead, inventing new ways to get the upper hand in a situation where I'm the one out of my element.

My words unlock a new facet to Carson. They lower their fists, laughing as they bite down on their lower lip, looking off into the middle distance. It's . . . *attractive*, to say the least. A bolt of desire shoots through me, setting me off-balance.

Maybe it's the way their hair flops down, short brown curls that look right no matter how they fall. I might be feeling envy over that kind of effortless ease.

Or it's their muscle tee, loose in all the right ways, showing me tattoos and skin and more of that damn glitter.

It could also be the unnerving playfulness I suddenly feel, a bouncy ball of excitement rattling around in my rib cage for the first time in years.

One sitting's worth of romance-novel longing has really gone straight to my head. This is direct proof I can't read them. It's too dangerous.

"What else did Tatum tell you about me, beautiful stranger who appears to be staying in her home?" Carson asks. "Did she mention my credit score has drastically improved as of late? It's in the mid–seven hundreds now. Perfectly respectable for a made-up concept." They crinkle their eyes, smirking, knowing full well their outward charm is effective.

Two can play this game. "I'm afraid I'm not at liberty to share what Tatum's told me," I inform them. "And I'd congratulate you on the credit score, but they want us to believe eight hundreds is the only braggable tier."

"I've been in desperate need of a tough-love reminder to aim higher, so thank you," they say.

"Anytime. I'm very fiscally responsible."

"I could tell from the way you held on to your wineglass even after I crashed through the window. You don't waste nice things."

"Who knew my judo-trained grip would be what gave away my credit score? And here I thought it was the scent of my expensive perfume."

Carson steps closer. Flecks of golden glitter sparkles fall off their skin. "That tells me something else," they whisper, inhaling.

"What?" I breathe, suddenly warm, my toes curling to grip the floor. Are they flirting with me?

They shake their head as they laugh again. "I'm afraid I'm not at liberty to share."

Touché.

"I'll tell you this, though," they continue. "Most of what you've heard about me is true, but none of it is relevant. I'm *very* good at playing by the rules when the situation requires it."

"I'll believe it when I see it," I say.

"You must be the one Tatum was breaking up with yesterday," they guess. "Looks like it didn't stick."

"That's not me. I'm single. Have been for a while." It sounds sadder than I intend, so I follow up with something risky, masking my vulnerability with the confidence I've spent years perfecting. "But that doesn't mean I'm opposed to enjoying myself every once in a while."

This gets an eyebrow raise out of Carson.

"Or enjoying other people," I add.

They take a small step forward. "What kind of . . . other people do you enjoy?"

"I've never been particular about that. I can enjoy any kind of person, if the circumstances are right."

The closer they get, the more I want to look at them, taking stock of the sinewy muscles in their forearms. A splatter of blue paint at the edge of their tank catches my eye, and the next thing I know, I ask, "Are you an artist?" unable to contain the question now that it's come to me, too overwhelmed with this urge to make sense of them. One minute in their presence and I'm almost believing I'm someone fun.

"Good eye," they say, looking down.

My eyes shoot to their hands, corded tendons flexing as they examine the paint that's made its way into their nail beds. *What else can those hands do?*

Their gaze moves again, this time landing on me, searching for some kind of cue that can tell them who I am in return.

"Are you a . . . judo master?" they ask.

"I made that up," I tell them, both of us somehow already at ease enough to laugh together. "I *have* taken enough reformer Pilates classes to make me believe my core could stay completely stable in the middle of a tornado, though."

"I see that for you." They pretend to pull a notebook out of their back pocket, miming the action of holding a pen to paper. "Tell me, though, if credit score doesn't do it, is there any special criteria you look for when enjoying other people?"

There's no uncertainty now. They *are* flirting. It's a white-hot spotlight of attention, and it does not make me wither. Instead I grow taller, eager to match the energy of this irresistible stranger who knows nothing of my life. Even if it's only for a night, I want to be a person someone else might miss after I'm gone.

"Good question," I say.

My eyes drag up Carson's frame. They're about as tall as I am, without any of the rounding I do, leaning over to keep myself closer to others. In the space they take up, I see a calculated confidence. A spine-straight way of staring into other people's souls. Even while covered in glitter and paint, they are as buttery and smooth as the smile on their face, melting away any of my reservations. The perfect person for a night of fun.

"I tend to like the troublemakers," I say. "The ones who stand too close. Stare too long."

Carson takes three steps closer. "Stand too close and"—they lock eyes on me—"what was the other thing?"

"Stare too long," I repeat, holding their gaze.

"Anything else?"

"I sort of have a thing for artists."

"Ah," they say, their eyes flicking down to my lips. It's a question. A request for permission.

I give it, pressing my lips against Carson's. Their tongue slips into my mouth as their hands grab my hair, tugging me in closer. My heart flutters with the thrill of unfamiliarity. There is so much I don't know about them. Every single thing, to be exact. Yet here we are, skin to skin, learning each other in real time.

Their lips sigh into mine as they move me toward the wall, pressing my back into the bookshelf. It's the exact kind of confidence I relish. There's no uncertainty between us, no tentative exploration or timid touching, even with all that's unknown. We move like we mean it. I wrap my hands around their torso, pulling them closer to me. This closeness feels like relief, my robe so featherlight between us it may as well be nothing at all.

"Glitter," they murmur.

"What?" I gasp out.

"I need to wash this glitter off me," they say, half-hearted in their attempt to create distance between us.

I'd forgotten about the glitter. It's all over me now too. I could ask where it came from, but that's not important. All that matters is getting back to what we're doing as fast as possible. The longer I have to think, the more likely I am to backtrack. I don't want that. Not tonight.

This is my first chance in years to be defined by anything other than my job, or my neighborhood, or even my personality. I can have desires and not have to worry about what they'll mean in the morning. Nobody here knows me, and they never, ever will.

"Go wash up," I instruct.

Without a second wasted, they move up the stairs toward the shower. "Are you coming with?" they ask, turning back to look at me.

I follow them up the stairs, making my first official decision since arriving here.

I will have sex with Carson tonight.

7

Tatum

I land in New York with June's hand in mine. It's such a shock I startle, shaking it off like a spider's crawled across my fingers. Obviously it's as simple as the fact that at some point in our flight, we both dozed off, and we grabbed on to each other without realizing. But why would my body do that without my permission? Don't I know better than to reach for the things I can't have?

Friends, I remind myself. That has to be my guiding light for this trip. My own friends and I have put up with each other's every anxiety and complaint for over twenty years. It's the only intimacy I have direct proof can last without souring.

June's still asleep, completely undisturbed by the landing turbulence. I'm wide awake, more alert than I've been all day. Nudging her gently, I whisper, "We're here." When that's not enough to wake her, I put more force into my next shake.

She comes back to the surface, her long lashes fluttering as she mumbles, "Where am I?"

"You're a deep sleeper," I tell her.

When she realizes it's me, she sits up straighter. "*Tatum*," she says, and it's hard not to feel charmed by the way her voice brightens.

She rubs her eyes and yawns. "Sorry. I took a sleeping pill. I have terrible flying anxiety."

"Wow, I didn't even notice. I was too busy worrying about the takeoff." All of this is easier to say now that it's over and I've survived it.

We're actually here. In New York City. Together.

"I figured that," June says with a gentle, sleepy grin. "When we were boarding, you looked like you'd seen a ghost."

It's all coming back—the long day of travel that's now behind us. All the anxiety and nerves in the buildup. I'd been so stressed that I failed to process what June's earlier body language had meant. My vision had snagged more than once on her shaking leg, bouncing up and down as she'd wrung her hands together, and I was too lost in my own concerns to put the pieces together.

I think now of what she said yesterday, about being bad at being alone. My heart softens—a tiny, dangerous space cracking open, clearing room for all I've yet to learn about her.

Friends. This is what they do. Learn about each other.

"God, I'm sorry," I say.

"Don't be," she says. "It was weirdly helpful. I realized that in the event of a crash, we couldn't both be scared. One of us needed to have it together. Unfortunately, I'd already taken the sleeping pill when I went to the bathroom before we boarded, so I slept right through all the brave protecting I was going to do. But in my mind, I definitely looked out for you." She reaches her arms up as she yawns, and I get a peek of her stomach, the barest hint of brown skin exposed beneath her loose tank top.

My face flushes. I make a point to look at the air vent above us as I say, "Thank you for your energetic protection."

"Anytime."

We deplane and make our way to baggage claim, bleary-eyed as we wait for our luggage to hit the carousel. I open my messages to text my group chat, ironically titled WE DON'T LIVE IN TROVE HILLS.

There are four of us in it—Presley, Nya, Emmett, and me. Most of us have known one another since grade school. Presley and I have been friends since kindergarten. All three of them moved away from Trove Hills for college, just like I did. Presley came back and lived with his parents for a few years, but he's gone again too, off to Vegas. Nya lives in Austin. Emmett's never in one place for longer than six months. He's currently in Nashville, not far from where my sister lives.

The chat title is a joking reference to their long-standing wish that someday I will leave Trove Hills too.

> TATUM: I've made it to New York in one piece.

> EMMETT: What did you guys talk about on the plane?

> TATUM: We both slept through pretty much the whole flight.

> EMMETT: So what are you going to talk about now?

When I told the chat about this trip, they were supportive, if deeply confused. They already know that June once asked me out and I said no. They know we still see each other at the diner all the time, and it's not weird despite my past rejection. Good friends that they are, they also know better than to press me too hard about it all.

They *don't* know why I'd take a trip like this on such short notice after years of only taking carefully planned vacations built around other events—visiting one of them for their birthday or spending a holiday like the Fourth of July together. And truly, I don't entirely know the answer to that either.

This is somehow the first trip I've ever taken that doesn't have a deliberate agenda, and it's with the one person I won't let myself date even casually. The chat obviously thinks it's because I want to make a move on June while I'm here. They don't understand how precious and important our diner interactions are to me. I already survived rejecting her, and then accidentally breaking up with her on her girlfriend's behalf. I can't push my luck any further and risk losing her presence in my life forever.

> TATUM: Thank you for your resounding faith in my conversational skills. We were both nervous about flying, so we haven't discussed much yet.

I look at June, hoping to prove Emmett's skepticism wrong by saying something conversationally enticing. A real dazzler of a statement that starts this New York City adventure on the right foot.

Maybe it's only in my mind, but it seems that our shared quiet has somehow turned awkward. It's become the silence of strangers stuck together on a long elevator ride. Of distant acquaintances at a dinner table waiting for their mutual friend to come back from the bathroom. We need the warmth of the lights at Rita's and the chaos of the line cooks inserting themselves into the daily humdrum. Without those constraints, there are so many options for what we could be talking about that I have no clue where to actually begin.

So, tell me about your childhood. Do you actually like the coffee we serve at Rita's? Do you wish it was your ex here instead of me? Why don't you like to be alone?

I open up the chat window again.

TATUM: Now you've psyched me out.

Emmett replies with one of those mischievous-looking emojis.

PRESLEY: You could ask her what she thinks about
soup.

This is his first contribution of the night, and it's as chaotic and strange as he is.

TATUM: Why would I ask about soup?

PRESLEY: Everyone always has a really strong
opinion about soup. It's a good conversation
starter.

NYA: I hate soup

Now that Nya's finally joined the chat, all four of us are present. It's nice to be together like this, even if it's just through text messages. It's the closest we ever get to actually hanging out. It used to make me sad, not seeing them in person very often. It happens once a year if we're lucky. I spent so long being upset about it that I wasn't appreciating the time we *do* have together. It was Nya who reminded me, gently, that we will never again be teenagers wandering around our hometown. We won't be able to all meet up at the twenty-four-hour pizza place at two in the morning. Even if it's one of us dropping life updates into the group chat for everyone else to dissect on their own watch, it's still better than nothing. And she is so right. This chat is proof that no matter what, we will remain friends forever. Across state lines. Year after year. We will always care about one another.

Nya is the busiest of all of us, going out in Austin almost every night. I don't even need to check her location on my phone to know she's at some bar with her friends, stealing a moment to read this while in the bathroom or waiting for another drink.

NYA: But hold on. Let me scroll up and find out
why we're talking about soup.

PRESLEY: See? A strong soup response.

"Do you like soup?" I ask aloud, shoving my phone back into my backpack for the time being.

June startles, pulling out a headphone I didn't even notice she'd started using. "Hmm?"

"Do you like soup?" I repeat, hating myself even more on the second round.

"Are you wanting to get some after we get our bags?" she asks, not understanding my question in the least. "I'm hungry too."

"What screams classic New York meal louder than a bowl of lobster bisque?"

She laughs, then rubs her eyes, like she needs to wake up even more to understand what's going on here. She's treating my obvious joke as a somewhat serious statement, which forces me to keep my face composed. My dignity is on the line. If a judge puts me under oath and asks about this moment during the trial for my honor, I will never be able to explain my actions. *Your Honor, the group chat made me, I swear.*

"I'll see if I can find somewhere that has soup," she says, taking out her phone to look online.

I don't stop her, because I need a moment to yell at the chat. After I finish transcribing the soup exchange to them, June's bag shows up on the carousel. Emmett sends a voice memo that I tell him I can't play, because I'm still sitting in the middle of the soupgate that he inadvertently caused by making me doubt myself.

PRESLEY: I never could've known you'd just ask
that COLD.

TATUM: Forgive me for not realizing I needed to
prepare a warm-up to soup-related inquiries! Now
she thinks I'm fucking obsessed with soup. Don't
be surprised when you see my posts. Expect an
ongoing series on New York's best split pea.

EMMETT: 😎 Tatum the soup sweetie thinking
about her upcoming liquid-based meals.

"Did you really want lobster bisque?" June asks, startling me back to the present.

"No," I admit. "I was trying to be funny. And then you believed me."

To my relief, she laughs again. "For what it's worth, *I* really like soup. I would've gone for lobster bisque with you."

Fighting embarrassment, I look down at my phone, furiously typing an update for the chat.

NYA: Hold on, hold on!! Why did you admit that?!
You should've carried the soup secret to the grave.
Like how we made Laney think there are dogs that
come out after midnight to attack coyotes.

TATUM: To this day she still won't sit in our
parents' backyard without warning us about the
night dogs.

I'm *almost* smiling. When we were in high school, we really did convince my then preteen sister that dangerous wild dogs roamed our hometown after midnight, and she, now a full-grown adult, somehow still believes it.

One by one, our fellow passengers claim the remaining bags, until there is one lone luggage piece on permanent rotation. Every time it passes, I convince myself it might be mine and I've somehow forgotten what it looks like. I even pick it up once and inspect it, as if maybe I forgot that I actually packed everything into a black leather duffel bag instead of a bright green hard-sided suitcase I bought on clearance at TJ Maxx last fall.

My phone vibrates with texts from the group chat, asking me for more updates. Texts from Carson come in too. And from my dad, telling me how excited he is for the coming week's activities. With the dread of losing my luggage blooming inside me, the constant vibration becomes an annoyance. I put my phone on do not disturb.

"I think I have to go file a missing bag claim," I finally say, choking back the threat of tears. I can't grieve what's packed in my luggage right now, caught in whatever liminal hellscape missing suitcases go to. It's too early to see this as a bad omen.

June gets to work calling us a ride as I give my information to the airline. Now that they've attached tracking to every piece of checked luggage, they're able to tell me where my bag is. Somehow it never made it onto our plane, but they assure me they will put it on the first flight out tomorrow. I can come back to the airport to pick it up, or they will have it delivered to me. I even get a travel voucher for the trouble.

So not a bad omen at all. Just a minor inconvenience. Nothing that will damage this adventure in any substantial way. And the voucher is kind of a win.

I turn to June and say, with a smile, "It really can't get any worse than that."

Enter Eleanor's home.

We knew her apartment would be nice. The place certainly delivers on that promise. The building is on the Upper West Side, twenty stories tall and overlooking Central Park, complete with a doorman in the lobby and only one other neighbor on her floor. Her unit has a small foyer entry with lovely herringbone wood floors, and ornate crown molding along the top of the walls, briefly fooling us into thinking we are in for a treat. Then we turn the corner into the main living area, where we are greeted with piles of empty delivery boxes and unwashed plates. Cat toys in various states of destruction. Storage containers. Articles of discarded clothing.

Oh, and old, rotting food.

I love clutter. A shelf full of your favorite beloved knickknacks, curated over decades? Absolutely. An unswept floor covered in the memory of every Amazon Prime order you've ever placed in your life? Significantly less appealing to me. The breathtaking skyline views from the windows almost make up for it, but there is only so much heavy lifting a view can do when it smells like old eggs in here.

"I thought she liked your perfume," I say, attempting something like humor again. "If Eleanor has enough taste to wear Lightbell, why the hell is her place such a disaster?"

"We can't stay here," June says, looking as horrified as I feel.

A fluffy brown cat slinks between my legs, meowing for pets. Syrup. I recognize him from the pictures. His presence feels like the tiniest mercy, and I bend down to pet him, swallowing back an urge to cry.

"I'm sorry," I say, because that much is true. If she were here with Vanessa instead of me, they'd be in whatever hotel Vanessa booked, not staying in the random condo of a very distant acquaintance.

This trip hasn't even started and it's like a slow-burn version of my worst-case scenario. It's exactly how relationship dynamics begin to change for the worse—a series of seemingly minor inconveniences compounding atop one another like hairline fractures that will one day break everything into a thousand pieces. How do I stop us from falling apart if I can't anticipate the exact places where we will first begin to crack?

I need to turn this around. And fast.

"It's too late for us to figure out a new arrangement now," I say. "Why don't we go out right now and experience this New York nightlife I'm always hearing about? We can even get some soup."

June pets Syrup, running her delicate hand along the length of his fluff. He starts to purr from the affection.

"We just need to feed the cats first," she says.

"Of course," I tell her. "We can do that much."

Problem solved.

8

Eleanor

Carson leans over the tub to start the water.

Whoever picked out the decor in this bathroom must have done it around twenty years ago, when everyone wanted their homes to look like an Olive Garden. I imagine a mother—Carson's mother, I guess—opening a catalog of tiles and combing through until she saw this one, with its warm beige tones and rustic finish, pointing to it with a manicured finger and saying, *This is it*. It's the kind of tile that cultivates a sense of escape. I'm sure I'm meant to feel as though I've ended up in an Italian villa. All it actually does is remind me of the strangers who live here, and all the unknown layers to their history.

What kind of tub would my own mother have picked out, if she could have afforded a renovation?

Carson looks over their shoulder and smiles at me, melting some of my concern. Now is *not* the time to think of my dead mother.

"How hot do you like the water?" Carson asks.

"It doesn't matter," I say.

They squint their eyes. "What if you're freezing?"

"I can handle the cold."

"What if you're scalding?"

"I'll move out of the way."

They sigh.

"What about you? Don't you have preferences?" I ask.

"The nice thing about me is I'm adaptable."

"Maybe I'm adaptable too."

They scrutinize me again. It's not unkind, but it is thorough. "You're not the type of person who walks into a restaurant and tells the waiter, 'Surprise me.' You've prescreened the menu before arriving, and you order exactly what you planned to get."

It's . . . alarmingly true. "I prefer the water to be about two degrees shy of burning my skin," I say.

Carson turns the knob to hot, leaning over the ledge to put their hand under the running water. The whole act is almost mundane in its simplicity. Like we're a couple in our bathroom, getting ready to take our nightly shower together. What a life that would be.

"Not that I want to ruin the mood, but aren't you still wondering where your sister is?" I ask.

"A beautiful woman just chased me up the stairs to shower with me. I forgot I had a sister at all. And I actually have two."

"You keep calling me beautiful," I note.

"Because you are," they respond. Some of the glitter on their skin swirls down the drain. "But I'll stop if you want. I can call you intellectual too. I contain multitudes. *An intellectual woman just chased me up the stairs.*"

"It wasn't a criticism," I say. "More of a shock. Most people call me intimidating before they call me beautiful. Or they call me tall."

"That's boring. Here, come feel the water. Tell me if it's right."

I kneel beside the glitter-covered stranger I just kissed, checking the water temperature. "It's a little too hot, even for me."

When I pull my hand back, my skin is already red. Carson

grabs it, holding it between their palms to cool me down. It's so tender that I flush, hoping it seems like it's from the warmth of the water. This is supposed to be quick and meaningless, and now Carson is clutching my palm like they're a wartime doctor who has just realized the burn victim they've been tasked with treating is actually their long-lost lover.

"Your sister is in New York," I say. "We swapped places for the week."

My admission is the first thing to cut the sexual tension in a real way. With impressive efficiency, even for me, I have ruined this fun, impulsive thing. It's for the best. Why would I sleep with a stranger connected to the place I'll be staying in for more than a day?

"I have a lot of questions," Carson says.

Good, I think. *Let the questions consume you.*

"I'll be honest, though, and say I don't need them answered right now," they continue, switching on the showerhead. "Just to be clear, Tatum won't be home tonight?"

"No. She won't be home for quite a while."

"Then I don't see any reason we can't continue this. Unless you don't want to."

"I do," I say, surprised by my own insistence. So much for putting on the brakes. "Do you?"

"Of course I do."

Their response resets the entire experience. The obviousness of their desire for me—no filter, no games—makes me more than willing to go back to our original plan.

With that, my mouth is on Carson's again. They give quick kisses that chase down my neck, then back to my mouth for something deeper. They pull us both up until we're standing again. Placing their hands on the knot of my robe, they press my back into the wall beside the tub.

"I'm just now realizing you're wearing this because you already showered," Carson says. They pull away, like once again we must renegotiate our terms.

The shower curtain is still pulled open. At this angle, a light mist of water sprays us.

"Yeah, and then some stranger kissed me, covering me in glitter," I say.

"What a fool," they mutter. "Though I think I was the one who got kissed, if memory serves."

I take this moment to put my hand along their face, half on their hair, half on their cheek. "Good memory."

Untying my robe for them, I let it fall to my feet, revealing my body in full. This part is usually awkward—just something to get through on the first go. I'm used to looking off into the distance, avoiding the other person's reaction. With Carson, I keep eye contact, daring them to wait. *Don't look down. Not just yet.*

They meet this challenge as they've met every other, watching me. Holding steady.

I kiss them again, hungry for their lips, wanting another taste of whatever it is I can't yet make sense of about them. This isn't something I'll be forgetting, but I don't even know what it is I'll remember. No hookup has ever been this charged, this spontaneous but somehow familiar.

"Who *are* you?" they say, pushing me back with light hands.

It's not a dismissal. It's more of a curiosity. Maybe they're feeling the same way I am, like they can't quite make sense of what this is.

Their movement has made space between us. Enough room for them to see me in full. The vulnerability rushes in, a whole new tidal wave of nerves making my legs begin to quiver.

"I'm the tall intellectual woman who's standing naked in front of you," I say.

"Ah, yes. That's right." They drop to their knees to press their hands to my hips. "So beautiful," they say as they kiss the skin of my thighs. "Excuse me, so intellectual."

This gets me to laugh, edging off the nerves.

Kiss. "Brilliant." *Kiss.* "Delicious."

Something strange happens. My eyes start to water, like I almost want to . . . cry?

It's so bizarre it thrusts me into action, my fingers weaving into the curls on their head to direct their attention to the heat between my legs. "Less talking," I command. "More doing."

"See?" they say, taking a moment to smile up at me. "You know exactly what you like."

Their smile turns ravenous now, pushed on by the thrill of the task. Whatever brief wave of emotion that had crested inside me is gone as fast as it came.

With a vigor previously known to me only by vibrators or my own hand, Carson begins the work of unraveling me. Their tongue presses down on my clit, sucking and licking until my panting builds into sounds.

"Yes," they encourage. Their hands grip the outside of my thighs so tightly that redness is already blooming, a fingerprint impression that feels like it could last forever. Like *this* could last forever. "Give me more."

My legs begin to shake all the way now, and Carson buries their tongue deeper, determined and attentive. Keeping my hands threaded through their hair, I hold their curls as they continue working.

I close my eyes, the tremble that's been building finally overtakes me, and I cry out, a violent crescendo against the patient, waiting thrum of the shower and the sweet, steady suction of Carson's mouth. They press and knead through my orgasm until the very end, when I've slumped against the wall, barely able to stay standing.

"I love the way you taste," they say, wiping the side of their mouth with their thumb and licking it.

In my dawning clarity, my desire does not rework itself into the shame I've come to expect. In fact, I'm still lit up, still locked in, hoping to keep going as long as Carson can withstand.

"Your turn," I say, reaching for the seam of their tank, running my thumb over the paint that's stuck there. Everything about this experience is new. Exciting. I'm eager to give Carson the same pleasure they gave me.

I pull off their shirt, and their bare chest wears two faint scars under their nipples, like smiling crescent moons. There is a tattoo all around the scars, large and intricate, weaving up from their belly button and stopping just below their clavicle. It fills up almost their entire torso.

"Wow," I say, in genuine appreciation of the art. My hands reach for the details, tracing the trees that live along their rib cage. Stray pieces of golden glitter have fallen onto the canvas of their tattooed skin. I brush some off to better appreciate the art. "This is incredible. Like a page from a storybook."

"I drew it," they tell me.

My life puts me in contact with a lot of art at all different levels. Theater sets, promotional graphics, fan art made from the shows we've worked on. And yet, this forest on their chest draws me in more than anything has in a long while. It's like looking at a memory I wish was my own. Like the feeling I used to get when I'd read fantasy books as a child, convinced for a few hours that instead of a young girl living in Pennsylvania, I was a displaced fairy waiting to return to my magical land.

I'm brushing off so much glitter that Carson puts a hand on me. "You know, I really do need to shower," they say with a sly smile.

They pull down their jeans and step into the water, leaving me on the outskirts, watching them. Admiring them, really, taking this distance as an opportunity to watch them take up space again. They sigh with relief as the water cascades down their long frame.

Jealousy flares up in me. I want to be the one who washes them clean.

I climb into the shower, reaching for the body wash I set out earlier. I pour a handful into my palm, sudsing my hands together. And then I make slow work of washing Carson, running my hands down their arms, across their chest, turning them to reach their back.

We say nothing. All the words I want to conjure don't have a place here, so I don't waste time by entertaining them. Instead, my hands turn the washing into massaging. Carson's sighs of relief turn into sighs of pleasure. It keeps me at work, kneading out the knots of tension in their neck, feeling their throat swallow back a sigh as I clean them of this beautiful, prismatic dirt.

"Who are you?" they ask me again with their back turned.

As much as I want to know what my name would sound like in their throat, I can't let myself give it over. "It doesn't matter," I tell them.

When the soap has rinsed clean, I let my hand wander lower, until they can't remember to ask me anything at all.

9

Tatum

What I thought might become a night of drunken debauchery—June and me downing expensive cocktails until we can't remember our own names—has turned into us tucked into the back corner of a quiet bar, sipping on artisanal beers and splitting mozzarella sticks. It's oddly peaceful in here, not at all what I expected from the New York I'd carved out in my imagination. I was under the impression this was a city that could swallow me up with its scale, way too big and bright for a small-town girl like myself. But this place reminds me of Rita's. It's intimate, with good drinks and great lighting. I feel contained here. Safe.

"Thanks again for coming out here with me," June says, grinning at me over her drink. "Sorry it's been such a chaotic start."

"I'm used to chaos," I tell her. "But really, thanks for letting me join you. I just hope you're ready to share your wardrobe with me in the event my luggage never actually makes it here."

"You can borrow anything of mine you want," she says genuinely.

"Oh, I was kidding," I tell her. "I can buy new clothes tomorrow if I have to."

"What? You don't want to sleep in my sheer paisley turtleneck and a corduroy overall minidress?"

She's joking now too, but the thought of me in June's clothes makes me blush too hard to maintain eye contact. I surrender to my phone for once, checking to see all the notifications that have piled up since my departure.

CARSON: I know what you're doing. Running all
the way to New York to get away from this reunion.
When were you planning on sharing that with the
class?

There is a text from my mom too, who doesn't yet know I've left.

MOM: Will you come over tomorrow morning and
help me set up the front lawn? Your father
somehow lost our folding chairs in the garage. We
need to figure out another way to seat all our
guests.

And from my dad.

DAD: Any chance you've seen the folding chairs?
Looks like I've misplaced them somewhere.

He follows it with a series of embarrassed emojis, and even a GIF of someone banging their hand on their forehead.

DAD: And I don't think the car thing worked. I'm
sorry, sweetie, but you're gonna have to show me
again.

Laney has texted me too. It's just a string of question marks. No words included. I know it means Carson's told her I've left, and she's wondering what the hell I'm doing.

The pressure of everyone's different expectations, wanting answers or actions from me, makes my head ache. I rub my temples, staring at the wood grain of the table.

"Everything okay?" June asks.

I startle, letting go of my head. I'd forgotten myself. Lost my sense of place.

"All good," I tell her. "Just been a long day."

"C'mon," she says. "What's really going on?" This might be the first time she's ever let me not get away with the pleasantries. It's too monumental for me to attempt to deflect.

"It's my family," I admit. "I'm supposed to be at a reunion with them tomorrow."

"Is that why you wanted to come on this trip?"

"Yes." I pause, weighing the options. Telling her this pushes me firmly out of waitress territory and into something much more human for us both. It's the kind of thing I'd never share during a shift at Rita's. Which is precisely why I do it now. We don't have the bubble of protection around us anymore. We have to figure out who we are without it.

We have to be real friends.

"My dad invited his son to it," I continue. "The guy is older than me, but my dad just learned of his existence, and now he wants all of us to know him too, since he's technically our brother."

June's jaw drops. "I had no idea what you were going to say, but it wasn't that."

"You thought I was finally going to tell you all of my real feelings on soup, didn't you?"

"I was hoping you would."

"Maybe someday." I look off, gazing at the strangers scattered around us, caught inside their own little conversational bubbles. "I don't really know what to do with the information. Having a secret brother is a little splashier than my usual drama. I need more time to process it." It's weird to speak all of this out loud. Freeing. "I don't blame my new brother, obviously. I just don't feel ready to know him. It changes so much for me, and I don't want to put all that onto this stranger who doesn't deserve it."

"That's valid. But you can't not know him forever," June says. "He didn't ask to be born into this either. I'm sure he's having a hard time too."

None of my friends have been brave enough to empathize with my new brother. Ben. His name is Ben. And I should use it. I feel this surprising swell of affection for June because of it. I like that she cares about Ben's feelings, that she'd fight for me to recognize his own struggles and humanize him. It's the exact perspective check I need.

"I know he didn't," I say. "I just have a hard time with change. I kind of panic. Because what I don't know is scarier to me than what's familiar, even if what's familiar isn't great. At least I know I can survive it."

"Ah yes, fear of the great unknown," June says. "Like you and me."

I school my face to remain composed, even though every alarm bell within me has been tripped by this statement. Is June about to relate what I've said to how I turned her down? *Of course not*, I assure myself. *You're projecting*.

"I was thinking about us last night before we left," she continues cryptically. "You and I have known each other for a while now, but we don't *really* know each other. Like, I have no idea what you do with your time outside the diner."

"Nothing exciting," I hedge, still burning with something like nervous embarrassment. "All my friends moved out of Trove Hills, so I spend most nights watching TV with my parents or forcing Carson to hang out with me."

"You don't have any local friends?"

"Just Carson. And the other people who work at the diner, whenever they invite me out to a trivia night at the bar or something. I mostly like to stay inside and read. Or if I'm feeling really adventurous, I'll surf the Great Wide Web."

"How dangerous," June says, playing along. "You dare to dabble in the dot-com?"

"In moderation, of course. My screen time is a comfortable eight hours a day."

"That's it? Personally, I strive for anywhere between twelve and fourteen."

"Wow," I say, biting back my laugh. "What *can't* you do?"

"Get you to go out with me," she says without breaking.

Now I'm really on fire, every limb sparking as I thrash about in my seat. "Oh, I . . ." I fumble for something to say. An explanation. Anything. "Like I said, it wouldn't be a good idea," I remind her again, echoing what I told her that day in the diner.

"I'm kidding. I know we're only friends," she says with an easy smile, no trace of the nerves that are threatening to turn me feral. "But I *have* learned some new things about you today."

"Like what?" She's moved us toward the danger zone and right back out of it with such fluidity that I'm actually a little dizzy.

"For one, you're courageous," she says.

"Courageous," I echo, caught between laughter and confusion. "No one has ever said that about me."

"They should," she insists. "You said nothing to me about being afraid of the plane taking off. You just sat there and handled your business on your own."

"That was more an act of embarrassment than of bravery, I promise you."

"It's not embarrassing to know how to hold yourself through something hard."

What is it? I want to ask, but I'm afraid the answer won't be one I like. Because it's probably sad. That's the real truth.

"You lost your luggage and you didn't raise your voice at that employee," she continues. "That's a feat. You just got the solutions from her and kept it moving. You walked into an apartment that smelled like garbage and pitched going to this bar to save it all. You admitted to writing my breakup text while I was embarrassing myself by crying over it. And you have possibly the strangest side job I have ever heard of. But I like that about you. You're just yourself, no matter what."

"Thank you," I say. It's a compliment tornado, and I'm swept up in it, blown away by how kind her lens is on me. "The cooks at Rita's will be thrilled to hear that the radical honesty they've taught me has led somewhere positive."

"I hope you didn't show them the perfume I made you," June says. "I got home and sprayed the rest of the sample. It smelled terrible."

"It was . . . interesting," I gamble.

"I don't know what happened!" She lights up in defense of herself. It's the kind of impassioned reaction that makes me want to stoke the fire, see her come alive even more. "I promise you I'm good at what I do!"

"I know you are," I assure her. "You always smell like a dream. And you were very courageous today too."

"Now, now. Don't you start trying to turn this back around on me. Take the compliments, Tatum."

I salute her. "Consider them received."

"I think something was rotten in the batch," she says. "I don't know how else to describe it. Or I couldn't smell it anymore after working on it for so long. I've made individual perfumes before, and this has never happened. I promise I've got about a dozen people who can tell you I've made them something unforgettable."

A dozen? That's good. I can tell my parents that when I see them again. How special can I be if she's done this a dozen other times?

"What do you like so much about perfumes?" I ask, hand on my cheek. It's fun to watch her like this, hearing her speak with such liveliness about the details of her life that always remained a little hazy during our diner chats.

"I like to smell good," she says.

"You always do," I remind her again.

She fights a grin as she continues. "Scent ties so strongly to memory. Like how Eleanor's apartment smelled. We're never going to forget that. If we're ever, I don't know, thrown into a dumpster, we will instantly remember walking into Eleanor's apartment tonight, and exactly how we felt when that happened. Which isn't something we want to remember, but we will. Because you don't forget the way things smell. I love that through my perfumes, I can play a role in someone else's life without actively having to participate. That's an ideal scenario for me."

"That's how I feel about ghostwriting," I tell her. "Or I used to, before I broke you and your girlfriend up." She laughs, and it fills me with relief. Maybe I didn't completely ruin her impression of me with my strange little side gig. "I'm good with words, and I know how to use them to help other people. As for myself? I think the less I say, the better off I am. I tend to talk myself into corners."

"I don't know, you're doing pretty all right." She steals a long glance.

"By the way, the ghostwriting isn't really one of my jobs," I tell her, needing, for some reason, to make that clear. "I don't get paid for it."

"So you spend all this time writing other people's messages . . . for free?"

"Yeah," I say with a weak smile. "I love to write, but I'm afraid of what people would think if I *actually* did it. You know? This way, I get all of the reward with none of the risk. It's perfect."

"You *are* actually doing it, though. It doesn't make it any less of a job just because you've decided not to profit from it."

This challenge is strangely thrilling, like she's pressing on parts of me that everyone else instinctually knows to leave alone, and instead of feeling defensive about it, I feel invigorated by her boldness. Either she doesn't yet know me enough to see the caution tape I've placed over these things, or she does, and she knows that it's just that—a flimsy barrier, meant to scare people away from everything I consider difficult.

"Why aren't you good at being alone?" I ask, attempting to challenge her right back.

June crosses both her arms and legs in the same moment, as closed off as one person can be. The flow had been effortless between us. Even playful. But the walls we'd shed go right back up, maybe even higher than before.

"I'm sorry. I didn't mean to make you uncomfortable," I say.

"It's okay," she tells me, still stiff.

It doesn't seem to be okay, but I don't have enough time to come up with a way to solve it before she's talking again.

"I wish I had a real answer," she says. "Sometimes I panic when there are too many people around me. I can't block out my awareness of their presence. It's like seven hundred different radio stations all playing at once, and I drown in the noise. It helps when I'm out with someone who knows me. Who can do things for me, I guess. I don't know. That's how Vanessa used to explain it when we'd fight. She'd say I rely too much on other people to get me out of spots I can't get out of myself, basically."

"That's fucked," I tell her. "Everybody needs help."

"Yeah, well, I'm just, I guess I'm always dating someone. Always doing something with someone else. Even this. I let you come with me on this trip, and like we just said, we don't even really know each other. But I was too afraid to come somewhere as daunting as New York all by myself. It's exactly what Vanessa said about me. I'll use anyone if I'm desperate enough. I want Vanessa to know I can be independent. It bothers me that she's right. And I want to prove it to myself too. That I can be alone."

"If she felt okay sending off my completely insensitive text message to break up with you, Vanessa's not the kind of person who really cared about you in the right way anyway," I say.

"I'd tell you I can't believe she did that, but honestly, I can," June says. "She told me once she'd let someone else brush her teeth for her if it meant she didn't have to walk to the bathroom one more time than necessary. It wouldn't have mattered what you said. She just wanted someone else to do the thinking for her."

"And she's the one who says you rely on other people too much?"

June cocks her head as she takes a sip of her drink. "It would blow her mind to know I made it here after all. I bet she thinks I'm in my bed crying. But no, I'm in *New York City*. And I didn't even get overwhelmed at the airport like I thought I might."

"She doesn't have to know I'm here," I offer.

"What do you mean?"

"We could make her think you're alone," I say. "She still follows you online I assume?"

"Of course. She wouldn't waste the time clicking 'Unfollow.' Maybe you could do it for her."

We share a smile. "Let's create the illusion of a solo trip."

"How do we do that?"

"Oh, June," I say, returning to a familiar shade of Waitress Tatum—the one who reminds her to put on a coat when it's cold. Who brings an extra lemon slice for the last dregs of her tea, knowing she wants every last sip to be tart.

Everything she'd dislodged earlier, telling me my writing is a real job, pushing the buttons about her asking me out, gets stitched right back up again, neat and contained.

"The internet is designed for this kind of con," I continue. "If we take pictures of you alone everywhere we go, they can look like selfies you've set up yourself. Caption them all about your newfound independence. Shit like 'Nothing tastes as good as having a slice of New York pizza all to myself.' I'll orchestrate the whole thing from the sidelines, never to be seen. I'm very good at that. It's basically one long variation of my other . . . job." I give her a little look here, a concession. "We write your own breakup response through the internet. We will make her think that not only do you not need her or miss her, she's completely misread you. You can be alone just fine."

"But I'll still be doing everything she said I always do," June says. "I'll be using you to help me."

"We can't change that part, now, can we? I'm not about to fly home after one day. I'm here with you in New York regardless, and I might as well be useful in the process, seeing as I'm the one who got us into this mess in the first place. What's important is *Vanessa* doesn't know I'm here. We have to take our wins where we can, don't we?"

"Okay," June agrees. "It's a little unhinged, but I can get behind it. I'm always up for some chaotic good. What can I do to pay you back, though? If you're going to do all of this for me, there has to be something I can help you with too. And don't say increasing your screen time."

"I'll have to think about it," I say. She has, rather unfortunately, read me like a book with the screen time joke. That's exactly what I would've said if she didn't call me on it first.

"You better." She touches my arm, and my whole body heats at the gesture. "I'm serious."

Looking at her, it's clear that she is, in fact, very serious. She's giving me the same focused intensity I recognize from her days in the back corner at Rita's, working on her laptop. She expects me to have an answer for her.

"I'm gonna get us another drink." She slides off her stool to head over to the bar.

Watching her lean over the counter, smiling lazily at the bartender as she orders, I give myself permission to imagine, for only a moment, what it was like to be Vanessa—the person June used to come home to at the end of each night.

She must have been excited. Proud, even. Watching June from a distance must have given her constant butterflies. How could she ever say all those cruel things about her?

A familiar sourness starts to churn up in my gut.

In the end, she still broke up with June. She still hurt her.

I can spot the problems in someone else's relationship without even needing to squint. June and Vanessa probably didn't last because they were never very deep with each other in a real way. No truly meaningful relationship could ever be ended by a stranger ghostwriting a breakup text. If Vanessa's view of June was that shallowly cruel, she'd never really seen her in the first place.

That's not my problem. I know June likes Rita's because it's small and quiet. More than once she's left when we've gotten a little busier than usual, and it doesn't surprise me to have her contextualize that as anxiety. As for the being-alone thing, she started dating Vanessa not long after she asked me out, so that's not new information either. If I think it through even further, she probably likes to look put together so she feels put together, doing whatever she can not to give space to all the things that make her overwhelmed. Smells comfort her because she can transport herself to a happier memory through a single spritz of perfume.

I have always seen her, and I've never once been put off by what she views as her weaknesses.

What I still don't understand, after twenty-nine whole years on earth, is why that isn't enough. Because my dad knows my mom. She knows him back. They've always been patient with each other's struggles, sensitive to their individual wants and dreams. But no amount of couples counseling or date nights have eliminated the simmering bitterness between them—Mom resentful that Dad cheated, Dad resentful that Mom hasn't let it go. Everything they've done on paper looks like a perfect recipe for repairing a broken relationship. And still.

It must be possible. I've filled my bookshelves with countless stories that tell me it is. Back in Trove Hills, I'd convinced myself I didn't need to experience it for myself to believe it exists. Some people never find romance—some people don't even want it— and that's okay.

Being here, watching June at the bar, I know I *do* want it. Into my bones I know. I need it, really. I need to know I'm more than my history, more than the oldest daughter carrying the family on her shoulders, more than the one who can't handle conflict. Who can't do hard things.

I need to know I can break their cycle. Break my own cycle too.

So while June is learning how to be independent, this trip has to be something very different for me. This is the safest place to experiment, because I'm so far from home that whatever I do here won't reach Trove Hills. I will dedicate this time to the hardest thing *I've* ever done—learning how to open myself up to real romance.

With anyone *but* June.

10

Eleanor

I wake up alone.

The pang in my gut confuses me. This is a relief. Carson is gone, and I can reset the start of this trip.

Except when I enter the kitchen, they're leaning over the stovetop. They have on last night's tank with an apron tied around their waist and a dish towel slung over their shoulder. Music plays from their phone, and they hum along as they grind salt over a sizzling pan.

My heart makes an unapologetic leap as I think, with relief, *There you are.*

I clear my throat to announce my presence, and they look back, smiling with the kind of warmth that drizzles into the pit of my stomach. Excited to see . . . me?

"Did you sleep well? I'm making eggs." They glance down at the pan in dawning horror. "Shit, do you eat eggs?"

"I eat eggs," I say.

Their smile returns. "That's good, because I have no alternative. What about bacon?"

"I don't eat meat."

"That's also good, because neither do I."

"You were going to make me bacon even though you don't eat it yourself? How was that going to work?"

"I've done it before. It's not hard. I put it in the pan until it looks crispy, and then I hope everyone is too polite to mention the quality of it."

"I'd tell you if it was bad," I say.

"Should I take it as a compliment that I received no critiques from you last night?"

The phrase *last night* usually precedes a departure. *Last night was fun*, or *We should do last night again sometime soon*. If Carson's whole game is confusing me with their forward charms, I refuse to lose.

"You performed well," I say.

"*I performed well?*" They bite back a laugh as they push a spatula through the eggs. "I'm gonna put that on my résumé."

"Under special skills? Experience? Am I listed as a reference?"

"You're asking all the right questions, Eleanor, as usual."

This is the first time they've said my name. It crossed my mind when they asked last night who I was, and again when I wished to hear them call it out, breathless and low as I worked them up. I wanted to know how *Eleanor* would sound in their voice. If I'd like hearing it. And I do. It's textured but soft, settling around me just right. Like velvet being brushed flat.

"How'd you learn my name?"

They push Tatum's welcome note across the counter. "My sister lied to you many times in this, by the way. I'm not pure trouble, for one. I'm just impulsive. Somehow I'm not the one in the family who flew to New York on a day's notice, though. And the banana cream pie isn't the best thing at Rita's. It's the apple crumble." They look at me with my arms wrapped around myself, and they sigh. "Let me fix the thermostat for you. Tatum is obsessed with keeping this place freezing."

No hookup of mine has ever stuck around to whip up breakfast, and they've never cared about my temperature preferences either. I despise myself for being impressed by it. I've gotten very good at cutting my desires off at the source, refusing to allow myself to want things I can't keep. That way it's not some sad show when I'm incapable of managing my own disappointment. Look what happened with me and Anthony Teller. I never even liked him that much, and I still managed to lose my job over him.

"I promise you I can handle temperature-related issues all by myself," I tell Carson, charging ahead to beat them to the thermostat.

They let me adjust it on my own, staying quiet as I turn the dial up. They continue to say nothing as we walk back to the kitchen. The nothing becomes its own conversation. They aren't going to challenge me on this, because I will challenge them right back. Even in this game, they have made the better move. They are giving me my space.

"Is this the part where you ask me about why your sister's in New York?" I offer, unable to withstand any more of this understanding quiet.

"I know why she's there." Toast pops up, and they plate it beside the eggs they've prepared. "She's avoiding our Ward family reunion. The one that starts today." My face must betray my surprise, because Carson smiles again, forever adept at getting the upper hand. "She didn't tell you that, did she?"

"This entire plan was completely last-minute and thoroughly under-researched," I say, trying to justify my own ignorance. "If I told you I don't know your sister at all, it would be an understatement. I hadn't even seen a picture of her until I arrived here.

I didn't even plan this with her. I planned it with June Lightbell, if you know who she is." Carson nods, not as surprised as I'd expect by any of this. "I'm alarmed by your lack of reaction."

"Tatum doesn't do well with change," they tell me.

"And that's why she flew to New York on one day's notice?"

"It's complicated. We're meeting our secret brother we just learned about." It reads like a joke, but there's no punch line. Carson prepares their own plate, then sidles up next to me at the island. "Ketchup? Hot sauce?"

"Butter."

"Tatum freaked out. Not sure how that resulted in your living in her cottage, but it's probably the happiest accident of this whole shit show." They hand me a butter dish. "I'm meeting our secret brother in an hour. My parents are throwing a little get-together in the front yard."

"The reunion is happening *here*?"

"Today's activities, yeah," they confirm.

"How many activities are there?"

"Oh, this whole thing is a spectacle. My dad is overcompensating in his usual way. This cottage is actually a past overcompensation of his. It's his pattern. I will say, in his defense, that this reunion is kind of sweet, in a roundabout way. Gotta make up for all the lost time with my bro, I guess."

I set down my fork. The last thing I want is to be involved in yet another person's personal drama. Even when I fled New York to a random Illinois town I've never heard of in my life, the energy followed me here.

"I should go," I say, like I'm the one staying over at their house. I guess technically, I am. "This was a mistake."

Carson shoots up, blocking my path to the stairs. "Hold on a second. You didn't eat my eggs. I want to know if they're good or not. I consider myself kind of a breakfast-food expert, but it's entirely possible people have been lying to me my whole life, and you're the only one who will be brave enough to tell me if they're bad. And two, even though I've managed to learn your name, I still don't know nearly enough about you."

My cheeks heat again. It's bad, this feeling. If Carson thinks they're the impulsive one, they're right, they *don't* know me yet. They didn't swap lives with a complete stranger on twenty-four hours' notice. They should not be stoking my interest in them by being curious about me. And I shouldn't be wondering about how they feel about the secret brother. Or who taught them to be this caring. Carson *is* trouble, just not in the way I expected.

Carson is the worst kind of trouble that exists—good trouble.

There was a time when I thought my situation with Anthony Teller was good trouble too. It's considered bad form to sleep with a producer when you're a press agent, yet Anthony and I managed to pull it off for over a year without incident. Up until learning about Kelsey, I considered our secret meetups to be a badge of honor. I knew how to bend the rules without making them break.

In the end, good trouble was my undoing.

"Besides," Carson continues, "I was hoping to spend a little more time with you. It'll be a nice distraction from the week ahead."

Their words help straighten out my internal spiral. It's not Carson who has gotten the wrong impression of this. It's *me*. I was reading this whole situation between us as something sincere, and it's not. Carson is trying to lock in a hookup buddy to pass the time during their family ordeal.

If there is one thing I know how to do in this life, it is how to be someone's hookup. That's where I thrive. Sometimes you need a body to keep you warm at night. It isn't even personal. It's primal.

"Are you dating anyone?" I ask, thinking again of Anthony.

"No," Carson says with obvious offense. "I would never sleep with you if I was in a relationship."

"That's what a lot of people say."

"If you keep staying here, my entire family will be around. You can stop any one of them throughout the week and ask if Carson Ward has a partner. They'll probably laugh in your face, but if that's what it takes to get you to spend more time with me, then so be it."

Another pang hits me, square in the chest. My brain and body are having their classic disconnect. Why does it make me ache that I'm not the first person to touch Carson's tattoos or probably even to wash them in the shower? After all, they're not the first person to get down on their knees in front of me before they've even learned my name. Maybe they're the best so far, but there's still plenty of time to find other contenders.

"Fine. I'll stay," I say.

They grin with a dangerous amount of relief in return. But now I know. That's just how they are.

"Now, move. I need to find out whether or not you know how to cook," I say.

Carson stops me. Plants one firm kiss on my lips. "Thank you."

For what? I almost ask, nearly choking on my own butterflies, but I think better of it.

It's better not to know.

11

Tatum

June stands behind me, mouth agape. "What did you do?"

"I couldn't sleep," I tell her, running the broom under the kitchen cabinets one final time.

"It looks incredible."

"I figured instead of us finding a new place to stay, it would be easier to stick around Eleanor's place. So I made her place livable."

June rubs her eyes in disbelief. I've been in such a flow state I haven't stopped to take it in myself. It's incredible in here without all the boxes and junk. There is an airiness to the living space that emphasizes how high off the ground we are. It feels like the exact kind of place everyone dreams about before visiting here.

"How much money does Eleanor have?" I ask. "This place has gotta be worth millions. Does she own it or just rent? How does it even work?"

June doesn't pretend to be offended by the question about money or to find it improper. Instead she gets out her phone and starts researching. The greenest of green flags, in my opinion. I love when people are just as curious as I am.

"She works in Broadway PR," June tells me. "That's not a luxury

New York apartment salary, though. And these are condos, so, yeah, she owns." She even starts walking around, examining the bookshelves and displays for some kind of clue as to how Eleanor has made all of this possible. "Are there any pictures around here?"

"For how much stuff was crammed into this place last night, very little of it was personal. The actual decor is almost sterile, actually. Like this is a show unit."

"She spends a lot of money on my perfumes," June tells me. "Though come to think of it, more than once she's messaged me to say she's lost a bottle and needs to order a replacement. She pays for it, by the way. She's not just asking for handouts. But it's happened enough that I've wondered how it's possible. Now I see." She gestures to the space, to the echo of what was there last night that I've spent the entire night erasing. "Her social media doesn't have a ton to go off of. Pictures of her cats and some shows she's worked on. And her LinkedIn just has the PR stuff."

"Google her full name plus New York," I say as I bust down the last of the living room boxes.

June is quiet for a while as she skims. When her first search doesn't turn up anything beyond what we already know, she starts taking information from Eleanor's social media, adding various names and places to her search until she gets a result that makes her let out a low humph. "I think her parents died in an accident."

She shows me an article from over a decade ago detailing a multivehicle crash with an eighteen-wheeler in Pennsylvania, and follow-up articles discussing the huge settlement that went to the affected families.

"Two of the victims named here are listed as a married couple, and I searched their name plus Eleanor and found their obituary, where she's listed as a student and communications major at NYU. It has to be her."

It's a grief too big to comprehend, so horrific that I have to stop myself from shutting out the tragedy of it. Instead, I think of my own family. The very family I've just run from, fleeing here to escape their drama. It suddenly seems so childish of me that I can hardly face my own shame.

"Fuck," I say. "That's horrific." All the mess Eleanor left behind offends me less than it did upon arrival. "Wish we knew this when we got here yesterday, so I didn't spend all night wishing her the worst."

"Seriously." June looks around at all I've accomplished. "Do you think she'll be sad to lose all her junk? I know some people see it as a comfort."

"I'll take the blame, I promise," I say. "I'll curate a special re-creation if she wants. I just need to order roughly sixty-seven different things on Amazon Prime and enjoy some food from every restaurant within a thirty-mile radius." Salt makes an appearance, meowing at my pile of deflated boxes. "I think the cats are the ones more likely to lodge the complaints, though."

June walks over and pets Salt on the head. "We're very sorry," she tells the cat. "We'll get you new boxes." Then she looks up at me, really looks, and it roots me in the moment.

What does she see when she does that? Does it make her stomach fizz the same way it does mine?

Do friends look at each other this way?

"I can help you take these last ones to the trash," she says.

"Oh, I got it," I say.

"Please. It's the least I can do." She follows me down the hall, on the path I've traveled countless times throughout the night and into the morning, headed toward the trash room, which now overflows with Eleanor's mess. "You're a very quiet cleaner."

"I think you're just a deep sleeper," I tell her.

"I must be, because it wasn't even the sleeping pill this time."

"I was banging shit around all night. I cleaned the office too, since it's my bedroom for the time being. I thought for sure you heard me in there. The walls aren't very thick for how expensive this place must be."

June's laugh echoes through the empty hall. It's musical and thrilling, and louder than both of us expect. We look at each other in a private, conspiratorial way, like two children disobeying their own bedtime.

"What are you two doing?"

June and I turn, surprised by the husky voice behind us. An older woman stands in the doorway of the unit across from Eleanor's. Weirdly, she looks familiar. She's got light brown skin and long white hair, and she's wearing a blue-and-green caftan with an incredible floral pattern on it. If I do know her, I have no idea why or how.

"I'm sorry," I say. "We didn't mean to disturb you."

The woman seems mad. Or she's just a fan of scowling. We weren't being *that* disruptive. Then again, I've been at this for hours. It's possible she heard me tell June I've been knocking shit around all night.

"I've never seen you here before," the woman says, not acknowledging my apology. She has her arms folded across her chest and one eyebrow arched up.

"We're friends of Eleanor," June offers.

"Eleanor doesn't have any friends," the woman responds, more skeptical than ever. "At least none that come by during business hours."

The mental picture I'm painting of Eleanor becomes more detailed by the moment. She's made her money through devastating means. She holds on to everything unimportant but she keeps nothing substantial. She has no real friends.

"That's our Ellie," I say, feeling compelled to spin a friendship story with Eleanor, if only so this neighbor will soften up. "She's a night owl. A very messy night owl."

"She asked us to cat sit for her while she's out of town," June adds.

The woman continues to examine us, offering no clues to her feelings about anything we've said. Just when I can't take it any longer, ready to keep walking, trying to match the baffling energy she's projecting, she says, "Come in."

"To your apartment?" I stumble out, confused.

The woman does not dignify me with an answer. June and I exchange a single look, deciding to go for it. It fills me with another swell of gratitude. June might not do well in crowds, but she doesn't shy away from knowing more about other people one-on-one. She's curious like I am. And the knowledge that she's doing it with me really does make me braver.

Maybe it makes her braver too.

We drop the last box off in the trash room, and we walk into the apartment across from Eleanor's.

Inside, it's a mirror of Eleanor's unit, with some minor layout differences. There's also a sense of personality in here that Eleanor's palace of beige lacks. The living room has an amazing dark orange wallpaper, patterned with white chrysanthemums, complimented by furniture in the exact shade of rich green I love the most. The glimpse of the half bath next to the entrance reveals a moody floral. It's the kind of carefully composed style that comes through patience and time. Each piece in here feels specific and right. I steal a glance down the hallway that must lead to the two bedrooms, just like Eleanor's unit, and notice movie posters lining the space between doors. Trying not to be too obvious, I attempt to catalog the titles to look them up later. *Twilight on*

Clarke Street. The Bridge. There are more, names I can't make out from where I'm standing, but there's a theme among them. They are all movies from the seventies and eighties.

Then it hits me.

This is Dawn Flores.

She was an actor in that time, best known for her work in horror films and dramas. One close-up of her melancholic face always set the mood better than any other movie magic could. There was a bone-deep sadness embedded in her downturned expression that never felt resolved, no matter the story's actual ending. Nowadays, she's one of those figures that appears in every "Where Are They Now?" listicle, with the answer being, "Nobody knows for sure."

All this time, it seems as though she's been right here.

Starstruck, I blurt out my thoughts, unable to contain them now that I've figured out whose home I've just entered. I've never been around a famous person. "When I was in high school, my friends and I got really obsessed with watching old movies because we wanted people to think we were sophisticated. You were in so many of them. I still watch *Twilight on Clarke Street* every fall."

"Are you calling me old?" Dawn asks, ignoring the rest of what I've said. That melancholy she's known for seems to have hardened into something rougher around the edges.

"No," I correct, hurrying. "I'm just . . . I don't know. I'm shocked, I guess. I love your movies. I didn't know you were—"

"Still alive?" she questions.

"No. I just didn't know you were *here*," I try, floundering.

"Everyone knows I'm here. They just don't care," Dawn says. She's *very* dry, I'm gathering, and I'm trying to adjust to her demeanor. "And I *am* old."

"You've aged beautifully," June chimes in. "Your apartment is incredible too."

"It's amazing," I say. "I love this wallpaper. Did you get—"

"Now that you're inside my home, it's only right that you stop lying to me," Dawn says, cutting off our train of compliments, which surely would have chugged on all morning if we were left to our own devices.

"You're right," June says. "We don't know Eleanor at all. We've swapped places with her for the time being. I have a meeting here this week, and she needed a place to go, so she went to stay where we're from."

"Illinois," I interject, receiving no reaction.

"I make Eleanor her perfumes," June explains. "That's how we know each other."

"That's why you smell so good," Dawn says to June.

"Thank you. I noticed your floral right away. Is it Penhaligon's Bluebell?"

June must be correct, because Dawn actually backs up a step, bewildered. "How the hell did you know that?"

"I have a good nose."

This gets Dawn to laugh, which strikes me as no small feat considering how rough she's been up to this point.

"Princess Diana?" June asks.

"Princess Diana," Dawn confirms.

Whatever *that* means.

Dawn has warmed to June much faster than she's warmed to me, which is to say she hasn't warmed to me at all, and she obviously feels different about June. Which I can relate to. June's presence is on par with the smell of cookies or the first bite of snow around Christmas. That's why she's a universal choice for favorite regular at any place she frequents.

"The problem is, we've never been here before," I offer.

"And you think I can do something about that?" Dawn asks.

It comes off as mean, but maybe it isn't. Maybe I've just gotten so comfortable in the shell of Trove Hills, always seeing the same people, always doing the same things. Talking to new people, experiencing a different place, is a shock to my senses.

"I think you can," I reply, trying on Dawn's style of delivery. Direct. Unfussed. "If you'd like," I add, softening. "We don't know where we are or what's good around here. Or anywhere. We could use our phones, but we don't even know where to start."

"I've taken the train into Chicago plenty of times, but it's different here," June tells her.

"It is," Dawn says. "But we don't need to start with that. We can start with walking around. Did you bring good shoes?"

"Yes," I say, even though I don't have my luggage yet.

"Get dressed. Meet me out in the hall at eleven. I'll show you what you need to know. But don't get me wrong. This is only one very small piece of one very big place. It's like showing you a single corner of a giant painting. Don't expect to understand it all."

"We won't," we say in unison.

12

Eleanor

Tucked away from the road, invisible to passing cars, this cottage is its own oasis. Until it comes time to leave. The only way out is down the long driveway, which leads me past the main house. In the front yard, there are folding tables set out under a tent. At least five people I don't recognize mill about, putting down colorful plastic tablecloths.

I'm used to walking past countless people without acknowledgment. That's part of the beauty of New York. You can go for miles without speaking a word to anyone. People might call out to you unprompted, but you can ignore them, and no one thinks it's strange for you to do so. Or you can stop and talk with a stranger for an hour, if the moment is right. The important thing is, it's a *choice*.

Here, one stray neighbor sees me booking it down this driveway, and my presence inspires an instant, enthusiastic comment from him.

"Hey there!" It's an older white man wearing a blue polo tucked into khaki shorts. He stands on his front step, not even pretending to do anything other than watch me.

I offer him a short wave and keep walking.

"Are you one of the Wards?" he asks. "We're planning on stopping by later today."

"Nope," I say. "Have a good one."

He heads toward the fence that divides the Wards' house from his own. "You're not here for the reunion?"

I'm here *because* of the reunion, but that's a technicality that doesn't even make sense to me. I stop and do my best to smile. I don't need a mirror to know it's coming off as more of a grimace.

"She's with me."

I turn, and there is Carson, walking up to meet me at the fence. There is that feeling again too. The *there you are*. They've put on a black short-sleeved button-down, left open to reveal their white undershirt, with a pair of light jeans belted at the hips.

Their presence sets me at ease, which then makes me nervous in a whole new way. They should not *set me at ease*. What am I, a fucking mattress commercial?

The neighbor accepts Carson's answer with a nod, walking back to his front door without further comment.

"How did you do that?" I ask, incredulous. "That guy was two sentences away from hopping the fence and settling in for a tell-all interview."

"That's why I rescued you," Carson says. "I'm very brave like that."

I fight off a laugh and start moving again.

"Where are you heading?" they ask.

"Rita's Diner," I say without breaking stride. "I've spent two days without working. There is way too much free space in my brain. I read an entire book last night. Very dangerous behavior. I need to crowd up my mind with tasks. Like applying for a new job."

"Rita's is almost a mile from here."

"Yeah. And there are plenty of sidewalks," I say.

"You know, this is a town where people live, not a town where strangers take a vacation. We don't walk places."

"Trove Hills is anti-walking? Interesting. I'll be sure to spread the word far and wide when I get back to New York. Heading to Trove Hills? Plan to sit your ass down and stay put."

"You're very cute when you do that."

My face flushes. "What, walk? And here I thought it was illegal. Like dancing in the town in *Footloose*."

"Carson, honey, will you help me set out the cheese board? I know you like that kind of stuff." A woman I assume must be Mrs. Ward walks up to us.

"Hello there," she says, stretching her hand out in greeting. "I'm Jeannette."

"Eleanor," I respond, grabbing her hand. Her shake is as strong as they come. In the silence that follows, a question is implied. *Who are you?*

"She's here with me," Carson announces for the second time in two minutes. Only now it's to their mother, not a neighbor with a somewhat sinister curiosity in my presence.

Great. My one-night stand, pure spontaneous fun, *who even are you anyway?* hookup has now introduced me to their mother.

Sigh.

"I didn't realize you had any new . . . friends," their mother says. It's awkward enough to make me squeeze my lips together, wishing for a way out. It does, however, confirm that Carson has no known partner.

"We've all got some fun surprises up our sleeves this week, don't we?" Carson asks.

"I'm actually about to head out," I say, wondering if I should acknowledge my presence in the cottage. Is it rude to leave without sharing that I am a guest in their backyard? Should I tell her I'll be back? Should I sneak around for days on end?

There isn't time to figure out a response, because if it's possible, someone whose presence is even more awkward than my own arrives.

The secret brother.

"*He's here*," Carson whispers. It's more for their mother than for me. Or maybe it's because it needs to be said. There are so few chances in life to lean into the theatricality of a moment, and Carson has correctly identified this as an appropriate opportunity for dramatic flair.

It's strange how even from thirty feet away, I can tell this man belongs to this family. The curly brown hair. The set of his jaw. Even the way he squints into the sun. He looks right out of one of the pictures along the stairway.

As the secret brother walks over to the front lawn, I wonder what it would be like to be him, having this many people care about me. It's a thought that strikes me as sad, detached from my own ability to feel it. I've never shown up somewhere and recalibrated an entire situation with only my presence. Come to think of it, I could make things awkward for Anthony Teller if I ever went to another one of the shows he produces. But I've certainly never filled an entire extended family with breathless anticipation.

I am the only child of two only children. My parents are long gone, and so are my grandparents. There is no family to wait for me at all.

"Hi," the brother says when he finally reaches us. "I'm Ben." He walks right up to Carson, maybe recognizing them from a photo, or feeling drawn in by Carson's easy charm.

Carson doesn't hesitate to pull Ben into a hug in return, and my eyes well with tears. It's one of the strangest things about me, the way I get overwhelmed with secondhand pride while watching someone else's life change. Every year, my coworkers laugh at me during the Tony Awards, because I weep for each winner like they're a close personal friend. It's one vulnerability I can't seem to school out of myself, no matter how much I try.

"Brother Ben," Carson says, releasing their brother to get a good look at him. Up close, I can see even more of an echo in their mannerisms—the way they both stand tall in their bodies while somehow managing to not look rigid or intimidating either. How they're both smiling out of the side of their mouth, maybe out of nerves.

"Brother Ben? Are you Catholic?" Ben asks.

"Nah," Carson responds, laughing. "Just never had a brother before. Felt like you deserved to wear the honor with a title."

The redheaded woman who arrived with Ben inserts herself into the conversation. "Brother Ben," she echoes. "BB for short."

Carson grins, pleased. "Exactly. You get it."

"I'm Dee," she tells them, stretching out her hand. "BB's wife."

"BB and DD," Carson responds, shaking it.

"What's DD stand for?" I ask, somehow involved enough to be curious.

"I don't know," Carson says. "I just say shit sometimes."

Next thing I know, Brother Ben and his wife are introducing themselves to me. *Me.* I am now meeting the secret brother. We shake hands, and bless Brother Ben for not asking who I am to Carson, or even to him. For all he knows, I am also a member of his new family.

Another one of my long-buried memories surfaces. I'd hidden it so deep I can't recall the last time I've come close to reflecting on it, and now here it is, reemerging as fresh as the day I first lived it. One night, not long after my parents died, I couldn't sleep. I was alone in the small apartment I used to have before the lawsuit. My brain wouldn't shut off, no matter what I did. After hours of tossing and turning, I finally found a way to lull myself to sleep—picturing my front door opening and guests pouring in to see me.

At first I imagined my parents returning. It didn't take long for that to become too morbid, reanimating them for my own little coping mechanism. I shifted to people I don't know, an imagined depiction of the rest of my family, all of them having recently learned of my existence. They carried in trays of food and presents—all little things they knew I'd need as a fellow Chapman. They wrapped me in their arms and pulled me into the fold. They didn't need to know my strengths or test my worthiness. They just wanted to shelter me through the worst moment of my life, loving me without reason.

In real life, this kind of moment is far less exciting. In fact, it seems to be an exercise in anxiety management. Ben doesn't know any of the people who have begun to arrive right behind him, at least four car doors opening at almost the exact same time along the street. People climb out carrying trays of food and drinks, waving at one another. He has no idea if they are his aunts, uncles, cousins. But they *all* know him. They pause and stare with jaws hanging open.

"He looks just like Andrew," one of them says, loud enough for us to hear.

"God, he really does," another confirms.

Ben's existence has sent a ripple through the whole family. Even Carson loses track of me to watch him.

I have a wide-open path to escape.

Walking the remaining bit of the Wards' driveway with my head down, it's easy enough to close myself off to the rest of the world. I am alone here, just as I always have been.

I am not a part of anyone's family.

13

Tatum

Dawn sounds wistful as she takes us through the Upper West Side of Manhattan, telling us about what's survived, what's been replaced, and what's been forgotten. She even points out cinematic landmarks, indulging us in some production gossip she's accumulated about the numerous TV shows and movies that have been filmed in this area. She knows so much it's like being in the presence of a personal Wikipedia engine. There is no area of show business she doesn't understand, including theater, though she tells us she hasn't been to a Broadway show in well over fifteen years.

"Where *have* you been all this time?" I ask her. "I googled your name when we were getting ready, and you haven't been in anything since 1987."

She stops, her serene expression growing serious. "What's your name? First and last."

"Tatum Ward," I stumble out.

She gets out her phone and speaks my name to her Siri. Her phone screen fills with massive text, set to the largest font size possible, as she combs through search results. "Do you work at Rita's Diner?"

"She does," June answers on my behalf.

"And you've lived at 143 Mandy Lane for the last, oh, twenty-nine years?"

"I deserve this," I say, understanding what she's doing. "Yes. I've lived there my whole life. Except when I went to college. But that doesn't really count."

June leans over, peering at Dawn's phone. "Is her address actually on there?"

"You should get that taken down," Dawn tells me. "You never know what someone can do with that information."

"Most of the websites have an opt-out feature. It's worth the extra time it takes to do it," June adds.

"Well, I'll still live on 143 Mandy Lane," I say, confused as to how I've become the target of an online security survey when I was just trying to ask the once-famous actress why she hasn't worked in decades. "Probably until I die. So if they know, they know."

Dawn points to a bagel shop. "Stay here," she tells us. "I'll be right back."

June and I wait on the sidewalk near the entrance, observing Dawn in her natural element. She has a long, *almost* sullen face, so distinct I can't believe I forgot who she was for even a minute. There's a uniqueness to her appearance that's matched by her personality and tastes. You see her and you just know she's *someone*. Even though she hasn't acted in well over thirty years, she holds the spotlight of the bagel shop the same way she used to captivate the screen.

"You think you'll live in your parents' house until you die?" June asks me, pulling my attention off Dawn and over to her. She's leaned up against the side of the building, thin black sunglasses perched just above the tip of her nose. She's wearing the sheer paisley turtleneck tank and overall dress she joked about loaning me, which I was moments away from actually having to wear, until the courier arrived with my luggage. And thank god. I never could have pulled it off. It's impossible how cool she looks, how *right*, like she was always meant to be lounging against brick walls in New York City as she asks people deep questions.

"When you put it like that . . ." I kick up a rock near the curb, trying to school my defenses. She's just asking because she's curious. It's not an accusation.

"Is that what you really want?" she follows up. Okay, maybe it *is* an accusation. Or at the very least, a request for me to expect more from my life.

If we were at Rita's, I'd tell her yes, it's exactly what I want.

Being here, free from the pressure of my family and the expectation I've created for myself to keep everything running, my deepest desires are starting to stretch out. Maybe it's the size of the buildings. Or maybe it's the knowledge that one single block here is probably filled with more people than all of Trove Hills combined. There is just *so* much room. Not only for my want for romance, but all my wants in general.

It's nice to take these wants for a walk, envisioning myself as the kind of person who could live here too, running down the subway steps to catch the train on my way to a coffee shop to write. Carrying a new fig plant up the four flights of my walk-up, excited to decorate my own space for the first time. Living on my own. *Really* on my own.

"It would be cool to have a dog," I say to June.

This gets one of her biggest, sparkliest laughs. "That's all that's missing? A dog?"

"I just think that having a dog is something you do when you're ready to create your own life."

"So you're admitting you haven't done that yet."

She's very good at finding the weak spots in my responses and pressing on them. It's hard to sit still and let it happen, but part of me wants nothing more than to let her keep going. To see how much I can take.

"I guess I am," I tell her.

She tilts her head up toward the sun, and the twinkle in her plum lip gloss makes her mouth sparkle. "Good. You're too talented a writer to stay waitressing at Rita's forever."

"How could you even know that? All you've ever read is my stunningly aggressive breakup text."

"I talk to you almost every day," she says, still basking in the warmth. "If the thoughts you write down are anything like the thoughts you say out loud, I know that you're as funny and observant in your writing as you are while waitressing at Rita's."

"I'm not a real writer, though," I reply, too quickly. There's my limit, I guess. "I don't charge people for my services, and I never could. I just do it because really, I like to be nosy. I get to know people's problems, and I get to come up with a way to fix them."

"I think that's what most writers do. They gossip about people's lives, real or made-up, and then they invent solutions."

I take my phone out of my purse and snap a picture of her.

"Here," I say, showing her. "For you to post. You know, for your independent-woman era."

She barely looks at the screen. "Ah yes. Of course."

"How are you doing, by the way? There are a lot more people out today than we saw last night."

"You know, it's funny. I don't feel nervous here. Not so far, at least. I think I like having something to prove," she says. "I don't know if it will work forever, but for right now, reminding myself that I'm more than my anxiety is helping. And pettiness. That's pretty motivating too."

We both laugh.

"It's extremely motivating," I confirm.

"I actually like the energy of the city so far. It's lively, but it isn't too much for me. I could really see myself living here."

My mind blanks, my personal panic button activated by her words. If the investors who want to buy into her business are from here, it would make sense that she'd move here too. But I hadn't explored the reality of her absence. It's almost impossible to picture my life in Trove Hills without her there, brightening up the corner of Rita's Diner.

Dawn returns with a paper bag full of the goods, stopping me from having to say anything at all. "Follow me," she tells us.

We end up on a random bench in Central Park, Dawn in the middle, as all three of us unwrap our bagels side by side.

"Everyone I know in the business has died," she says.

It comes so far out of nowhere it takes me a second to connect it to the question I asked her earlier, about where she's been. Afraid to startle her off the topic, I lift my head to show an interest in listening further.

"It's kinda funny, that I can still be here, but I'm not really here at all," she continues. "My older sister never had any kids, and neither did I. So when she died, I really just had nobody. This is where I've been the whole time. The same city I've lived in since I was born, surviving on the money from my youth and all the stuff my dead relatives have left me."

"Surely someone's tried to reach you, though," I say. "You're a legend."

"When I was a little younger, my phone used to ring with requests. I'd just let those calls go to voicemail. I thought I didn't want to talk to anybody. Now my phone never rings at all. I should probably get rid of my landline. But I like knowing it's there."

It's weird to feel like I relate to her. Because I've never been a famous actor, but I *have* spent all my life in one place. And up until now, it's been easy to imagine me forty years from now, still there, pretending it's exactly how I want to be living, while knowing way, way down—in the deepest chambers of my wants—that it's not true.

"Do you want to act again?" I ask her.

She waves me off. "No, no. Of course not. I'm way too old for that now. I've been too old for a long time. I'm ancient now."

"No, you aren't," June protests. "Not at all."

"How old are you guys?" Dawn asks us.

"I'm twenty-nine," I say, right as June answers the same way.

Dawn flicks her wrist, as if to say, *You wouldn't get it.*

"Have you not noticed the way everyone we pass looks at you?" I ask.

"They're looking at me because I'm a crotchety old woman who might get in their way."

"They're looking at you because they recognize you, and they want to know where you've been," I tell her. "They're waiting for the next Dawn Flores slasher flick. Or some meditative Guy Cicero project with you as the lead. He's very big into reviving the careers of old starlets."

Dawn waves me off again, this time with less effect. "Stop flattering me. I get too full of myself." She points to my food. "How's the bagel?"

"It's incredible," I tell her, meaning it. "Puts to shame every bagel-related item we serve at the diner."

"You work at a diner?" Dawn asks. "Oh yeah. That's right. Rita's. Damn. See? I already forgot what I learned about you from Siri. No way I could remember my lines at this age."

"The diner is where Tatum and I met," June says. "And now she's here helping me."

"June makes perfumes," I remind Dawn.

"That's right. You told me that too, and I already forgot. I was even gonna say when we sat down that one of you smells very good. But I'm not much for compliments. Same reason as above. Can't have anyone getting full of themselves. Does you no good."

"It's definitely June," I say. "She's here to hopefully sell her business to an investor. She's about to be one of the biggest names in perfume."

"It could be Tatum, though," June rebuts. "She's wearing a gourmand that's perfect with her skin chemistry. She smells like a glass of whiskey served with a batch of fresh cupcakes."

"That's really a compliment to her, because she lent me one of her perfumes this morning. She also picked out this outfit for me because my luggage arrived about thirty seconds before we met you in the hallway, and I couldn't make a game-time decision that quickly. So if I look good, it's only because of June."

"Please," June says. "Yellow is your color."

Dawn clears her throat. "Anyway," she says pointedly. "So June is here for her perfume business. What are *you* doing here?" she asks me.

There are a handful of ways I could answer that would be true, if not particularly detailed. Something tells me Dawn wouldn't like that. She'd want the risky answer, the jagged truth I've only just started to acknowledge.

"I think I'm here to figure out what I want from my life," I say.

"She's in her Saturn return," June adds.

Dawn nods sagely.

"What's that mean?" I ask, feeling out of my depth, remembering how June and Vanessa could talk about this kind of stuff with familiarity.

"You're entering the next stage of your life," June tells me. "There's upheaval. Change. You're looking back on everything you've learned in this first third and thinking about what it means for the next third." She leans closer. Drops her voice to a whisper as she adds, "Don't worry. I'm going through it too."

"You know, I'd tell you it's all bullshit, but I got divorced for the second time and moved to LA in my late twenties," Dawn says. "Went through more changes than I could count. Some didn't stick, obviously, since I'm back here. But most of it was good. I needed it."

"Is that why I kind of want to go on a date while I'm here?" I ask her.

June shoots me a look that could cut through steel, while Dawn glances back and forth between us like there's something she thought she understood that I've just invalidated.

"June's change is that she's in her single era," I add, trying to answer the questions they're both asking with their eyes, reminding June that she's trying *not* to date while simultaneously telling Dawn we are not an item. "I've *been* in my single era. But being here has me thinking about changing that. I'm not looking for anything serious. Just dipping my toes into the pool. Do you know where I go for that?"

"Well, shit," Dawn says, clapping her hands together. "Of course I do!"

This is the first sign of true delight she's shown me, and I feel weirdly proud of it. She springs up from the bench, waving a hand at us to follow.

"I didn't mean right now," I say, realizing it's already too late. Doing this in front of June is mortifying. I'd rather scrub this park pathway with a toothbrush.

"One of the best places in the world to find a date is in the park," Dawn says, ignoring my protest. "If you see someone you like, all you have to do is give them *the look*."

"What's *the look*?" I ask.

"Oh, Tatum knows *the look*," June says to Dawn.

Dawn tips her head into her shoulder, batting her eyelashes.

"I've never made that face in my life." My ears are getting so hot that I have to cool them down with my hands.

"She's exaggerating the look," June tells me, as if that helps. "It's more like this." Her eyes soften, both lids closing in on each other, little crinkles appearing at the corners. Her chin does tilt, but barely. And she doesn't *quite* smile. It's more of a quirk, a comma of an expression, incomplete but inviting, making you want to finish what she's started by smiling all the way in return.

"You could be an actor," Dawn tells her.

Just like that, the expression is erased, replaced with June's usual demeanor. "I think I'm good with sticking to perfumes."

"When have I ever made that face?" I ask.

June laughs. And so does Dawn. Like two coconspirators who have known me all my life, when really, I just met Dawn a few hours ago, and June only knows me through the diner, where I'm apparently inviting every guest to date me.

I want to defend myself, but there's part of me that knows June must be right. The first time I ever saw her, I went out of my way to be impressive. It wasn't often we had a customer around my age showing up all by herself, and I wanted desperately to have her come back again. I refilled her coffee cup more than she needed. Bussed her plates myself the second she took the last bite. Brought her out a complimentary slice of pie that I actually charged to my own tab and paid for myself. She'd come in with a laptop and notebooks, spread out all her things across the table to work. And as I watched her that first day, I thought, *What are your secrets? Where do you go when you're not here?*

Who are you? Who are you? Who are you?

I wanted to know her, to invite her back to our charming little diner so I could see her as much as possible. It's been a while since I thought about those beginnings, shutting all those memories down the moment she asked me out. When she did that, she turned the fantasy into reality, acknowledging what I'd spent so long tiptoeing around, pretending it was all in my mind. And it was too real to me, too vivid to see through.

With every other woman I'd been with, I'd been willing to give dating a shot, even though inside I felt worried—maybe they'd be too much, or maybe they'd be not enough. But I was willing to try, curious to see what would happen.

With June, I never felt worried. I felt scared. Scared of what could be on the other side of the diner. Scared of how much we might mean to each other, how long we might talk if we never had a timer on it, never had working hours to hold us back. Scared of what she might find if she got to know me better—that I didn't know how to love right. That all the years of trying to make everyone else around me better had made me forget how to be myself.

"Who are we looking for?" Dawn asks, scanning people as they pass us.

"A woman," I say. "I'm a lesbian."

When I don't elaborate, Dawn waves her hands impatiently. "And?" she asks.

The question makes me want to crawl into a ball. Because I look at June—who is currently admiring a tree—and I think, *Someone like her.*

Instead I spout off a list of qualities that I find attractive, careful to dance around anything that's too specific to June.

Dawn rebuffs me the second I finish. "Oh really? You want a woman who is smart, funny, and kind? Well, shit, why didn't you say that sooner? That really narrows down the field."

I've already grown fond of how Dawn handles me. It's a comfort to not be coddled. "What can I say? I'm a visionary."

We walk for a while longer with me turning down everyone

Dawn suggests. "Okay. I give up," she says. "Let me know when you're ready to be helped. Then we can do this properly."

"I am ready to be helped," I protest, but we all know it's not true. "Fine," I concede. "I will make an attitude adjustment, and we can try again."

"Good," Dawn says. "And make sure we do something fun beforehand. So I get something out of it too."

14

Eleanor

The muggy afternoon heat blows a hot breath into Rita's Diner every time the door opens. The other customers here give me loaded glances when they sit down to eat and again when they exit. Is it because I've taken up a booth for several hours with no signs of leaving? Or is it that I'm here with a computer and a coffee, disrupting the small-town Americana charm of this place with my electronics?

Maybe they've noticed how unpolished I am in my black leggings covered in cat hair and my gray tank with the tragic but faint coffee stain over my left boob. There was very little time for me to pack, and even less time to do laundry before this trip. The other patrons here have gotten ready like the day matters. I look like someone who has lost her purpose.

If that's what they're seeing in me, then they are right.

"Need anything else?" my server asks me. Denise, according to the name tag clipped onto her faded blue apron.

"A slice of the apple crumble, please," I say.

"We don't have apple crumble," Denise tells me.

"Really?" I confirm, shocked by the casual way that Carson

lied to me. Who lies about apple crumble? "Then the banana cream pie?"

Denise nods.

At least Tatum told me the truth about the desserts in Trove Hills. But I won't mention her name here like she said to do. I can cover my own slice of pie. There's no need for it to be on the house.

Denise heads behind the counter, and I return to my laptop. An email draft to Atlas Theatrical, Garber and Link's main competitor, sits open on my screen. Basically any Broadway PR job that doesn't go to Garber goes to Atlas. For as large as New York is, the theater scene is not very big in comparison. Working at Atlas would be easy and obvious. I know for a fact they're in need of another upper-level press agent over there, and I've also known everyone on their team for years. We get along as well as I got along with my old colleagues, which is to say, we are perfectly cordial.

My email to Atlas sits with the appropriate address plugged in, the body already written. It's the title that stops me from following through. The idea of my name appearing in their inbox with something like "Job Inquiry" as the subject feels like a betrayal of Garber and Link, knowing all the meetings I sat in on where Atlas was discussed at great length—the press opportunities they secured that we'd kept track of, finding their work to be insufficient, or the shows they'd gotten assigned to that were offered to us first. It's not a flashy rivalry. *Rivalry* is too strong a word—it's just a constant, competitive awareness of each other. Which is why it still feels disloyal somehow, trying to work for the other side. How I have any loyalty left for a place that fired me, I don't know. It's yet another piece of my life I have to unlearn.

Instead of emailing Atlas, I decide to log in to my Garber and

Link work email one last time. Maybe it will help me let this go. I can see if anyone's checked in on me, or if I've been accidentally bcc'd on any company-wide notifications about my dismissal.

If they're rude about what happened, I can feel smug. If they're sad, I can feel prideful.

My log-in fails. For some reason, I try again, like it's a matter of faulty passwords. It fails again. It's been two days, and they've already removed my account. When I check my phone notifications for the first time since last night, there are no new texts or DMs from coworkers or acquaintances. Anyone who reached out to me on day one to express their shock about my firing has already gone silent. They were only looking for gossip, and they've surely found it through other sources by now.

It's over. Just like that. All the countless hours sacrificed to talking up rude producers, to finessing the wording to make boring show announcements sing, to battling with personal publicists over what their actors are willing to commit to in the name of promoting their latest theatrical endeavor, to every other thankless task I've taken on in my years at that job—none of it matters anymore. This isn't even counting the endless hours I spent showing up to random events solely to keep friendly relations with other industry people, all in the name of making sure Garber and Link stayed on everyone's radar.

This is the downside of being the person who does the most. I am the only one who understands exactly what I've sacrificed for my work.

I used to believe that knowing my own worth was enough. That I didn't need it recognized or appreciated by anyone else. But this experience has shown me none of that was true. Now that I'm gone, I can see how long I've hoped for someone else to tell me that my work really does matter more than my personal life. That giving everything up is worth it.

The end, though, is just like the beginning and the middle. There is only me.

Denise drops off my banana cream pie. I take one bite, sighing into the taste. It *is* good. Tatum was right. It's creamy and sweet, with just the right amount of banana, and wafer crackers that have gone soft without getting soggy. Closing my eyes, I tilt my head back to think.

Within seconds, someone blocks my light, looming over me.

"What are you doing here?" I ask, eyes still closed.

"How do you know it's me?"

"You're the only person I've met in this entire town," I say. "Unless you told law enforcement I dared to break every rule by walking here, no one else would have a reason to get this close to me unprovoked."

I open my eyes right as Carson slides into the booth across from me, taking my fork off the plate and having a bite of my pie. "I was on my way to the station to report you," they say, chewing. "But I figured I should grab something to eat beforehand."

"I don't remember saying you could have some of my food," I tell them. "And you lied, by the way. They don't serve apple crumble here."

"Did you ask Denise?" Carson holds the fork up, staring at me with hopeful eyes until I give a permissive nod. They take another bite of my pie. "Denise doesn't like to give the crumble out to people she doesn't know. That's how good it is."

"Yet another backward business model in Trove Hills. First there's no walking, now no one here can enjoy the menu's best options? I have to say, as someone who works in publicity, this is the worst way to make your town appeal to outsiders."

"The Eleanor lore expands," Carson says. "Publicity? That's cool."

"It was, until they fired me."

"You got *fired*? I know you said something about a new job earlier, but I assumed you quit and you were here in Trove Hills on some kind of exploratory small-town vacation before returning to your bustling big-city life. How are you not the one who does the firing wherever you worked?"

"Are you about to tell me I have firing energy?"

They swallow back their words.

"You paint such a lovely picture of me," I say. It's a joke, of course. These are all jokes. I can dish it out as much as I can take it. So I'm not sure why an edge of truth cuts into my intended playfulness.

"I was just trying to make you laugh," they say. "I like it when you smile. Feels like winning a carnival prize."

They have a way of finding the right thing to say that turns me from defensive to impressed. It's an unfamiliar problem. Most of the time I spend with people I'm sleeping with involves me actively ignoring my own standards in the name of keeping the situation afloat.

With Carson, it's a matter of finding their weakness. There must be something unappealing about them, some way they would pull up short that would remind me there's no point in letting them occupy any of my idle thoughts. Anything other than the obvious fact that they live here, in Trove Hills, and I live in New York City.

Once I fix my ignorance on the subject—the subject being Carson—my personal interest will disintegrate, and I will be left with only physical attraction, which is much more manageable.

"What do *you* do?" I ask. "I'm quite light on the Carson lore myself."

"I do a lot of things," they tell me. They take a sugar packet and rip it open, pouring the contents onto the table. "I build furniture, but that's not consistent. I only make things when people ask." They pause, staring at me.

"I have no plans to expand my furniture collection at the moment," I say.

"That's what you think now. But you're going to get home and realize you've always wanted a *credenza*, and next thing I know I'm spending my every waking hour carving tree details into cabinets for you."

"Who says I want trees?"

"I remember the way you touched my tattoo."

"Maybe that had more to do with the subject than the art," I say. It's supposed to be my defense, but it's really a compliment, and Carson takes it in with visible pleasure.

Their ego could be off-putting, but that's never been a turnoff for me. I like when people know their value.

"How are you surviving on building a few tables a year?" I ask.

"I told you. I do many things." They take their pointer finger and begin to rearrange the granules on the table, shaping the pile of sugar into some kind of art. "I've been commissioned to do some of the murals you can find around town. If you want to see my work, I painted the side of a shop that's down the street from here. They asked me to do a gigantic sentient doughnut."

"Should I credit you with the nightmares it might give me?" I ask.

"Believe me, it wasn't my idea. But I still think I made the prompt work. You'll have to tell me if you agree."

"If anyone could sell me on a sentient doughnut, it's probably you."

They smile. "Luckily, that job led to the park district's reaching out about doing a town-themed mural for their lobby. They're in the process of a whole revamp over there. It's still in the early stages, and it could definitely fall through."

"How does a park district go about revamping?" I ask, genuinely curious.

"Well, our new mayor has kick-started this whole movement around putting emphasis on what makes Trove Hills so special. He wants to highlight local talent, and if you can believe it, he even wants to put an emphasis on the arts."

I gasp in performed shock, even though it is an actual surprise to know they might care about art. A good surprise.

"I know," Carson says. "Supporting creativity? Who could believe it? The park district even secured funds to restart our community theater. They could probably use somebody like you to help with that. You know, get the word out."

"Oh, really?" I say. "Not to fire people?"

"*Anyway*," they say pointedly. "If I had to sum it up, I'd say I'm this town's Swiss Army knife of building and crafting."

"That explains the glitter."

"I was making something for Brother Ben."

"With glitter?"

"It's a surprisingly versatile substance."

"That wasn't a judgment," I say. "Sorry. That came off too harsh. Like, say, a person who fires other people for a living."

Carson grins. "I'm very sorry about the firing comment. I see now that you would never fire someone. They would fire themselves, because they'd realize you are infinitely better at everything than they are."

"Correct," I say.

"I made Ben a snow globe of Trove Hills. My parents fucking love snow globes. We all get one every year for Christmas. I figured making Ben his own was a fitting way to initiate him into the Ward clan, even in July."

"That's very cute."

"Yes," Carson confirms. "Downright adorable. I used cardboard to cut out an outline of the main street. I spent a few days painting it, making little replicas of places like Rita's and the doughnut shop. Had to get my own work in there, of course. Then I put the models inside a real glass globe. My biggest mistake. I should've used plastic. Or I shouldn't have used glitter for the snow. When I finished, it looked super fucking cool, though. I was driving over to my parents' house to drop it off before the big first meeting. It broke in the car. Glitter everywhere. You can't believe how much."

"I believe it," I say, last night once again leaping to the forefront of my mind.

"Denise," Carson calls out, keeping their eyes on me as they do it.

Denise appears at the table. "You can't have any more of our old plates. We're out." For as blunt as she is to Carson, it also seems familiar. Like how you'd pester a sibling. "And please tell me you plan to clean up after yourself with that." Denise points to the table, where Carson has dumped out yet another packet of sugar.

"Lucky for you, I don't need any plates today," they tell her. "I heard you told my Eleanor that you don't serve apple crumble here. You and I both know that isn't true, don't we?"

My Eleanor is a slip of tongue. I do my best to ignore it, as does every other party in the conversation.

"We don't have any right now," Denise maintains.

Carson rises from their side of the booth. "You're telling me if I walk into the back and I open up the freezer, I won't find an entire apple crumble in there?" They're already heading toward the kitchen.

Denise follows at a frustrated clip. "You better not. Customers are not allowed back there!"

Carson breaks into a run. Denise does too.

"Eleanor's worthy of the crumble! I'm willing to risk my role in this establishment to get it for her." Carson slides across the counter that separates the customers from the employees. It's so smooth it looks choreographed.

Denise looks back at my table with unguarded disdain. "You should've told me you know a Ward."

"I know Tatum too," I say, having fun with this game.

Her face falls. "You're the one who's staying in her place."

"Eleanor," I offer.

"Why didn't you mention that? I wouldn't have put the pie into the system. It would've been on me."

"Tatum told me you'd do that," I say. "But I don't need any free pie. I'm happy to pay."

Carson returns from the freezer, breathless, holding an entire apple crumble. "Where do I heat this up?"

"None of the cooks stopped you?" Denise asks.

"I cannot confirm or deny the involvement of the cooks."

"Do you really want a piece of the crumble?" Denise asks me.

"I think I have to have it now," I tell her.

With an eye roll, she takes the dish from Carson. "This will be on the house. But not because of this one. I need to heat it up. Sit tight."

When she's gone, I lean in. "What did you do to that woman?"

Carson sits again, returning to their sugar packet creation. "Nothing," they say. It's a blameless tone, not at all playful.

"That can't be possible. She reacts to you like you once toilet-papered her house."

"Maybe I should. Kind of weird to do as an adult. I could pass it off as an art installation, though. That's what the plates were for. I was trying to do something about how diner food is the backbone of our society. It didn't really work."

"You're deflecting."

Carson looks up. "I thought I was the one who gives risky observations around here."

"That's also a deflection."

They lean back, studying the walls behind me. "Can I tell you something honest?"

My instinct to keep it witty doesn't match the moment, so I shift to genuine. "Yes."

"Some of the Trove Hillians, love them though I do, don't totally know what to do with me," Carson explains. "Which is fine. I don't know what to do with them either. I can't relate to being a fifty-three-year-old mother of four who has been married to a pipefitter named Ted for thirty-one years, and Denise can't relate to being a thirty-four-year-old genderqueer artist whose most serious relationship lasted four months and involved a custody battle over a gecko."

This gets a belly laugh from me, which incites another glare from Denise as she stands in front of the microwave.

"I think Denise treats me like this because it's easier than admitting that she doesn't understand me," Carson continues. "She doesn't understand what it means to be nonbinary, though she and everyone in Trove Hills has been very nice about it, all things considered. No one understands my job, though I'm the first person they call when they want to get someone a unique birthday gift or they need, say, a sentient doughnut on the side of their building. They're in this state of perpetual confusion when it comes to me. For people like Denise, it shows up as annoyance."

"Why do you stay here, then?" I ask.

"Because I like it," they say insistently. "People like to think I'm a fan of complicating things. They see some of my personal art pieces and think it's more proof that I try to make the world as muddled and glittery and weird as possible. And really, it's the opposite. My art is where I'm trying to iron things out. Put a name to a feeling, or sometimes just put a feeling to rest. Get a thought out of my brain and onto something else."

They gesture to the view of the town beyond the window. "When it comes to Trove Hills, it's a place that has always made sense to me. It's small, and cozy, and just far enough removed from Chicago to feel like it's somewhere different, but close enough to have access to interesting, big-city things. I make sense to me here, because this is where I've always been, and I'm quite fond of who I've become."

"I get it," I say, meaning it. "And for what it's worth, you make sense to me too." Their cheeks redden, and they lose track of whatever they're doing with their sugar packet creation. "My god, have I done it?" I say. "Have I made *you* blush?"

They clear their throat. "God no. Sorry. I was remembering how hot the water was yesterday."

I blush too, heat rushing into my face so quickly that my ears burn. "It was a nice shower."

"A very nice shower," they confirm.

This is my favorite kind of flirting. Fun, risky, a little unfamiliar. In general, I don't flirt beyond the first interaction with someone. There is no need to keep it going once we figure out what our situation is going to be. Carson and I figured that out this morning, so I don't know why I'm trying to out-charm them still, as if we haven't already crossed the barrier between us and gotten physical. I'm acting like I still have something to prove.

"How was time with your brother?" I ask.

"He's really nice," Carson tells me. "His wife is very cool too." They pause, slowing. "It makes me sad that Tatum is missing this. She'd like him too, if she gave him a chance."

Carson's continued vulnerability catches me by surprise. My instincts to banter have to be continuously rerouted, honoring the spirit of this conversation. "What do you miss about her?"

Carson goes on to describe their sister in such generous terms that all I can do is put my face on my hand and lean forward to listen. They're not always kind. In fact at least a minute of their discussion gets dedicated to how annoying Tatum can be, explaining how stubborn she is without realizing she's stubborn. But the love still shines through all of it. And that's what I appreciate. How much they love their sister while still being acutely aware of her faults.

"Do you have any siblings?" Carson asks me.

"Nope. Just me, myself, and I."

"Don't be too sure of that," Carson warns. "Your parents could very well have a secret love child appear at any moment."

"My parents are currently dead, so any connection to love children will have to happen through me. I've yet to take any genetic tests, so all mysterious Eleanor Chapman relatives will be dying before they ever learn about our relation to one another."

Denise appears with a slice of apple crumble. "If it's not good, blame this one." Her eyes narrow on Carson. "It hasn't been properly thawed out. I don't know if the microwave reheat process has been as effective as it could be." She sets the plate down and leaves us, and silence blankets the moment.

"It's okay," I say to Carson preemptively. "You don't have to go through any of the pleasantries. It happened fourteen years ago. I promise I've heard them all by now, and I know your heart is in the right place."

"I'd still like to say something, if that's okay," Carson tells me. They *do* go through the usual fare, albeit with a sincerity that does stir something deep inside me. Then they stop, and they put a hand on mine across the table. "I'm glad they made you."

To my embarrassment, tears leap into my eyes, so fast acting I have no time to stop them or deny their existence. "Well, thank you," I say, wiping them away. "Now, stop being nice to me. I need to have some apple crumble."

"I'll stop, only if you promise me one thing," Carson says. "Come to the family picnic on Tuesday."

I swallow hard, pushing down the last wave of my tears until I'm back to my usual self. "Don't the people in your family have to work?"

"Ben is a teacher, so he has the whole summer wide open. My job is on a case-by-case basis, as you now know. A lot of my aunts and uncles are of a retirement age. And Dad had everyone else take the week off," Carson answers. "By the way, the family was asking about you after you left. Even one of my aunts who only saw you for a second. She was like, 'Who was that knockout?' I said, 'Oh, the woman daring to walk in Trove Hills? Is she out of her mind? Does she want to get arrested?'"

"I'd only believe that she thought I was off to run an HR mediation over someone's employment status. Maybe audit strangers' taxes for sport. Certainly nothing complimentary was said."

"Okay, fine," Carson says. "My aunt didn't say anything. But Brother Ben really did ask about you after you left."

"Was it just to make sure I wasn't another one of his long-lost sisters?"

"He could definitely tell that you're not my sister, Eleanor."

The way Carson says it, so matter of fact, sends my thoughts once again to their mouth on me. It feels a bit like I'm back there, powerless to their ways.

"I know you don't want to be thrown into this whole affair, but the picnic should be a pretty casual event," they tell me. "Definitely more casual than the dinner I'm supposed to be at right now. My dad rented out a banquet hall."

"I noticed you looked nice," I say.

This makes Carson smirk. "And yet I've received no compliments?"

"You don't need me to tell you that you look good."

They put their hand on their chest in performative shock. "Of course I do. How else will I go about the rest of my night without you?"

I return their playful look until the joking crystallizes into something deeper. Something real.

"I'll go to the picnic," I say, taking a bite of apple crumble to break the pressure of our gaze. It's every bit as divine as Carson said it would be. "Now, leave me be."

"I will." Carson stands up, pleased. After taking a couple of steps, they backpedal, remembering something. "I won't be able to stop by the cottage later. I have to pick up my sister, Laney, at an ungodly hour. But I'll see you as soon as I can."

"Sounds good," I tell them. "You know where I'll be."

They leave me alone in the booth to enjoy the apple crumble. And suddenly, it's not as enjoyable anymore, being here by myself.

Suddenly, I'm wishing they'd invited me to the banquet.

It's only later, when I'm standing up to leave, looking back at the table one last time to make sure nothing's been left behind, that I see what they've created with the sugar packets—a portrait of me with my eyes closed, head tilted back toward the ceiling. I look peaceful, somehow. Content. Not at all like the image of me I see in my own mind. And even though it's just sugar—a quick sketch they've done to pass the time here—I like the way they've captured me.

15

Tatum

Eleanor keeps a paper calendar in her office, the space that has been acting as my bedroom. There's a comfortable couch in here and a good amount of room for all my belongings. Searching Eleanor's desk for something resembling a bobby pin, hoping to pin my too-long curly bangs back to keep them out of my face in this July heat, my eyes land on a Post-it beside her desktop computer. It just says *Save Hannity Banks?* in bold red letters.

Google tells me *Hannity Banks and the Great Escape* is a new Broadway musical about a young woman from the 1920s who accidentally time travels to the future through a magician's trick. The production pictures show me simple staging that emphasizes lots of bright, eccentric costumes. When I google Eleanor's name plus the show, it pulls up a PR website's information link, where she's listed as a contact. Her picture is on the website under the TEAM tab.

I stare at it for a long while. June showed me her picture when we first came up with the plan, and again when we were looking into her financial situation. This time, it's just me and Eleanor locked in a battle of gazes. She wears a crisp taupe suit with her arms folded across her chest. She has long, sharp features, and the kind of smile that's more like a searing gaze than an expression of joy. She looks like the type of person who does cold plunges for fun. If I saw her on the street, I'd guess she sleeps on ironed sheets. Yet I know, living in her apartment, what no one would ever suspect. I know that I would've been completely wrong about her.

According to the website, she's been at her firm for over ten years. It even lists her as one of their most valued press agents.

To me, having a job doing publicity for Broadway shows seems glamorous and intense. It conjures up images of *The Devil Wears Prada*, which was about working at a magazine, but seeing as this is more of a vibe-based assessment, it still works. I see Eleanor in chic coats rushing between cabs to make meetings with important figures, battling with the powers that be to get the best coverage for her show. Seeing how wrong my impression of her picture was, it's probably not at all what her job is actually like either.

I wonder what it is she sees when she looks at my pictures in the guest cottage. Has she met any of my family and plugged in gaps from my life through knowing them? What has she gotten wrong about me?

My phone vibrates with another message from my dad.

DAD: We really missed you today. Carson told me what you did. I wish you'd talked to us. But I hope you enjoy New York.

He sends a single sobbing emoji afterward.

It's so comical that it staves off some of the guilt that threatens to swallow me up.

> TATUM: I hope it's going well. I just need some
> more time. You're the one who said I seemed
> disconnected. I guess I'm trying to figure out why.

He sends another crying emoji.

On impulse, I buy three tickets to *Hannity Banks*, thinking of Dawn telling us she hasn't been to a show in years. And her request that if we're going to try finding me a date again, we do something fun beforehand. I doubt these three tickets will help save *Hannity Banks*, as Eleanor's Post-it requests, but maybe I'll learn why it's tanking at all. I'm always better at seeing why things fall apart than I am at figuring out how to keep them together.

My credit card bears the weight of this decision, but that's another problem for future Tatum, who will certainly be carrying the weight of so many of my choices here.

"I thought of something fun for us to do tonight!" I declare to June, who sits on the couch brushing Syrup's long fur. "We're going to take Dawn to see a Broadway show, and then Dawn can take us to that bar she was talking about yesterday. So I can meet someone."

"Awesome," June says, remaining placid. It's the same flat affectation she's had since yesterday afternoon, when we wandered through the park with Dawn. She's as steady as a ruler. So unflappable it's starting to become unsettling.

"Is everything okay?" I ask her.

"Of course!" she says, using the exact kind of cheer you use when it's not true. I know I've thrown her for a loop by saying I want to date. I've thrown myself for a loop too. But she's the one who needs to experience independence. Our wants don't align.

It can't be us.

I head across the hallway and knock on Dawn's door.

"Who's there?" she calls out.

"No one can get up here without the doorman's permission," I say. "You know who it is."

"Go home," she tells me. "I'm too tired."

"I have a surprise for you."

Dawn unlocks her bottom lock but keeps the chain lock secured, peeking at me through the sliver of doorway. "I don't like surprises."

A little more versed in the art of Dawn-speak, which amounts to her lying as a means of protecting herself, I trudge on, undeterred. "You asked for something fun, so I got us tickets to see a Broadway show!"

The door closes all the way.

I stand bewildered.

To my surprise, it opens up again fully. Dawn's standing in a bathrobe, trying her best to conceal a smile. "What time do we leave?"

HEADING INTO TIMES SQUARE FEELS OBVIOUS IN ITS tourism. At the same time, everyone here has something to do that matters to them, whether it's taking a great picture or getting home from their job. I don't know if I've ever consciously wanted to have it, but being in New York, I recognize a sense of purpose as something I *could* want. It's fun to look around and wonder, *What if this was my life? What if every morning I woke up needing to be somewhere important?*

This part of the city is so overstimulating it actually helps to dull the nagging ache at the back of my mind, thinking of Trove Hills and my family navigating this unfamiliar time without me. I'm only one person, I remind myself. One person in an unfathomably large sea.

I can't always be my family's glue. I am allowed to have a life away from them.

"This is a lot," June whispers softly.

It's quick, but it's enough to know she's struggling with the overload of sights and smells and people everywhere.

I grab her hand, squeezing tight. "I've got you," I say. "We can find somewhere quiet."

"That's okay," she says, small.

"Remember, you're proving the doubters wrong. Pettiness is powerful." I give her *the look*, just to try to make her smile.

"Don't you dare do that." She offers me a weak version of the smile I'd hoped to get. "I might go getting ideas."

"Don't you dare do *that*," I counter, echoing her tone.

"Just keep holding my hand," she whispers, her breaths short and sharp.

"Of course. Anything for you."

There's no need to overthink the intensity of what I've said, because her safety is the priority. We continue weaving through the endless throng with Dawn leading the charge. The whole way, our hands never break apart.

When we get inside the theater, the lobby is quiet and deliciously cool, pumping with high-quality air conditioning. There's a cushioned bench along the wall, and I guide June over to it, with Dawn right behind us.

"What do you need?" I ask June.

"Water would be good," she says softly.

Dawn takes the cue, heading to the concession stand.

I press a hand to June's cheek. She's warm, but so are we all, thanks to the mid-July humidity. "Anything else?"

She gives me another small smile as she takes long, intentional breaths. "I just need a few more minutes."

Dawn comes back with two waters. "One for your neck," she

says. She sits on the other side so we are bookending June, who continues taking stretched-out breaths. I hold the other water bottle along the back collar of her shirt as Dawn fans her face with a piece of old mail she's extracted from her purse.

"Thank you," June says after a while, most of the color now returned to her cheeks.

I give her hand one more quick squeeze. "Anytime."

THE SHOW ITSELF IS BIZARRE. IT'S NOT A PROBLEM OF the performers or even the production itself. The actors are very good, and their voices are great, but the actual music is brassy and chaotic, and the plot is incoherent. It's like watching someone reenact a dream they had without trying to fill in any of the logic gaps that have sprung up.

At intermission, June, Dawn, and I put our heads together to discuss what we just watched. June's all the way recovered now, back to her usual self, and the relief I feel barely overrides the concern that nearly consumed me earlier.

"This show reminds me of when I took acid," Dawn says.

"I've never done drugs, but I can imagine it's similar to this," I confirm. "The story makes no sense."

"I like it," June says.

Dawn and I both gasp. It's the first time we've been united against her, and it's a surprise for all of us.

"I have no idea what's going on," June continues, "but the costumes are fun, and everyone seems to be giving it their all."

"What a nice way to see it," I say honestly.

"You're making us look like assholes," Dawn tells her. With me sitting between them, she reaches across me to nudge June's arm. "Assholes who are right, though." She nudges my arm next.

"I wonder if Eleanor liked the show," I say. The whole experience is not giving me the glossy-stilettoed *Devil Wears Prada* energy I expected.

The theater itself has fewer than a thousand seats. In fact it's so close that for a lot of the first act, June's foot stayed pressed against my shin, her leg crossed toward me and her elbow leaned onto the arm rest closest to my side.

I liked that part, comforted by being able to feel her stay relaxed and engaged.

While the show is chaos personified, it's also not an easily identified disaster either. There are a lot of good individual elements. They just fail to make something cohesive.

"How would one go about saving something like this? Especially from a promotional perspective. Eleanor can't exactly rewrite the show," I say, thinking again of her Post-it.

"I could text her and ask," June tells me.

"Do it," I say.

"I need to stretch my legs." Dawn gets up to walk around, leaving June and me alone again.

June angles herself my way, crossing her leg in my direction again as her foot grazes my shin once more. These small touches are starting to build, all the emotional ground I spent so long leveling between us rising so much faster that I can control.

"What would you change about the story?" she asks me.

Taking a beat, I comb through the first act again, gathering up the loose threads and examining them for the biggest fixable flaw.

"For one, I wouldn't make the future so vague," I say. "Hannity doesn't know where she is, and neither do we as the audience. That works in the very beginning, because we get to experience the disorientation alongside her. But by the end of this act, we should have a sense of what this future place is supposed to represent. I'm guessing they want it to be a stand-in for all her unfulfilled hopes and dreams, but they haven't quite accomplished that. Everything she's encountered has been great so far, so it doesn't make sense to end this act with her getting really emotional over believing she's stuck in the future forever. They needed to do more to make us believe that's a bad thing. We don't know what she left behind."

June nods along, following my every word with careful attention. When I finish, she grins, like she's figured out something herself.

"What?" I say, reddening. "Do I have something on my face?"

She stops me from reaching for my mouth, grabbing my forearm as she lets out one of her gentlest laughs, a lullaby to my nerves. "No. It's just funny that you don't think you're a writer. I didn't notice any of that. I was looking at their costumes and thinking about how I should wear more monochromatic outfits."

"And I didn't notice the monochrome," I tell her, attempting to turn this into a compliment for her instead of a revelation about me. "You could pull off head-to-toe orange."

Dawn returns, flopping back into her seat with her usual weariness. "Doesn't look like this showing is sold out. The balcony is pretty empty."

I tell her about Eleanor's Post-it, which requires further explanation, because Dawn knows so little of her neighbor, she didn't even realize Eleanor was a press agent. In return, Dawn plugs in some details about Eleanor that we haven't yet learned. Mostly that she has occasional *late-night visitors*, as Dawn calls it, all different ages and genders.

"And I mean, good for her," Dawn concludes. "At least someone on our floor is getting laid."

We all laugh. It's a perfect segue to reminding Dawn of our next step after Hannity ends. "Don't forget," I say. "You need to find me a place to pick up women."

"I can't make promises," she says. "I haven't dated anyone in a long time, much less a woman. But I know a few places that should be good."

"Dawn, you've dated women?" June asks, slapping her lightly on the arm.

"Honey, of course I have. I may not get out much anymore, but I still know about the finer things in life." She looks to me. "Which gives me an idea. What if you tell me about the women you've *already* dated, and we can figure out what to avoid?"

"Yeah," June says, eyes glinting with mischief. "Tell us about your exes."

I get that squirming sensation again, struggling under the pressure of the spotlight. I'm wishing for some of June's water from earlier. "They've all been great."

Dawn rolls her eyes.

"I'm serious," I say.

June leans forward, cupping her face in her palm. "Then what happened?"

"Me," I tell her. "I happened. I cut things off before they could get too serious. It was better that way."

"Why was it better?" she asks.

"Because it would only hurt worse the longer we let things go on."

"Forgive me if this comes off a little harsh, but I'm begging you to just say all of what you mean at once," Dawn interjects. "Listening to you talk is like reading a poem. And I like poems, but sometimes, you just gotta say it."

"Tough but fair," I tell her, my neck starting to itch. If I get a stress rash right now, I'm going to fist-fight myself. "I mean that I have this fear . . . that I will do to someone else what my dad did to my mom. Not exactly like him. I know I'd never cheat on someone. But that I'd betray them somehow, even when it goes against what I know of myself, or even what I actually want. My dad loves his family. He's so proud of us, so proud of being married to my mom. And he's always been that way. But he still did it. He still cheated. And I get scared that kind of betrayal is in my DNA somehow. Or that it's the only way I know how to love at all."

June reaches out her hand. Grabs mine the same way I held hers when we walked over here, squeezing tight.

Just then, the house lights flicker, a sign for everyone to return to their seats for the second act to begin.

Dawn just nods, finally understanding me enough to stop pressing.

And June, soft, whispers, with her breath on my cheek, "It's not in your DNA, I promise."

It's simple. Probably obvious. Something anyone would say to me. But it matters more to hear it from her. To know that she believes in me.

I find myself wishing it could be her. That she wasn't trying to be single right when I'm ready to open up. It's a terrible kind of luck, that the ways we need to grow work against each other.

When the show starts again, I don't let go of her hand.

At least we have this.

16

Eleanor

It's now been twenty-nine hours since I last saw Carson. I wouldn't say I miss them. We have known each other for such a brief period that it can be measured in *hours*. Plus this alone time has been beneficial. Of course, I could argue that most of my private life is alone time, and what I need might be social time. That sounds like the kind of argument no one wins. Why bother making it with myself?

Missing my cats, I zoom in on the photo June just texted me. They're stretched out side by side on the sofa, as content as can be.

ELEANOR: That's a rare occurrence. They only do that about once a year.

JUNE: I took that before we left to see your musical. We just got out a little bit ago! Hannity Banks is so fun! Do you like working on the show? Tatum wanted me to ask you.

Hannity is one of Garber's biggest flops to date. One critic called it "the most ambitiously bad musical in decades." Everyone at the office has gotten so used to thinking of it as a failure, I forget that anyone can still deem it enjoyable.

As with every show I've worked on, there was a time when I believed *Hannity* could be the next big thing. That's half my job. Selling everyone on the dream, including myself. Then the reviews came in, and the critics were all united in their distaste. It was a good old-fashioned flop. Just like that, the dream dissolved.

When a show goes off the rails, it's almost impossible to get it back on track without the help of a big-name star joining the cast or, frankly, some sort of viral online content that makes people curious enough to buy a ticket. *Hannity* has neither. It's as good as dead. Anthony Teller and his fellow producers just have to pull the plug.

If my old boss, Mark, and I were having one of our weekly debriefs, this is the exact kind of text I'd mention to him to prove that sometimes, people in the arts have their nose stuck in the air when it comes to what's fun, and maybe we weren't wrong to root for *Hannity* in the first place.

What makes good art anyway? I'd ask him.

We'll spend our whole careers trying to figure that out, Mark would tell me.

But I don't work there anymore. I don't have to say anything cheeky and self-aware to June in response, like *Wish more people agreed with you*, or *If you told that to a thousand of your closest friends, we might be able to make it to the end of our original run!*

> ELEANOR: I'm glad you enjoyed it. I'm happy with the press we secured for it. We got our lead on morning television last week, which is always nice. Can never control what people think, though. Hope New York is treating you well.

JUNE: It is! We've even made friends with your
neighbor Dawn. She's hilarious. She's taking us to a
bar right now.

Sifting through the minimal interactions I've had with other people in my building, I search for a Dawn. Is it the woman with the fantastic lipstick choices who lives a floor above me? Or the man who owns several dogs and takes the entire pack out for walks every few hours? It's embarrassing to have June know more about my building than I do. It also doesn't surprise me that two people from this town would show up and attempt to make friends with my neighbors, but most of the people in my building are old-money New Yorkers who aren't typically looking to expand their social circles.

Another text from her comes in, preventing me from having to own up to my ignorance.

JUNE: Are you enjoying Trove Hills?

ELEANOR: I am. It's not what I expected. In a
good way.

She heart reacts to the message.

ELEANOR: Give my kitties a kiss from me.

Setting down my phone, I continue reworking my email to Atlas Theatrical. The more I tweak it, the closer I get to being brave enough to give it a subject line. My earlier drafts were too casual. Dismissive, even. That's not the way to approach my former competitor and ask for work. Still, I can't bring myself to do what I know I should—write something sincere.

There's a knock on the cottage door, and it takes everything in me to school my response. It might not even be who I think.

But it is. Of course it is.

"You've learned how to use doors," I say when I open up, fighting the smile that's desperate to break free.

Carson's wearing an oversized button-up shirt hanging open to show today's tank, with a backward ball cap containing their mop of short curls. They look so effortlessly good, my attraction is almost jealousy—that's how deep it goes.

"In my defense, you weren't answering me when I knocked last time." They step across the threshold to close the space between us.

"And if I hadn't answered now?"

"I would have crawled through the window. But this time it would have been to make sure nothing had happened to you." They take this moment to grab me, pulling me in as if in rescue.

"How heroic," I say.

"I do what I can."

Then they kiss me, so deep it makes my feet rise off the floor as they squeeze me close. I give in to the feeling, holding them as if I've missed them just as much, letting myself, for just a breath, pretend that this is my life, not some vacation cosplay I've been enacting. I wrap a hand around their neck, my fingers tangled in their hair as their own fingers press hard enough into my skin to leave a mark.

"And here I thought I was someone you were going to use to pass the time, but I haven't seen you in an entire day," I tease.

"Are you trying to tell me you missed me?"

"How could I miss someone I don't know?"

"Right, right. We are pretending we don't know each other at all. Sure. That if I do this"—they put a hand on my upper thigh, squeezing the bare flesh—"it doesn't make you let out a gasp."

I do, as stated, gasp. "Anyone would."

"What would anyone do if I put my hand higher?" they ask. "Would *anyone* say my name?"

Their hand wanders up to the hem of my underwear. "*Carson*," I whisper, their fingers slipping under the edge of the fabric.

"Aha," they say, pulling back. "You *do* know me." They kiss me again with a newfound fervor, returning their hand to the inside of my thigh. "I've been waiting all day for this."

"Me too," I admit.

"I love the feel of you," they tell me, continuing to coax out my involuntary gasps. We're only three steps from the doorway, which is still open a sliver.

"The door." My words are faint, barely winning out over my need.

Carson makes quick work of reaching back, closing us off from the rest of the world. They press me up against the closed door, everything much more serious than it was ten seconds ago. With escalating urgency, they continue working me up, their fingers slipping under the fabric and onto the slick heat of me, where I do little to repress how good it feels. I can't. Not when they have this uncanny way of finding what I want the most.

They kiss at my ear, keeping our bodies pressed together.

"Good," they whisper as I begin to shake. "That's what I want to see."

Turning the tables, my hand undoes their buckle, reaching inside their pants without much ceremony.

"I can't always be first," I tell them, composing myself enough to get out my words.

"I like it," they say.

"What if I like it too?" I ask, my hand resting on their underwear, waiting for permission. "What if I want to see you come for me? What if that does it for me even more than your touch?"

It's never been true before, wanting to see someone else fall apart ahead of me. It's a miracle if I get to fall apart at all. But Carson, so sneaky, so good at hiding their desires behind my own, doesn't get to run this whole show.

"I—" They falter.

My hand stays still, resting on their pelvis, waiting. It goes on long enough that I start to pull back, never wanting to overstep.

"Yes," they say.

Carson, for once, becomes pliant under my touch. And the fabric-tearing passion that we've shared softens into something so gentle it's almost weightless. I take them to the couch, undressing them layer by layer while keeping on my own clothes. They are in their tank. Then they are in only the pants.

Then nothing at all, in broad daylight on the couch in the cottage, all mine to undo.

My fingers trace their stomach tattoo again. They tuck their hands behind their head.

"You have me, Eleanor Chapman," they say. "Do anything you dare."

"Adding in the last name," I notice. "Did you google me or something?"

"Of course I did," they tell me. "I'll be insulted if you haven't done the same."

"I can't confirm or deny doing such a thing," I say.

They reach up to kiss me. "No need to. I can see it on your face anyway. You know me."

Even when I think I'm the one in control, their naked body underneath me as I sit atop their pelvis, they find a way to throw that into question. I press my lips to theirs, silencing my thoughts along with their words.

"No talking," I remind them.

Then we do what we're best at—we unravel each other.

17

Tatum

Dawn has indeed picked a place where there are a lot of women. A lot of people in general, packed in for what they're calling a queeraoke night here, where people sign up to belt out show tunes, big ballads, and everything in between.

By a stroke of luck, we're able to grab seats along the actual bar. A disco ball hangs from the ceiling, scattering circular light over the bartenders as they race back and forth to make enough drinks to accommodate the crowd. It's loud in here, but bearably so, and the groups ebb and flow, providing countless candidates for Dawn to pitch as a potential date.

"Is this okay?" I whisper to June. "It's busy."

"I'm good," she tells me. "I promise."

"What about her?" Dawn shouts, pointing at a short, pretty blonde who has just finished singing a warbling but very committed rendition of "Leather and Lace," opting to cover both parts of the duet.

Before I can answer, the blonde walks up to a brunette in the crowd and kisses her hard, which makes the small group around them erupt into a second round of applause, even louder than the one the blonde got for singing.

"Taken," I say, like we all can't see that already.

Dawn, undeterred, scans for more options.

One by one, I shoot them down.

It's not intentional. I can just look at someone's face, or the way they take up space in the room, and know it isn't right. I can even imagine the smell of their breath in the morning, or what loyalties they have to people in their life that they shouldn't, and it's enough to shut down any inkling of attraction that might exist within me.

"These women won't work for me because I won't work for them either," I say to Dawn. "No need to waste our time seeing if that can miraculously change."

Abruptly, June announces she plans to sign up for karaoke. She threads her way through the crowd, heading toward the performance area, where twinkle lights and a single mic stand set the scene. It's a raffle, and every person drops their name into a bowl with the hopes of being picked before the night ends.

"I'm glad she's feeling better," Dawn says.

"Me too."

June smiles at the DJ, who smiles back twice as big. There's a sick little tug in my stomach at the sight, and I shove it down, running through the list of reasons it can't be her, finding it less and less compelling each time I do so.

"Let's try a different approach," Dawn says, forcing my attention back. "My *third* attempt at making sense of this, mind you. And look, I understand all your fears. I really do. But since you're willing to work through them, surely there's something specific you look for. A certain type. Like for me, when I was going for women, I liked the butchy ones. Is that still okay for me to say?"

"Butch is still a term, yes," I tell her.

"What's your thing?"

"I don't really have a thing," I say. Knowing Dawn is one hefty sigh away from berating me, I force myself to continue. "All my life, I've just been drawn to the energy of certain people. When I was a kid, I was obsessed with Martha Stewart. I don't know if it would be considered a crush. I never wanted to kiss her or whatever. I just wanted to watch her all the time."

"So you like older women?" Dawn asks, not following.

What the hell am I saying? I'm digging my own grave.

"No," I say, too quickly. "Not that you're not beautiful. Or that you're old."

Dawn puts a hand on my arm. "Stop floundering."

"I just mean that to me, liking someone has more to do with how I feel around them than how they look, I guess," I say. "And I didn't ever want to date Martha Stewart, but she's the first person I can remember in my life who made me understand that for me, love is fascination. And I've never felt that way about any man. Only women."

It's a testament to Dawn's resilience that she doesn't give up on me altogether. "Yes, I haven't forgotten that you're a lesbian. That's about the only clear thing going on."

It's funny enough to get a laugh out of me.

"All right," Dawn concedes. "If it's about feelings, then how do you like to feel around a woman?"

"I kind of like to feel a little uncertain of myself," I say. "I like to feel like when I'm with her, I can't predict what will happen next. I'm a little too good at figuring situations out. It's kind of my curse. So I guess I'm looking for a woman who surprises me."

"I don't know how the hell to look for that, but that's nice to know," Dawn says. June returns, and Dawn wastes no time looping her back into the conversation. "What do you look for, June?

Maybe that'll help our friend over here. The one who specifically asked me to help her get a date."

"Remember? I'm not trying to date anyone right now." June readjusts her short pleather skirt so that it covers the tops of her thighs as she settles onto the barstool. The thrill of seeing her upper thigh makes me linger on her legs too long.

Not her, I remind myself again.

"I just got dumped," she continues. "I need to learn the art of being single. I'm far too prone to wanting people I can't have."

My heart goes into my throat.

Dawn asks June for more information on her breakup. June starts by explaining who Vanessa is and how they got together, details I was never able to gather during my time as their waitress. They met on a dating app. They were together for five months, and Vanessa helped June find the investors she's here to meet. They'd been discussing moving in together, but June was worried about it, because Vanessa is very particular about a lot of things, and June anticipated fights over how to load the dishwasher and all the little things in between. Still, the breakup came out of nowhere for June. There were no signs leading up to it that indicated Vanessa might dump her.

I spend the entire time preparing myself to hear her explanation of the ghostwriting angle. I almost miss the fact that June doesn't mention it. She just tells Dawn that Vanessa breaking up with her unexpectedly stung on principle, but it didn't hurt in any deeper way. Even though it ended very fast, it was more of a relief than anything else.

"You know, that's a blessing," Dawn says when June finishes. "If she's capable of doing that, she's not the one for you anyway."

"I know that," June replies. "I think I always knew that. I just liked having the company."

"Never mistake the comfort of company for actual feelings. I did that with my first husband, and he slept with my best friend. Got her pregnant too. May he rest without peace," Dawn says, laughing.

We join her, although much more tentatively. "I'm sorry," I offer, wanting to be sure I've said it.

Dawn waves me off in her usual way. "Don't worry about it. I was more pissed off at my friend than I was at him. Because I realized I didn't even like him. Certainly didn't want to bring his children into the world. I just didn't like to be alone." She stops, registering her own words. "*Ha.* Look at me now."

It's a journey that makes sense to me—Dawn tricked herself into thinking she loved him because he was the person who was there, who was convenient. It was the life she thought she should have. And in the end, she probably let her bitterness and her fear get the best of her, keeping her from dating and acting altogether, because that made sure she never got hurt again. All that got her was a version of her life she never wanted—one where she's no longer doing the job she loves, no one to pass the time with either. Sometimes you can be right about every single thing, and it does you no good. Life doesn't reward your observational intelligence. There's no grand scoreboard that gives you bonus points for avoiding hypothetical obstacles.

"Two vodka cranberries with lime," someone calls out, so loud and commanding it forces my acknowledgment. It's the blonde karaoke woman, shouldering her way into an open space along the bar.

"Nice performance," I tell her, unable to let the moment pass without inserting a compliment now that we've made accidental eye contact.

"My girlfriend bet me a hundred bucks I wouldn't do it," the blonde says, pointing to the woman she kissed. "I don't lose bets."

"Good song choice," Dawn tells her. "I used to party with Stevie Nicks when I'd go out to Los Angeles."

The blonde doesn't know what to make of that, doesn't realize she's talking to a legend of sorts, but she nods in appreciation. "Awesome. My name is Stevie too, so she's always my karaoke choice," she tells us. "We're here for my birthday trip, visiting some of our friends who live out here. Garland surprised me with it." She points again to the other woman, like we might have missed her the first time. "She's currently pretending she's lost the stack of twenties I watched her stuff into her purse before we left for this place. She doesn't want to pay me."

"Happy birthday," June offers.

"Thanks," Stevie replies. "It was actually in the beginning of June, but I believe in celebrating all month long."

"It's the end of July right now," I tell her.

"*Shh*," she says. "Anything is possible if you believe it hard enough." She's fun, vibrant. The kind of person who can talk to anyone about anything.

"We're visiting too," I tell her, gesturing to June. "We've never been to New York before. Our friend Dawn here has been showing us around. Taking us to all the good spots."

"They don't know I'm just looking up places on my phone like everybody else," Dawn stage-whispers.

"Your secret is safe with me," Stevie stage-whispers back. The bartender returns with her drinks. Stevie pulls a wad of cash out of her bra to pay her tab. "Well, I hope we get to hear you and your girlfriend sing."

The comment hangs in the air after her departure, lingering over the conversation.

Dawn, never one to miss an opportunity, says, "Now, that's an idea," looking between June and me.

"Oh," I say loudly, "I hadn't even thought of that."

It's the most panicked untruth that's ever left my lips in all twenty-nine years of my life. If the cooks could see me now, they'd banish me to the back room for my least favorite task, ladling our homemade dressings out of the giant vat they're made in and into the squeeze bottles we use. I'd deserve it too.

"Well, that's a lie," Dawn says, uniquely good at making this situation worse.

In the fog of my mortification, I'm distantly aware of June. How she's not saying anything either. She hasn't challenged Dawn or laughed it off. She's as awkward as me right now, and it's the only thing keeping me from walking out of this bar and wandering the city until my legs can't carry me any farther.

"What is it, you guys already slept together and it was bad?" Dawn continues, undeterred.

"*Dawn*," I say, using the same low, stern voice I employ on my parents when they come to bingo night at Rita's Diner and embarrass me in front of the other players by telling some story from my childhood. It's probably the tone they used on me as a toddler when I'd say something to a stranger in the grocery store, far too curious and not yet versed in the appropriate pleasantries of the world. The universal message behind it is the same, no matter the reason—*Shut the fuck up, please.*

The karaoke DJ reaches into the bowl of names where everyone's submitted their song requests. "Up next, we've got June Lightbell!" they call out, reading the scrap of paper.

Yes, I think with relief. *Thank you to any and every higher power for providing us with a way out of this moment.*

"And Tatum Ward!" the DJ adds.

My eyes shoot over to June, who has folded her lips together. "By the way, I signed us up for a duet," she says weakly. When I don't stand, she's forced to get closer, putting a hand on my leg. "It's not the kind of song I can sing alone."

This gets me to move. At least it puts us away from Dawn,

who seems to have an entire arsenal of awkward questions she's more than willing to ask us.

I follow June through the crowd, and we pass Stevie and Garland, who hold up their vodka cranberries. "Hell yeah!" Stevie says. "What are you guys gonna sing?"

"It's a surprise!" I tell her.

Understatement of the century.

"I'm Whitney," June whispers before the song starts, providing me with my one and only clue as to what we're about to perform.

In a matter of milliseconds, I comb my brain for Whitney Houston duets, only coming up with "When You Believe," the song she did with Mariah Carey for *The Prince of Egypt*. There's no way that is what June has picked for queeraoke night.

Right?

A disjointed piano line kicks in, and the title flashes onto the lyrics screen in front of us—"If I Told You That" by Whitney Houston.

It's not a song I know very well, though it's familiar. June plays a lot of Whitney on the jukebox, and this is certainly one that I've heard. Enough to fake my understanding of the melody as I follow the words on the screen.

"I don't know when I'm supposed to sing," I whisper quickly.

"You don't know the George Michael duet version?" June asks in genuine shock, right before she puts her lips to the mic and begins the song.

To say she commands the crowd is to undersell her transformation. She becomes a *performer*, pointing her finger and walking back and forth across our three feet of open space, playing to the small crowd of bystanders around us as she sings her way through the opening chorus. She does a confident pivot, head tucked into her shoulder as she nods to cue me for the first verse.

I miss my entrance, part confused at the required melody and part transfixed by her presence. The lyrics fly by so fast they activate my speed-reading brain, where I can pick up a novel late at night and scan the words as fast as a computer downloads information. My voice is no prize, but I've never been the type of person to worry about that when it comes to karaoke. And I certainly wouldn't strand June up here on purpose. There is just so much happening, all at once.

It's only halfway through the performance that I process the actual lyrics—this is a song about revealing your feelings for a friend.

What would happen if I told you I had feelings for you? Would it ruin our friendship?

It feels like we're having a conversation up here, telling each other we both know this is more than we're acknowledging but that neither of us wants to ruin what we are.

Friends. I remember that pledge at the diner.

We are that. But it's not enough. I want another layer on top of it.

I want June.

I want her so bad I could scream. Or sing. Again. Sing forever. Stay up here performing karaoke until the bar closes down, just to get all this feeling out of me, express it through every song I can find.

I want to know what she's like up close, to run a finger along her jaw. To hold her body to mine and feel her breathe. To press my lips to hers. To be the one she comes back to after a long night out.

I want to go on trips with her. See the world through her lens. Hold her hand through the bad things. Stand beside her through the good ones.

I want all of it.

When we finish, Stevie is the first person to cheer out loud.

"That was the gayest thing I've ever seen in my life!" she calls out, clearly loving it.

Her friends join her. There are two men who look to be identical twins. They both drop to their knees. "We're not worthy," they say in unison, waving their arms up and down in dramatic bows of worship.

We return to Dawn, whose skeptical expression has only grown stronger since our karaoke endeavor. If something changed for me during this performance, it also changed for her, because she doesn't have the bulldog-aggressive curiosity anymore. She even goes so far as to yawn.

"Look, if you're not gonna make a move on anyone tonight, we should be getting back," she tells me. "It's way past my bedtime."

Make a move on who? I want to ask, but I don't have to. Because I know who she means. And so does June.

"Of course," I say to Dawn. "Let's go home."

It's only on the drive back that I realize I've called this place my home.

And that I liked the way it felt to say it.

18

Eleanor

Sometimes I loop my thoughts, as if repetition will convince me to believe what I'm thinking. Which is why I remind myself, over and over, that renting a car for the day has nothing to do with Carson joking about my walking everywhere. Walking is great. So is public transportation. I just want to cover more ground than my two feet will let me, and I don't want to be limited by train or bus times.

It also has nothing to do with trying to find a way to pass the time until tomorrow's picnic, or about distracting myself from wondering what Carson is doing with their day.

This is all about me.

An employee hands me the keys to a bright orange hatchback. It's a hideous vehicle. Bright, oddly shaped, demanding of attention. It makes me even more determined to have a real spectacle of a time somewhere other than Trove Hills. Maybe I'll spend the day driving the part of Route 66 that begins here. Who knows? Cue the Shania Twain and *Let's go, girl*.

It doesn't take long to discover that cars have changed a lot since the last time I drove one. Which was . . . twelve years ago?

I've kept my driver's license current for moments like this, which are few and far between. Nonexistent, to be more specific, but this kind of spontaneity is what the license is for, and I'll be damned if I don't use it for once.

The first change to throw me off is the ignition. I've seen this from the back of cabs and ride shares. It's a whole new thing to experience as the operator of the vehicle. There's no place to insert a key. I press a button with my foot on the brake, and somehow, the engine turns on?

Then there are the sensors. They are *everywhere*, shouting at me for failing to buckle in as soon as I shift out of park. Beeping whenever someone comes near me in reverse. Chirping at me to stay centered in the lane as soon as I make it onto the road. The speed limit here is thirty-five, but driving it outrages the other vehicles around me. Drivers honk in frantic succession, then speed past me like I have sought to personally offend them.

I make it all of one block from the rental lot before I panic.

Cutting over as hard as I can, I pull off onto the grass beside the road. To my right, oak trees stretch as far forward as the eye can see, a forest of lush green unknowns. On my left, cars fly by, as rude and loud as they were when I was operating one alongside them. It's a nightmare. Why would anyone want to operate a vehicle every day?

"You're okay, Eleanor," I say, hands still death-gripped around the steering wheel. "You're okay."

Forcing myself to problem-solve instead of continuing to waste time by freaking out, I reach with shaking hands for my phone. How do I get this car back to the rental property without having to drive it? Do Lyft drivers do that? Maybe if I pay them extra?

The knock on my window startles me into a scream, and I drop my phone in the space between the seat belt and the middle console.

It's Carson.

Somehow, it is always Carson.

I roll down my window, caught between relief and terror. "How are you everywhere I am?" I ask, breathless.

"I followed you," they tell me.

"You *what*?"

"I went over to my parents' house to see you," they say. "I pulled up right as you were getting into the back seat of a car. I don't have your number, so I couldn't text to ask where you were going. So I followed. Which, yes, that was weird of me. I just do things, I'm telling you. But I was thinking about how you don't know anyone here, and sometimes you hear scary stories about what happens with rideshare drivers. I got worried."

A blush begins crawling up their neck, like their nerves are somehow as potent as my own.

"Anyway, when you got out at a car rental place, I was invested," they continue. "I told myself I'd leave when you did, and I wouldn't keep track of you after that. But you gunned it out of the lot like a twelve-year-old who'd gotten into their parents' car without permission. I started to wonder if maybe you were drunk or something. You cut off a bus to swerve onto the grass. And yeah. I knew you needed help."

"I don't need help!" I shout. It's so emotional and untrue that I almost break down again. "I'm sorry." I slap my cheeks to stop myself from crying. "I'm not drunk. I just haven't driven a car in a very long time. I thought it was like riding a bike."

Carson reaches in through the window and unlocks my door. They pull it back, then step into the open space, squatting down beside me. Before I know it, they've grabbed my hands, stopping me from touching my face.

"Eleanor," they whisper, voice so tender it coaxes my suppressed tears back to the surface again. "It's okay."

"This is ridiculous," I say, eyes welling. "I'm embarrassed that you're seeing this."

"Don't be," they reply. "I just told you I followed you here. I'm winning the embarrassment Olympics."

"Why on earth did you follow me?" I ask.

"You were getting into a car when I pulled up, and—"

"No, I heard all of that. I mean, why do you care what happens to me?" Carson reacts like they've been sucker punched. "I know, I know, we all deserve care and attention," I say, stumbling in pursuit of a joke that will take me far away from this accidental vulnerability. There is no space in my life for their pity. "And you're a good person. You'd do this for anyone."

"No, I wouldn't," they tell me.

"You might not rescue your parents' intense neighbor, but I bet even Denise from over at Rita's Diner could get you to invest in a low-stakes car chase. If the situation was juicy enough."

Carson stands up again. It's a drastic improvement to piercing my soul with a devastated gaze while holding a perfect heels-flat and ass-to-the-grass squat. "Here's what we're going to do." They reach over me and unbuckle my seat belt, taking my hand again and guiding me around the front of the car and over to the passenger side.

They aren't being forceful. I'm being compliant. I could resist, and they'd stop without hesitation. Part of me wants to. But another part of me wants, for once, to have someone else think on my behalf.

"I'm going to drive this orange monstrosity back to the rental place with you in the passenger seat," they continue. "We will return it, explaining what happened. If they still make you pay, we can figure that out too."

"I don't care about the money," I say.

"Cool. Then we will return this and walk back to my car. Hopefully the boys in blue don't see us doing it, but if they do, we will be brave and defy them by continuing to walk. And then we will find a big, empty parking lot, where I will teach you how to drive."

"I know how to drive," I tell them.

"Okay. Sure. Let's just practice getting you more comfortable behind the wheel."

"I'm not uncomfortable, I just—"

"*Eleanor.* Please. It's clear you're going to go through this kicking and screaming, but I promise I won't tell a single soul that you have weaknesses." They lower me into the passenger seat, even going as far as to buckle me in again.

"Thank you," I say, doing my best to accept the help I know I want, even if my actions don't seem to match my desire. "The sensors would've screamed at you if you didn't do that part. They're very sensitive."

"Just like me," they say.

"Not me, though."

Carson picks up the conversation once they've gotten seated in the driver's seat. "No, no. You're a pillar of insensitivity. You definitely haven't committed to distracting me from my family for the week or anything thoughtful like that. You've never left a one-hundred-dollar tip at Rita's Diner for no reason either."

It's helpful to be reminded I've agreed to be their distraction. It re-centers me. Deep down, I know there could be more than that between us—that there already *is* more than that—but what good would come from giving that any headspace? I'm just a visitor here.

"Who told you about my tip?" I ask.

"My sources are confidential."

"By the way, my phone's stuck," I say.

"Of course it is."

"Nothing's ever easy with me."

"It's not that difficult either."

I sigh. "Just drive. Please."

19

Tatum

June busts open the door to the office, finding me in a pile of blankets, my eyes still crusted over with sleep.

"Let's take a walk," she says.

"It's seven in the morning," I tell her, still tasting the tang of last night's drinks in my mouth. We didn't have very many, but what we did have, combined with the adrenaline rush of the karaoke situation, has made it hard for me to get anything out of my system—alcohol, feelings, lingering dread about what's happening back in Trove Hills without me.

I've now read the lyrics to "If I Told You That" so many times that if I'm ever thrust into another impromptu performance, I won't need to look at the screen. I could even perform it like a spoken-word poem if necessary. Dawn would hate that. It would be amazing.

"It's actually 10:53," June says. My hands reach for my phone. She is, somehow, right. "Could you be ready in twenty?"

Her nervous energy is so potent it pulls me off the bed and into action. "Sure," I say, moving with more intention than I expected.

By the time we make it to the door, June is looping circles around the entryway as we make sure that Salt doesn't try to make a run for the exit once the door opens. She's put on a mono-chromatic outfit, though it's lavender, not orange. It's an athletic set and matching ball cap, with ankle-high socks and a pair of vintage sneakers that have lavender accents on them too.

"Inspired by *Hannity*?" I ask.

"You know it."

"You look good."

"Thank you," she says, not meeting my eye. "I'm stressed about the investor meeting."

She's deflected my compliment, which *should* be a good thing. She's not overwhelmed by us like I am. She's overwhelmed by her meeting.

"Nerves are good," I assure her, attempting to slide into a role I know well—Tatum the advice giver. "And we can take some pictures of you on the walk with some captions like 'Dreaming of big things to come' or whatever. Vanessa will be sweating."

Invoking Vanessa is a pressure test. What does her name mean between us now?

After all, June has stopped maintaining the ruse on her Insta-gram. Gone are the solo shots with the pointed captions about enjoying New York alone. When we got home last night, she even tagged me in a story. Right when I'd almost been able to drift off to sleep, the notification came in. It was a picture of us from the bar, taken by Stevie and sent to June through DM. June even put the Whitney song over the story.

She has to feel what I feel.

She has to know.

"Who cares about Vanessa?" she asks.

I could kiss you right now, I think. *I could press you up against this wall.*

"I'm more worried about whether or not the investors will like my presentation," she finishes.

"The presentation, right," I say, putting my thoughts back on track. This is *not* about kissing. "You know, something that always helps me is to flip my worries on myself. Instead of asking what happens if it all goes wrong, I ask myself what happens if it all goes right. What's the best-case scenario here?"

I almost never *actually* do this for myself, but it's great advice to give someone else.

We're out the door now, heading down in the elevator. "They agree to keep me on as creative director, and I'm still making the perfumes I want," she says. "But I have real support behind me, and I don't have to oversee every single step, down to the printing of the receipts and the tracking of the packages." She looks at her reflection in the mirrored ceiling above us. I watch her there too, gazing at us from this height, seeing all the people we could become. She looks infinite here, prismatic. Only she could look flattering under these circumstances, so lovely and soft.

As we walk through the park, we run scenarios together, playing out all the ways the investor meeting could go. We're good at this, just like we've been good at everything else we've tried. I think again of the kiss, wondering more than ever what it would be like if we just gave in.

Wondering if maybe—just maybe—it really is us.

"Do you feel ready now?" I ask her.

"I do, thank you. I just wish time would speed up and I could get past the meeting." She squeezes my hand again, and it's exactly what I need to urge me forward.

"I know one thing that might help with distracting you," I say. "I finally figured what you can help me with. How you can pay me back or whatever."

"Do tell."

"I think last night, I couldn't follow through with asking anyone out because I'm so good at talking myself out of things. If you let me, I can find the flaw in almost anything," I say. "But I'm tired of trying to find what could be wrong. I'd rather figure out what could be right. So this is me going for it. This is me asking you."

Her eyes crease into curious slits. "Asking me what?"

"On a date."

She steps away, waiting for the catch. "You want to go on a date . . . with *me*?"

"Yes," I say, holding my ground, even as a nervous quiver begins working its way through my system. "I know you're trying to learn the art of being single, so I obviously understand if it's a no. I just . . . I had to ask."

"I thought you said we'd be a bad idea," she reminds me.

I've planned for this comment. I've read the Whitney lyrics like scripture. "I'm not so sure I believe my past self anymore. And I think my exact words were that we wouldn't be a *good* idea. Which means maybe we're a *great* idea instead."

All her skepticism washes away, cleansed by the hope of my words. It's in the way her eyes widen, her nose crinkling with delight.

In this shift, we linger on each other, a new gate of possibility suddenly opened up.

"Wait a second," she says. "I asked you out first. I should get to take *you* out."

I expected her to challenge me, but only on the concept. Not on the specifics. "I thought this was my favor."

"You can cash in your favor later," she tells me. "Because I'm the one who will be taking you out tonight."

When my mouth opens to protest, she presses a finger against it.

"It's not negotiable," she tells me. "I'm going for a jog. See you tonight. You can get ready at Dawn's. I'll pick you up at seven."

Then she leans in, kisses my cheek, and takes off running.

20

Eleanor

D riving is fucking inane," I say, gripping the steering wheel so tight the tendons that stretch over my knuckles are visible. We're in the parking lot of a middle school. The very middle school Carson, Tatum, and their youngest sister, Laney, all attended, according to Carson.

"Don't tell me you use big words like *inane*," they say. "It's too sexy for me to handle while my blood pressure is this high."

"You're making fun of my vocabulary now? What's next? My inability to execute a three-point turn?"

"Oh, sweetheart, I don't think we're getting to three-point turns today. You swear you got your license honestly? You didn't pay off the person running the exam?"

"I failed it twice beforehand, but no, on the third time, I passed without incident." We hop a tiny parking curb. "Sorry. I didn't see that."

"You didn't see the curb that surrounds the only tree in this otherwise wide-open parking lot?"

"Do *you* want to drive?" I ask, throwing the car into park. When I look at their face, they're smiling, head cocked to the side, beholding me as if I'm worthy of wonder. "Stop making that face. You make me want to be nicer."

They fix their face into something serious. "Is this better? Because I love it when you're feisty. Your ears start to turn purple."

My hands reach for my ears, which are indeed warm.

"Don't cover it up," they continue. "I like seeing my effect on you."

We are still beside the tree, sideways in front of the curb I hopped. The tree provides the perfect amount of shade, blocking the high-noon warmth from getting in through Carson's sunroof.

"I don't think I'm making any driving progress," I say.

"You're not," they tell me, deadpan as ever.

I shove them. "Fuck you."

"Sounds good to me," they say. "But I think public indecency is a bigger crime than walking. Though I'm willing to risk it."

"I'm not fucking you in your middle school parking lot."

"If I had a nickel for every time I heard that . . ."

"You'd have one nickel," I say.

"Exactly."

We laugh.

"Was it a good school?" I ask, looking out past the tree to see a tall brick building, attempting to paste a young Carson in front of it.

Carson thinks for a while before offering up a very mild, "I guess so."

"Wow," I respond. "Don't hold back or anything."

This cracks them open, letting me in on the best version of their smile—the shy, slinky grin that slowly lights up their whole face. "It's where I learned to love art, so I can't hate that. And no one was ever *that* mean to me. Everyone was mean to everyone in seventh grade, but I think that's kind of par for the course."

"That was eighth grade for me," I interject. "But go on."

"High school was harder," they say. "I knew I liked girls, but I didn't know why knowing that wasn't enough to make me feel complete. I thought figuring out my sexuality would, like, unlock this path to inner peace or something. But it didn't. I got into a lot of trouble." They start to tap a random beat atop the glove compartment. "While breaking countless hearts, of course."

"I've seen the pictures of you," I say, thinking again of the framed images that line the staircase in the cottage. "I would have had a crush on you. Add me to the list of the broken-hearted."

"I'd have totally claimed your attention running cross-country at six thirty in the morning."

"If you can believe it, I was in Ecology Club in high school," I say. "So I'd have been out there collecting rainwater samples from the imprint of your running shoe in the mud."

"It's all coming together. Eleanor the walking enthusiast, examining the ecosystem."

"And Carson the track star, running from the trouble they've caused."

"It's a funny exercise, wondering if we'd have liked each other," Carson says.

"I already told you I'd have had a crush on you," I remind them.

"Yeah, but that's just something you're saying because you think I'm irresistible now. Ecology Club Eleanor would not have been looking twice at the gangly swamp creature that was teenage me."

"I think being a member of Ecology Club proves I would be very interested in a swamp creature."

Studying their profile, I notice a gloss over their eyes. It surprises me to see how close I am to hitting a nerve when all I meant to do was make them laugh. They swallow and lean their head back, moving their gaze from the school to the roof of the car.

"This trouble you used to get into," I start tentatively, wanting to explore this new, tender side of them the way I've explored every other. "What kind of trouble are we talking? Because I was also on the debate team my junior and senior year. I bet my well-considered arguments could've gotten you out of some tight spots."

"I used to steal shit," Carson tells me.

"Never mind," I reply, coloring it with a light laugh, still figuring out what level of depth we're excavating. "Couldn't help you with that one."

"No, I wasn't easy to help in those days."

"What did you steal?"

"I'd go to the grocery store and stuff my pockets with small things. Candy, gum, makeup. I didn't even want it for myself. I'd give it to my friends as gifts. It was months before I got caught. The time they busted me, I had two packs of sour candy and a container of hair gel on me."

"The usual supply," I interject.

"Exactly. I got taken into the police station, and they made me spend the night in a holding cell. Turns out they'd been tracking my behavior at the store for weeks. They knew exactly how much I'd stolen. That's where a lot of this 'Carson is trouble' mythology began."

I want to brush a curl out of their eye, overwhelmed with the need to touch them, but I stop myself.

"I've talked a lot about it all in therapy," they continue. "Probably too much, if I'm honest. I kind of feel like I've thought holes into all of it at this point, trying to figure out what I really wanted. I've pretty much landed on the fact that it felt like everything was out of my control. My parents were unhappy with each other but sticking together anyway. And it was confusing to learn what my dad did. He and I had always been really close. He liked teaching me things on his off days. Suddenly I felt like I didn't know him at all, and nothing had even changed. I just learned something from his past that I didn't think fit with the guy I knew in the present. It kind of blew my mind that people could walk around with earth-shattering secrets all the time, and they were still the same people. So I started racking up some secrets of my own, I guess."

"That makes sense," I tell them.

"Yeah. Add onto it that my body at the time didn't feel right for the life everyone told me I was supposed to live inside it, and I didn't have the understanding then of what I wanted it to be instead. And look, I know I fucked up a lot. I don't mean to excuse what I did. But I think if I had a kid who started acting out the way I was, I'd have tried a little harder to figure out what was making them do all that instead of scaring them into stopping while ignoring all the reasons why it began. I just wanted someone to see me, I guess."

A single tear rolls down the slope of their cheek, leaving behind a glistening river. This time I can't help myself. I do reach out, resting my hand atop theirs and giving it a squeeze.

"If I learned anything from that time, it's that all the rules we create for ourselves about how life needs to work, none of it is real," they continue. "And yeah, maybe I could have taken a neater road to figuring that out, but it did help me understand that I didn't have to play any part the world assigned to me. I've spent the rest of my life trying to put that feeling into my work. Building, painting, drawing it into existence, how it feels to understand that everything is all made-up, but somehow, being alive is kind of a marvelous thing anyway."

When I don't respond right away, they force their usual grin, morphing before my eyes from someone vulnerable into someone careful, putting up the same shields I recognize from my own arsenal of defense.

"Sorry," they say. "I shouldn't be laying this heavy shit on you."

"No apologies necessary." I squeeze their hand tighter. "I understand more than I can even say. I'm somewhat allergic to the lighter fare myself. You know, child of dead parents and all. I'm sure if someone was around to care about me after they died, they'd have started calling me trouble then too."

There it is. Another slip.

I'm planning all my rebuffs, ready to make a stunning case for my lack of support, workshopping how to mention the squirrel-psychic thing in a way that's funnier than it is sad, when Carson leans over the seat.

"*Trouble*," they murmur in my face.

"Hey now," I say, playfully shoving them back to their side of the car. "I don't qualify anymore. I've aged out of the bracket."

"You qualify," they say. "I've been over to the cottage more times in the last three days than I have in the last three years. That's the work of a true menace to society."

In the startling quiet that follows, a need possesses me. To show them more than I can put into words. I lean over the seat.

They give me that look, the permissive grin, and I know my instincts are right. With fragile pressure, I press my lips to theirs.

We've already kissed. We've done a lot more than that. Now the urgency between us holds the weight of our past. I know some of their vulnerabilities, and they know some of mine in return. To kiss them here is to accept them for it.

This kiss stands in for all I don't know how to say. *Be nearer to me*, I tell them with my tongue, dancing with theirs as our hands untangle the knots of each other. *Tell me all your secrets.*

It's only when I put my hand on the steering wheel to push up, needing to get even closer, and the car lets out a loud, disruptive honk, that we separate.

"Jesus," I say, startled by the sound.

Carson laughs, falling back into their seat. "Fuck," they whisper.

I'd meant to spend this day without them. When I'd rented a car this morning, I'd intended to get out of Trove Hills. But here I am, in the parking lot of Carson's middle school, clutching the steering wheel as we're parked under a tree, and I don't know how I could ever be somewhere else.

"We should go somewhere," I say.

"Where?" Carson asks.

"What about home?"

I don't mean to say it like that. It's not *my* home. But it's the fastest way to communicate what should be next. We shouldn't be in public. That's all I know for sure. And it's better than sitting here in the middle school parking lot, talking about who we used to be. That's not getting me anywhere productive.

"Yeah," Carson says with a smile. "Let's go home, Trouble."

THE GUEST COTTAGE GETS FANTASTIC LIGHT DURING the day. Even during summertime, there is a hazy, sun-drenched filter over everything that makes it feel as though you've stepped into your favorite memory. I could do nothing here and somehow, for once, be content with that.

"Were you and your siblings ever in a fight over who got to live here?" I ask as Carson follows me through the front door.

"Not at all." They plop onto the couch with a practiced familiarity. "No one used the cottage until Tatum moved in."

"You're kidding," I say, taking off my shoes and settling beside them. "Why not? It's perfect."

Carson explains to me the origins of this cottage. How it got constructed when the affair came to light, which was years after the affair had actually occurred. I listen with my head drifting toward their shoulder, magnetized by the idea of being able to feel their beating heart as they speak.

By the end, I am nuzzled into them, looking out the very window they tumbled through a few days ago. It offers a perfect view of the main house, a back door leading out to a wooden patio, and a long garden path that connects the two buildings.

"Tatum has to like living here, though," I insist. "It's charming."

"She likes that it doesn't make this place a family joke anymore," Carson explains. "Everyone had a different reaction to the affair. Tatum wanted to undo it, I think. And the fact that our mom won't step foot in here unless she's forced to made it really hard for Tatum to scrub the affair from the family conscience. If anything, Dad building this cottage made a lot of things worse. I don't think Tatum has any real love for it beyond the fact that now no one can call it Dad's Bad Apology Building anymore."

"If the vibes are that bad, why doesn't your family move to a new house?" I ask.

"There was a time when they discussed it, but my parents have lived in the main house for almost forty years. They've accumulated so much stuff that they don't want to go through yet, so the hassle of moving everything out isn't worth it to anyone. But Tatum should absolutely go, yeah. I've been telling her that since she moved back after college. Her friends have too. We all want it for her. She just can't bring herself to do it."

"I'm always team leave home," I say. "I moved out when I was eighteen. Practically ran out the door." There's a catch in my throat, something beyond me nudging out a deeper truth. "I can't say I regret it, because no one could have changed my mind then.

But losing my parents so young did make me wish I'd spent more time with them before I left."

I never press these emotional bruises, knowing the tenderness of the touch is not worth exploring. Why speak to the pain in myself that can't ever be healed? But something about Carson makes me willing to acknowledge it. Being away from the life I know makes it safe enough for me to open up.

"Do you have a favorite memory of them?" Carson asks.

"It's funny," I say. "I've spent so long missing them that I forget to remember what happened when they were still here."

"How long has it been?"

"Fourteen years in November," I tell them. "My mom wasn't very good at expressing herself, and my dad never had a lot of patience for anyone trying to find themselves in the world."

"That sure sounds like a recipe for a young Eleanor," Carson says, stroking my arm.

"Oh yes. It was very important to me that they saw me as an expert at existing," I say. "I spent a lot of my childhood searching for ways to impress them. That was the fastest way to get my mom to say she was proud of me and to make sure my dad didn't get frustrated. If I was bad at something, I'd quit before there was any kind of recital or game, so I didn't have to sit in the car and hear about how I could be better at it." My filter has been so far removed that it's only after I'm done speaking that I realize what I've said. "That's not an answer to your question at all. There were a lot of good things. I don't know what made me tell you that. We went to Disney World every summer. That was fun."

Carson laughs, not in a pitying way. "Disney World is fun. But so is being bad at things." They pick up a strand of my hair, running it through their fingers. "If I'm allowed to brag, I'm pretty good at being bad at stuff. If you ever want someone to show you."

I sit up straighter, leaning back to look them in the eye. "Please tell me one single thing you are bad at. You managed to use the sugar packets at Rita's to make a *Mona Lisa* of me."

"That was easy though," Carson says. "Who wouldn't want to draw you?"

My body tenses, unpracticed in accepting this brand of fondness.

"I frequently misjudge the severity of things, for one," Carson continues. "I think I know what's serious and what's for fun, but I'm usually wrong."

We've just shared what we think are our fatal flaws—my inability to fail and their inability to assess something. Our worst flaw might be that neither of us wants to be incorrect about what's going on between us. Which makes it easy for me to go for the physical. The part that doesn't have to be explained. We've understood it from the very beginning, before Carson even knew my name. It's the first rule we established in this strange little game we've been playing, and it's the only thing I'm sure I understand.

I can kiss Carson like I planned to on the entire drive over. They can put their hand under my leg and tug me on top of them. We can get lost in each other's bodies until the sun starts to move across the window, shining golden-hour light through dust-covered panes.

There's an expiration date to all of this. That's what I need to keep in mind. The more we speak, the less I'm able to keep track of what this is supposed to be.

So we won't speak anymore. Not about anything real.

We can hold each other instead.

21

Tatum

June picks me up at seven on the dot. There are three short knocks on the door, and a long stretch of silence afterward. Dawn makes no move from the couch where both of us sit.

"You can't be serious," she says, staring me down.

"I was kind of hoping you'd get it," I whisper.

"It's not *my* date," she says back loudly.

I spring up, smoothing down the yellow shift dress Dawn has lent me. She even curled my hair for me, taming my curls into loose tendrils that flow away from my face. I haven't gotten put together like this in years.

I look nice.

There's a moment when I'm caught, standing with my hand hovering over Dawn's doorknob. Opening this door changes everything. That should scare me. I've spent a whole year believing it would. Instead I'm exhilarated, almost too eager for my own good.

Everything's already changed anyway. It's time for me to take charge of the direction.

I throw the door open.

June holds out a bouquet of flowers. "Coral roses," she says, thumbing one of the soft orange petals. "They represent a first date."

"Did you learn that on the internet?"

"From my mom, actually."

I stare at the flowers, so nervous about seeing her face that it's easier to put all my attention on the roses first, needing to take in each detail. "They're really pretty."

She hands them over. "I told you. Yellow is a great color on you," she says.

My whole body flushes. I was hoping she'd notice. That she'd put together why I chose this. "It's Dawn's." I twist from side to side to show off the dress at every angle.

"Looks perfect." Her eyes linger on me so long that the hairs on my arms prick up.

She wears a black silk tank tucked into dark jeans. The low cut of the shirt accentuates her collarbone, where she's put a shimmering highlight. She has her bob slicked down, hair tucked behind her ears to show off her collection of studded earrings. There are stars, moons, and gemstones, with a small hoop at the top of her left earlobe.

"You look . . ." I search for the right words. They never come to me with June. Because to see her is to understand what it means to be speechless. "Perfect," I decide.

Still, she blushes, tucking back a piece of hair that needs no actual adjusting. We call out a goodbye to Dawn, then take the elevator to the ground floor, where the doorman we've come to know gives us a nod.

"You first," June says, waving me inside the vehicle. I crawl into the driver's-side back seat, making room for June to get in next to me. My hands are so slick with sweat that they leave a damp imprint on the leather seat. "We're going to an Italian restaurant. I figured the best first date is a classic one, so I'm trying to check all the boxes."

She is so assured that it has the magical effect of making me relax a bit myself. This night can go in so many directions that I find myself wanting to sprint, eager to find out where we will land. June has a way of grounding me, showing me the value in taking each moment as it comes.

She takes me to an Italian restaurant not very far from Eleanor's place, where the tables are made of a sturdy wood, covered in red-checkered cloths, and the decor does little to detract from the purpose of the meal, which is to enjoy pasta and drink wine. It isn't what I expect New York to look like, but my vision of this place has always been a skyscraping, jet-setting stereotype. People taking work calls during dinner inside sexy, smoky restaurants. I think I thought all of New York was like Times Square. And it's really not. It's so many different things. It's whatever you want it to be, really.

June pulls out my chair, then tucks me back in before taking her spot across the table.

"You're really giving me the red carpet treatment," I say.

"I've been on a lot of dates in my life," she tells me. "Not many of them have been good. This is my chance to try to do for you what so few have ever successfully done for me."

When she settles into her seat, we lock eyes again, and it's the kind of feeling I want to bottle. The promise of this beginning. Because we're both going for this with the same hope, the same care, that we give each other at the diner. I don't know why I thought that was some sort of courtesy she paid me because I was her server. It's just who she is. Who we are to each other, really.

"You're already leagues above the rest," I say. "And that's not just flattery."

"I think it *is* flattery. But I guess now is a good time to tell you that I like being flattered."

"Good thing I have a lot of compliments for you that I've never said. I didn't think it was right to tell you how beautiful you are after I was the one who turned you down. But you're so, so beautiful."

This has the effect I hoped it would—June's eyes darting to her hands and then back to me.

"And quite excellent at first-date selections," I continue. "The first date I ever went on was my junior year of high school. This girl wanted to rent out a movie theater for us, but she couldn't afford it, so instead she made us skip school to have our date at ten a.m. on a Wednesday. She thought nobody would be at the theater then. Instead the entire place was packed with senior citizens. Filled to the brim. Needless to say we didn't really have the hot-and-heavy experience we both imagined. Not for us, at least. Some of the seniors were having a good time, though."

"My first date was going to a movie too," June tells me. "No heavy petting between the elderly though. Not that I noticed."

"A movie date is really the classic high school move," I say.

"My first date was actually right after I graduated."

This takes me by surprise. For some reason I assumed June would've started dating in middle school or something. Probably because I'd guess everyone would want to ask her out.

"We saw *The Fault in Our Stars* in the theater," she continues. "I cried so hard that a rash broke out across my entire face and neck. My eyes swelled up until my lashes started to stick together because my mascara was so tacky with tears."

"Relatable."

"If that wasn't bad enough, I was out with a guy I didn't even like," she says. "I just felt so behind then, I agreed to go out with him to catch up to my friends. Even though I'd cried enough to look like I needed to be admitted to the emergency room for an allergic reaction, and we'd said maybe ten words to each other before and after the movie, he still kissed me in the parking lot of the theater."

Before I can process my own reaction to this, June puts her hand on mine.

"Don't worry, I told him he could," she assures me. "But it was a very bad kiss. Although it did confirm that I prefer girls, so that was nice of him. It also proved that I really didn't need to be in any kind of rush to date someone. I wasn't missing out on much."

"Didn't you tell me you're a serial monogamist?"

"Yeah," she confirms with a sad laugh. "Just because I knew that doesn't mean I followed it." She gives an even sadder laugh this time. "I proceeded to date that same guy for an entire year. I haven't been single for longer than a month since."

I believed her when she told me she wasn't good at being alone, and that she was always dating someone. I just didn't conceptualize it fully like I am now, understanding the exact expanse of time she has spent partnered with someone else. All the life milestones she's lived with another person at her side. The same ones I've spent in avoidance, not letting someone live them with me. Looking back at it, I feel acutely aware of how long that time has stretched on, how far I've let this go. And for the first time, I'm wondering if I've really planned to live this way forever.

Is that actually what I want? To be alone for everything?

As we eat our meal, we swap stories of our respective high schools. June grew up a few towns over from Trove Hills, and we have enough overlap to be able to appreciate the shared language of the area. She talks about a few more of her past relationships. Another guy after high school. The first woman she dated.

By the time we've finished our food and closed out our bill, she's telling me how one of her girlfriends actually proposed to her when she was twenty-two, and she had to say no. This is less surprising to me, that the people June has dated would want to be with her forever.

"I can't believe you didn't go through with it," I tease. "If for no reason other than getting to pick out a dress."

"I know," she says, not at all offended. "The thing is, I was obsessed with hats then. I wore them all the time. I probably would have gotten married in one. And that would be tough to look back on now."

"Are we talking like a beret, or a newsboy cap situation?" I ask.

"I hate to say it, but it was a full-on Willy Wonka situation."

"*June*," I say, scandalized.

"I know. What about you? Any proposals?"

"I haven't let any of my ex-girlfriends get anywhere near that question," I say. "I like to scare them off in that sweet spot after we've spent a lot of fun time together, but right before they tell me they love me."

June cocks her head. In this appraisal, I know she's recalibrating me again, placing this information beside all the other pieces I've given her. It's hard to take the pressure of this change. At the same time, it's the truth.

I gaze back, handing her a piece of my fragile, jagged trust, understanding that she will care for it the same way she's cared for everything else.

"What would you have done if they said it?" She's leaned into the table, head resting in her hand the way she usually looks at her notebook at the diner. Now I'm the problem she's solving, and her face even wears the same scrunch of concentration I recognize from years of observing her at a distance.

"Probably told them it wasn't a good idea," I joke, a callback to my rejection of her.

"Love is rarely a good idea," June challenges. "That's not the point. There's always going to be a reason it won't work. There's always going to be some baggage to work through. But what I love—*ha*—about love is that you're asking someone to do it with you anyway."

"What if the journey has too much unexpected turbulence? You're afraid of flying . . ." I peter out, not sure why I'm trying to relate this to us. We're not talking about us. How could we be? This is only a first date.

"C'mon," June says gently. "Let's go get dessert. There's an ice-cream place not too far from here."

She comes around to my side of the table to pull my chair out. It's over-the-top, even a little ridiculous, but I still love it all the same. She offers me her arm, gesturing for me to thread my hand through her elbow, so we can walk out side by side.

Off we go, through the restaurant and out the door. No one in Trove Hills associates us together, but all these strangers in New York are getting a snapshot into a life where June and I are linked. Where I'm the person June orders drinks for. The one she comes home to, even if the home we have here is temporary. It's still ours.

I hold her tight, breathing in the scent of her, basking in a closeness that doesn't have to be hidden behind pretending to want to smell her perfume, as June makes plans for us to visit some of the places we pass. What is this future she speaks of, where she and I will be back here in New York together?

Still, I commit to it, even if I don't understand the hows or whys. It's not difficult to do, sketching the outline of my life here. Every location she pitches for us to try, I'm in. Doesn't matter that the amount of time it would take to do all of this far exceeds the time we have remaining here. It's easy to imagine a world beyond right now, even if it's not what's true.

When we make it to the ice-cream shop, we learn it is, tragically, closed.

"Shit," June says in disbelief. "I checked on Yelp and everything."

"It's okay," I tell her. "This date is still the best first date I've been on. No ice cream required."

Under the soft glow of night, with the endless hum of traffic surrounding the ice-cream shop, June spins me toward her.

"You know, you were never going to be my friend," I say, my breath catching as she steps one of her feet between mine.

"I've always been your friend." She brushes one of the wavy tendrils off my cheek. "And hopefully, I always will be."

The word *but* hangs in the air.

She doesn't say it. She looks at me, her purpose clear, gaze flickering from my lips to my eyes.

"But you want more?" I fill in. She tilts her face down. Before her lips can touch mine, I press my finger there, keeping a single inch between our faces. Her breath blows gently onto me.

"You've been single for only a few days," I whisper.

"And you're afraid of hurting me," she whispers back. "We could go through an entire list of reasons this shouldn't be right now." She places her hand on the small of my back, pulling my body against hers. "I think we've spent far too long doing that, don't you?"

Instead of answering with words, I take my finger off her mouth and place my lips there instead.

Kissing June, I become alive with want—with *need*. I run my hand up and down her back, gliding between the silk of her shirt and the softness of her skin. When I land on the spot behind her neck, she lets out a faint gasp, so I hold her there, cradling her head as my tongue slips into her mouth with a sigh.

She moves her hand to my chest. That pressure keeps me steady. My heart beats against her hand. All hers to have.

Why did I ever fight this?

And how did I hold off this long?

"I don't know where we're going," I say, not sure if I mean right now, or altogether. The words fall out of me, almost panted, like all this time I've been running, and only now, for the very first time, I've stopped to catch my breath.

"Neither do I." She moves her mouth to my ear. "But let's keep going together. Let's find out."

I don't know what comes next, but I know I want to keep feeling this way, like I've been cracked open, and all this bright, frantic need is pouring into me, filling all the dark places where I've kept my desires hidden away, forcing them to the surface.

I want June in every way I can have her.

22

Eleanor

When we meet the Wards outside a forest preserve, Carson's dad is the first to notice me.

"Eleanor!" he calls out. "Seems like I'm the last person in the family to meet you. I've heard nothing but good things." He kisses me on the side of my face.

I kiss him back the same way, the corners of my lips coming closer to his temple than they do to his cheek. "You must be a fan of women named Eleanor staying in your guest cottage, because I don't know what else you could've heard about me."

He laughs, looking at Carson with a knowing face. "I heard you were funny and likable. I'd say that's ringing pretty true."

Taking in his khaki shorts and button-up Hawaiian shirt, it's hard to imagine him as the man who quietly tore apart his family with the revelation of his affair. He's harmless-looking, dorky even, if that's a way people are even allowed to be classified anymore. Everything that Carson told me in the car yesterday makes more sense. Seeing this man while processing his choices feels impossible to do.

Anthony Teller springs forward in my thoughts, another man

whose role has been rewritten in the postscript of our relationship. If you can even call it a relationship. Situationship is more accurate. I wonder what's happened with his fiancée. If they've survived the message I sent, and the revelation that's come with it.

I don't know what's worse—they don't have the kind of love that could survive infidelity, or my actions have contributed to the same kind of pain that's rippled through the family I am picnicking with today.

"You can call me Andy if you want," Carson's dad tells me.

"Or Dr. Ward," Carson chimes in. "He loves that, but he wants to seem humble to you right now."

"Why go through all the trouble of getting a title if no one's going to use it in your everyday life?" I say. "Thanks for having me, Dr. Ward. I hope I haven't been an inconvenience."

"You've got our kid showing up on time and bringing the approved dish." He points to the sherbet Jell-O cake Carson spent the morning making. "I think we could be throwing this whole shindig in your honor instead. Or maybe we should save that for convincing Tatum to come back for some of this." His eyes gloss over as he shrugs his shoulders. "Ah well, what can ya do? Anyway, it's a pleasure to have you."

"I hope Tatum sees some of this too," I say, as if I know her at all. It feels like I do. I can see her in the space between everyone else, the weight of her absence forming her shape. She seems to be a lot of things to a lot of different people. My attention has always been best served when it's focused on one thing. I was good at my job because that was the place where I gave all my attention and effort. But everywhere I go in Trove Hills, someone knows Tatum. Relies on her.

Carson and I head for the picnic shelter, which houses several tables full of family members of all ages. The faces from the stairway, as I'm starting to think of them.

"Your cake is a pastel vision," I say, waving off flies as Carson sets it down on the food table. The air is thick with a wet, heavy heat. Sweat trickles down my neck. I can feel the pressure of the stairway faces watching me.

What am I doing here, at this family's party? Who the hell do I think I am?

"They make me bring this to every function," Carson whispers, looking over their shoulder to be sure no Ward is listening. "Thanksgiving, Christmas, Fourth of July. No one ever eats it."

"What would they do if I cut myself a piece?"

"There's gelatin in it. Neither of us can eat it."

"What if I pretend? Cut a slice and mimic the act of bringing it to my mouth?" I ask. "What happens then?"

"Impossible to say," Carson tells me. "My whole family might disappear. Entire bloodlines could vanish into thin air."

"A cake that could cause a rapture," I say. "What power you have."

"I know. Heavy is the head, et cetera, et cetera."

To be safe, we leave Carson's Jell-O masterpiece untouched. Carson takes me from table to table, introducing me to more aunts, uncles, cousins, and miscellaneous relatives than I could ever remember at once.

"Where are you from?" one of the aunts asks me.

Before I go to my default—which is to say New York—I pause, considering the truth. Being here has excavated so many pieces of myself I've allowed to be buried by time and distance, including the home I haven't been back to since my parents died.

"I grew up in Pennsylvania," I say. The syllables sound unnatural, like I'm speaking a language that's foreign only to me.

"Uncle Paul and I go up to Pittsburgh every few years to watch the Pirates games," the woman tells me. "I'm Irene." She gets up to kiss me on the cheek the same way Dr. Ward did.

"Your family loves a kiss," I whisper to Carson.

"Tell me about it," they whisper back.

"So, Eleanor, what do you do?" Irene asks.

"She's a press agent," Carson offers.

Irene lights up with genuine interest. "What's that mean?"

"It's just a fancy word for a publicist," I say. "I work for a firm that handles some of Broadway's plays and musicals. We don't represent the individual actors. We represent productions. Basically, we're the ones who get write-ups about shows in magazines or online. We book the leads for interviews and press opportunities with various media outlets. That kind of stuff."

It's all such bullshitty PR-speak nonsense that it takes me a while to realize that I've said it in the present tense, forgetting once again that I got fired. So much of my life has been spent giving this exact speech, I don't even know how to work in the fact that it's no longer true.

It occurs to me that in all of my life, I have never met someone else's entire family. No partner of mine has been serious enough for us to spend the holidays together. I haven't had friendships deep enough to merit traveling out of the city and into whatever random town they've come from either.

I'm an imposter of the highest form. My life used to be my job and my cats, and currently I have neither at my disposal. It's hard to make small talk as is, but right now, nothing about my life feels very small anymore.

"I'm actually in between agencies right now," I add, patching over this unintentional gap, even though I'm the only person who understands how wide it is. "I'm hoping to head over to my last firm's competitor."

"That's just fantastic," Irene says. She has to be one of Dr. Ward's siblings. The kissing, for one. But also, she has the same earnestness, though her exterior is more serene than it is dorky. "What a fascinating job."

"It's really not as glamorous as it might sound," I tell her. "It's a lot of emailing people saying things like, 'Just circling back here,' or 'Checking in on this one again.' Being a professional nuisance, really."

"I still think it's cool," Irene says. "And what a beautiful young woman you are too. Very smart and composed. You're just lovely."

"She really is," another aunt adds. "I'm Fran," she says, rising for the kiss I've now come to expect. "You've got the nicest shade of blond in your hair. Could I take a picture of it? I wanna show my stylist. She always makes me too brassy."

"Oh," I say, my surprise genuine. "Sure. And I don't think your hair looks brassy, for what it's worth."

As Fran fumbles with her phone to set up the shot, Carson puts an arm around me. The surprise of it makes me offer up a bigger smile than I mean to give.

Fran turns her camera around to show us the image, she and Irene murmuring another round of praise for me as she does so.

While I've never before thought of myself as lovely, Carson and I do look lovely together. We used to talk about this kind of thing at Garber and Link, how certain actors just look *right* when photographed together. Even though I feel sticky and over-cooked, it doesn't come through in this picture. Carson has their eyes squinted, giving a sly expression, and I've got my head angled toward them while still holding the camera's gaze. I'd done this to show off my hair, hoping to catch the blond in sunlight. In the photo, it creates an intimacy between Carson and me. We look like we have secrets that only we know. Which is true, in some ways.

Even stranger, I look . . . happy.

"Look at you, Trouble," Carson says. "You're glowing."

Irene grabs the phone from Fran. "Eleanor, you could be a movie star!" She turns around to look at one of the other tables, where several of the Ward men are chatting in low tones. "Paul, honey! You gotta come meet Eleanor from Pennsylvania! You're gonna love her!"

Her admiration is so sincere it pricks my heart deeper than I expect, letting in more sadness than I've made space for in a long, long time. Maybe it's that she looks to be the same age my mother would be, if she were still alive. Or it's the way she doesn't need to know much about me to decide I'm worth liking.

"Excuse me for one moment," I say, unable to staunch the flow of tears that's begun to surface.

I wander into the trees and the breath of heat that's stuck between them. Holding myself like I have countless other times in my life, I walk until I can no longer see the picnic tables, so I can whisper the words that have always comforted me in times of unexpected distress—the mantra I have for me and me alone, my last line of defense against whatever threatens to overwhelm me.

"You're okay, Eleanor," I say. "You're okay."

It's never enough, but it's usually something.

Right now, for the first time, these words devastate me. How many times have I soothed myself back to a false state of normalcy? How many struggles have I endured all alone, no one around to care for me except myself?

I'm so tired of being brave and self-sufficient. I don't want to wipe my tears and paste on a smile.

I just want a hug.

"Eleanor," Carson calls out. I can hear branches crack under their feet, their pace frantic. "Where are you?"

"I don't know," I call back.

"That's okay," they assure me, their voice already growing closer. "Just keeping talking to me, baby. I can find you."

My tears flow hard enough to induce snot. "I don't really know what to say."

"How about you count out loud?"

The hiccup in my throat fights me with each number.

It takes Carson nine seconds to find me. I fall into them, my arms wrapping around their torso, holding on like they might disappear if I don't squeeze tight enough. They might be a dream—one of those romance novel fantasies—and I can't let it evaporate.

They match my pressure in an instant, squeezing back in the exact way I hoped they would, letting me melt into the assuredness of their arms.

They are real. They are here. For me.

"What's going on?" they ask, rubbing soothing circles into the fabric of my shirt.

"I hate that you keep finding me like this," I say. "I swear this doesn't normally happen."

"I hate that it keeps happening to you now." They put my face in their hand, and it's the exact kind of gentle I want the most. It undoes me, rips off the last paper-thin barrier that stands between me and the truth—I care about them. Way more than I should.

I lean back into their embrace, letting myself be held. Their arms are unyielding, grabbing me without reservation. My head fits so nicely into the crook of their neck.

"I'm not used to having so many people interested in me," I tell them. "It's just overwhelming."

"It's not hard to care about you," Carson whispers into my ear.

If the hug was my undoing, these words are my reshaping. They form me into someone I have never met, reinforcing the softness within me that's been desperate for a safe place to land. I want to find something adequate to say back, but words can't match the way it feels to be seen.

After a while, it's enough to make me stop crying.

"I'm ready to go back to the picnic," I say, stepping back.

Carson laughs. "No, you aren't." Their thumb reaches for my face again, wiping under my eye to show me a wet smudge of mascara. "You do not want to go see my entire family looking like a raccoon. Not that you don't pull it off. But something tells me we'll get a little distance from this event and you won't want the proof to be on your face like this."

"Okay," I say.

And so Carson walks me to their car, parked away from the event, so I can get a tissue and adjust my face.

Years of grief have taught me to school joy. My every success has been measured against what I've lost. There are so many barricades around my heart that it's become commonplace for me to work around those obstacles, moving farther and farther away from the core of me—the wild, beating dream of desire inside my chest that reminds me the sun is out and the sky is blue. I've been living in my stomach. In the acid that gurgles and stews. Only now do I realize that I've been crying so much because for the first time in fourteen years, I'm starting to find my way out.

I care. A lot. Too much. I care that I am good at my job and I lost it because of my own recklessness. I care that no one ever meets my standards.

I care that I'm lonely.

And maybe, for the first time in my life, I care enough to do something about it.

23

Tatum

It's been almost an entire day since I kissed June under the lights of the ice-cream shop. We had to break apart eventually, lips swollen, to walk home together so June could get some sleep before her investor meeting. We could've kept going. We could've stayed up the whole night together. But I knew better than to let her show up for her meeting without a good night's rest.

We slept one wall apart—me in the office, her in Eleanor's room. It might as well have been a thousand miles. Still, I found myself listening for her, my spine straightening at every creak in the floorboards, hoping against my better judgment that she was coming in to see me.

In the end, she made the right choice by staying away.

Dawn and I have spent the morning and afternoon going through her closet, a task she tells me she's put off for over a decade. My work in Eleanor's apartment has inspired her to tackle it. As we open box after box, Dawn shows me relics from her past—awards she's won, dresses she wore to premieres and to nightclubs. Knowing how closed off she was when we showed up last week, it isn't lost on me to have her be this open now.

"This," she says, showing me a long slinky dress made of a liquid-looking silver fabric, "was what I wore when I got invited to the Golden Globes in 1979. It was very scandalous. I showed a lot of shoulder."

It doesn't take long for me to find the picture online. "Dawn, you look incredible."

"Better than Martha Stewart?" she asks.

"Way better," I tell her.

"Good. And I haven't gone to jail for insider trading either."

Sifting through the pieces of her life, Dawn tells me stories from her earliest New York days. It makes me sad to think of how long she's been in this apartment alone, no one to collect this amazing wealth of information. The problem, I know, was also on Dawn, who hasn't let anyone get close to her either. Still, it seems criminal that she's been here all by herself, sitting with these beautiful clothes and amazing memories, believing no one cared enough to experience any of it.

When we get on the topic of the women she dated, she becomes shy, especially considering the way she treated me at the bar when we discussed my own dating history.

With lots of coaxing, she finally tells me about someone named Paula who she used to go clubbing with in her early twenties, before her big break.

"Paula didn't take shit from anybody, which I loved," she says. "All kinds of seedy men would hit on me at the clubs, and Paula could give them one look, and they'd leave me alone for the rest of the night. It was amazing. But with me, she was soft, which I loved too. She'd call me sweetheart, and she'd make sure I drank enough water after we'd been out all night. I always liked having somebody who took care of me. And Paula liked having someone to protect. We worked well in that way."

Dawn explains how when she booked her first role, she had to stay in Los Angeles for six months. By the time she got back, Paula had moved.

"We'd both agreed when I went to work on that movie that it would be too much of a distraction to keep talking to each other," she tells me. "I think back on that now, and I just want to smack myself. But I was young and ambitious then, and I didn't want anything getting in the way of my acting career. Paula said she understood. I really thought she did too. I was always a little oblivious like that. When I finally got back to New York after the shoot wrapped, I showed up at her apartment and got greeted by a man and his pet parakeet. Paula had moved, and I had no way to reach her. We only had landlines then."

"Didn't any of your other club friends know where she was?" I ask.

"I asked them, of course. And everyone was cagey about it, telling me Paula moved to Brooklyn, then saying, no, she actually went to San Francisco, or you know, maybe it was London. Nobody would give me a straight answer. Next thing I know, I've got another acting job lined up, and I don't have the time to look into it further, because I'm flying back to Los Angeles. I could kick myself now, I really could. I just let her slip away, and I told myself that it didn't matter to me as much as my acting did. But I look back, and I miss her more than I miss acting, that's for sure."

Hope blooms in my chest, thinking of getting the chance to orchestrate Dawn's happily ever after.

"Do you know her last name?" I ask.

"She died in 2004," Dawn says, shattering my fantasy before it can even take root. "I found that out a few years ago when I thought to look her up online. She lived in Washington Heights. Five miles from me, the whole damn time." She sees my eyes welling and snaps her fingers in my face. "Don't you do that," she warns. "I can't do crying right now."

"I'm not," I say. "I'm just allergic to dust."

"I know it's sad, but you know what? It's what happened. And it's my fault, but it was Paula's too. I think we could've really been something, but that's all it is—a thought. Nothing more."

"It still bums me out," I admit.

"Am I allowed to ask you about June again, or are you gonna get up and perform another song instead?" She gives me her challenging glare, the one I recognize from all her best roles. She really could still command a screen. Her presence has only strengthened in the years since she last worked.

"We're friends." My lie falls out not as a defense but because what we have seems so precious, so new, that to talk about it feels like I could somehow startle it away.

"Bullshit," Dawn says, unwavering. "She took you on a date last night. You've been randomly smiling all day, staring off at the wall. The world's changed a lot, but I still know what it looks like when someone's smitten."

"Fine," I concede, fighting the smile that's bloomed just from thinking of June again, my hand cradling her neck, pulling her to me. "We had a very nice date last night."

"And . . ." Dawn says, waving a hand at me, like, *Get on with it already.*

"And that's all I know right now!" I protest.

It would be easy to spout off all the things that could go wrong. That's kind of my whole thing. But I think back on this week, and how it's all managed to go very, very right, and it seems too pessimistic to scrape together a case for all the ways it wouldn't work.

"I really like her," I continue, leaning into the optimism. "I really think we could have something."

"Have you told her that?" Dawn asks.

"It's a little intense for a first date," I say.

"Please. That wasn't really a first date. You two have been circling each other like hawks for a while now. This was a territory marking for you both."

I laugh. "What a stunning way to describe romance."

"Not many people appreciate me for my comedy. They think of me as a dramatic actor. But I'm funny when I want to be."

"You are," I assure her.

"Anyway, I think you should tell her all the gushy stuff," Dawn says. "I think she's been waiting a very long time to hear it from you, and I bet you've been waiting just as long to hear it back. Isn't that the whole point you took from my sad story? That it's never worth it to wait?"

Telling June how I feel would've been an impossibility for the old me. But that Tatum never made it onto this trip. She got left behind in the airport with my checked bag, and when the airline finally delivered the luggage to me, it was too late for that Tatum to join in on the fun.

"Maybe I will," I say to Dawn.

"Hey," she says, her tone completely changed. "What if you spent the night here tonight? I haven't had a guest in about a million years."

"Really? Me, not June? We both know you like her better."

"I do," Dawn says. "Which is why I gotta try with someone more annoying. Make sure I can tolerate it." She smiles. "You've inspired me, what can I say? I want to see if I can handle having another person in my space again, even just as a guest. You're my test run."

I stick my hand out for a high five that she does not permit. "I'm in. Let's have a sleepover. I'll pop over to Eleanor's before June is back so I can tell her, then I'll come over here after." I clap my hands together, oddly excited. It feels like the times I used to spend the night at my grandmother's.

I'm not the only one changing for the better.

IT'S DARK WHEN JUNE FINALLY COMES BACK FROM HER meeting. My pulse is up the moment she walks through the door, secondhand interest making me feel like a personal shareholder in her company myself.

"Well?" I start, searching her face for clues.

She's placid as she removes her shoes, placing them beside mine at the entrance. Syrup comes to her, rubbing against her legs, and she bends over to pet him, cooing hellos.

"You're killing me," I say, still waiting.

After a quick kiss on Syrup's head, she looks at me. Her face breaks open, the joy filling in every inch.

"You got it!" I scream.

"I got it," she confirms. "They want to invest in me!"

And I throw my arms around her, so infected with joy that I have to share it. She matches me right away, and the comfort I feel in her arms has a sinking, sagging satisfaction to it. This is a place where I could live. These are the arms I always want around me.

We stand waist to waist, wrapped in each other.

And I do it again.

I kiss her.

She presses back, hungry, devouring the moment with fervor. My hands begin to explore her, searching for new ways to fire her up. She bites my ear and lets out a soft sigh of satisfaction as my hands find the buttons of her blouse.

"Yes," she whispers. "Keep going."

I do, ravenous with that need, staved off last night so she could rest up for her meeting. But the meeting's over. The good news received. June has secured the investors. All that's left is this.

I'm flicking each button of her shirt open like a woman possessed, using every bit of control I have to keep from tearing the fabric to shreds. When the last breaks free, her chest is bare, no bra beneath her shirt.

Which is exactly when Dawn knocks on the door.

"I heard you come in," she calls out. "I wanna know how it went!"

June and I lock eyes, bursting into laughter.

"She does have impeccable timing, I'll give her that," I say, breathless. Then I steal one more kiss.

June hurries over to the mirror in the living room, buttoning up her shirt and tidying her hair. I wait until she's presentable, enjoying this moment of just *being*, seeing her piece together the careful facade, knowing I was the one to muss it up. It didn't last nearly as long as I'd like, but I can't be too mad. Not when my heart feels this light.

Once June gives the all clear, I open the door for Dawn, who says, "What took you so long?"

June and I laugh again.

Dawn gives us both a look. "Well? Did you get them to sign on?"

"I did!" June tells her.

"Very good. Very, very good," Dawn says firmly. "Tatum's spending the night in my guest room."

"Sorry, yes, I am," I say to June. "I didn't have a chance to tell you yet."

This time, we hold in the laugh. But only barely.

"Am I not invited?" June asks, tipping her head down to give me *the look*.

"Dawn's choice, not mine!" I tell her.

Syrup takes this opportunity to try to run out the door. June catches him only a few steps out into the hall.

"Well, I'll be waiting for you, Tatum," Dawn says. "I ordered pizza."

Beneath her rough exterior, I know Dawn is excited. Me sleeping over there means more to her than she'd ever say. I wonder when exactly she last had a guest. Has it been years? Decades?

She excuses herself back to her side of the hall, leaving June and me alone.

"I don't think I can cancel," I say once Dawn is gone.

"God no," June tells me. "I wouldn't want you to anyway. This feels like a big deal for her."

"I thought the same thing," I say. "Tell me everything first, though. Walk me through the whole meeting. No detail is too small."

We plop onto the couch together, and June recounts the whole affair, indulging my desire to hear about every sight, sound, and sensation she felt. I cup my head in my hands, watching her, feeling so much pride. These investors saw the light that I've always seen, the shimmer around her that tells you she's someone you should know. They believe in her and her business the same way I do.

"It's a lot," June says once she's run through it all, looking down at the way our fingers have threaded together. "It's going to be a massive change."

"Saturn return," I say jokingly.

"But really, though," she responds. "I started this perfume business in the garage of my parents' house. Now I'm gonna move to New York City for it?"

"Wait," I say, sitting up straighter. "You're *officially* moving here?"

"I have to, if I want to stay involved."

"When?"

"Pretty much immediately."

I still can't envision my life in Trove Hills without her. All I see are gaps, places where I'd miss her, long to be around her. That space doesn't make me as sad as it could, knowing how much it means to her to see this dream realized. It's the kind of letting go I understand. She needs to be here.

"I'm so happy for you," I say.

This time when I hug her, there is none of the charged energy of earlier. This time it's something deeper, our arms wrapped so tight around each other that it feels like we're one body. I breathe in the smell of her, not just her perfume, but her skin, inventorying each detail for safekeeping.

"We have terrible timing, don't we?" she whispers.

I feel something damp on my shoulder. That's when I realize she's crying.

"Don't say that," I tell her, pulling my head back to kiss her cheek. "Let's just appreciate right now. We still have this trip."

It might be all we have, but for now, it's enough.

24

Eleanor

Have you ever played pickleball before?" Carson asks, looming over me in bed.

"I love pickleball," I say. "I'm actually the reigning Broadway Press Union Pickleball Champion for two years running."

If they look up Broadway Press Union Pickleball League, they will know I'm bluffing. Until then, this narrative survives on the strength of my convictions.

"Really?" they ask, making no effort to hide their disbelief.

"Oh yeah. Give me a pickleball ball and a paddle and I'm in my paradise."

Carson kisses me once, quick but meaningful. "That's fantastic news, because that's what we're doing with the family today, and we're one person short to make complete teams. It would be very highly appreciated if you'd join us."

My face gets hot. My lie was supposed to be playful—a subversion of expectation. "Only if you're my teammate."

"Nope. It's actually for my dad." Their bright, uncensored grin shows me they're enjoying this. Too much. They know they've got me cornered, and they're milking it for all it's worth. "My mom's sciatica has been flaring up, and she can't play. It's a pairs tournament. There's no way to redistribute the numbers without having someone compete twice, and that defeats the point. Everyone will really be devastated if the teams aren't even." They point at themselves.

"I see," I say. "*Everyone* will be devastated. Brother Ben has surely been sobbing for hours. Aunt Irene can hardly get out of bed. How brave you are, being able to come to me and ask this."

Climbing back on top of me, they collapse in performed grief. "It's been really tough, getting through the morning, not knowing if our family's first ever pickleball tournament would be completed. Now that I know I'm in the presence of a champion, I feel the peace my heart has been seeking." They blow a raspberry onto my neck. "Get dressed, champ."

THERE ARE SIX PICKLEBALL COURTS SIDE BY SIDE AT the park district. Each one has a Ward lingering about in sportswear. In a strange twist of fate, Dr. Ward and I match, both of us wearing the exact same shade of mint green.

"Would you look at that?" he says, gesturing to our shirts. "We were meant to be a team!"

Then he hugs me in the same way my own dad used to, from the side but squeezing tight. After yesterday, I thought I was done being reminded of the parent-shaped holes inside my heart that can never be filled. And here is Dr. Ward in his mint-green polo, making me remember.

Thank god I don't cry again. Three days in a row would suggest a new emerging behavior.

We're up against Sister Laney and Brother Ben for our first match. They make a fun pair themselves. Laney hands Ben a hot-pink headband that matches hers. He puts it on gamely, letting it sit on his forehead the same ways hers does.

"I hear you're good," Ben calls from the other side of the court.

It takes a second to register that he means *me*. "I might be," I tell him. Not a lie. I really might. Who knows?

"Not as good as us," Laney says, puffing her chest in what must be an attempt at intimidation.

Ben, reading Laney's cue, folds his arms across his chest. "Definitely not," he adds.

I have to laugh. "If this is supposed to be trash-talking, both of you are terrible at it."

"You just *wait* until we start playing," Laney says. "Even the night dogs fear us."

"I don't know who the night dogs are, but if your trash talk is anything like your pickleball skills, there won't be much waiting to do, because Dr. Ward and I are going to be too busy mopping the floor with you both," I tell her.

Dr. Ward fist pumps. "Now, that's some good old-fashioned smack talk!"

"Dad, *please*," Laney warns.

We flip a coin to see who will start. Our team wins, earning us the first serve of the game.

"We're playing tournament style," Dr. Ward says as we walk to our positions. Not knowing what tournament style means, I nod. "You want to serve first?"

"Sure," I tell him. Challenges have never ruffled me. There's nothing for me to hide, even if I don't actually know what's going on.

I can feel the pressure of Carson's gaze, watching me from two courts over. They are curious, I know. To see how far I will take my lie. To find out where I will buckle.

Which is why they gasp when I smack the ball across the

court with power and precision. Laney, my diagonal opponent, is not fast enough to get a return shot.

I wink at Carson.

I don't play pickleball, but I *do* play tennis.

"Really nice, Eleanor!" Dr. Ward says, thrilled. He gives me a thumbs-up, then leans over the net to get the attention of Laney and Ben. "Sorry, kids. *We're* winning this one."

Seems the trash-talking abilities might be genetic too.

As our match progresses, it becomes clear that Ben might not be a pickleballer, but he *is* an athlete. He's fast, with good instincts and fullhearted commitment to the game. Laney is equally committed, but she's clumsy. Her passion makes up for it, though. She's unbelievably enthusiastic—clapping for Ben, cheering on his every serve and success. It inspires me to take this as seriously as possible.

I may not sing with every serve like she does, and there's no chance in hell anyone is going to catch me doing a jazz square to celebrate scoring a point, but I can scowl and huff, pretending to be one of the brilliant, tortured tennis greats.

Eleanor Chapman, a brilliant, tortured pickleball great.

The real surprise of the day is how good Dr. Ward and I are as a team. We have this weird simpatico that again reminds me of my own father. My dad and I couldn't always talk about things, but we could usually enjoy a harmless activity together without conflict. We'd look at each other after a trip to the grocery store and say, "Ice cream?" in unison. And it would be March in Pennsylvania, during the bitterest of colds, and we'd both still be excited to have had the same idea.

With Dr. Ward, I see his confident stance and his deceptively casual demeanor, and I can feel what choices he's going to make on the court. He looks harmless, maybe even slow. He is neither. He's *patient*. It doesn't surprise me when he makes a quick dive for one play. It doesn't surprise him either when I pounce on the next, slamming the ball over the net.

Soon the entire court becomes a symphony of pickleballing. Grabbing a sip of water between serves, I take a peek at the other matches. Thanks to yesterday's picnic, I can recognize a decent amount of the participants now.

There's Uncle Gary, who hates coffee, paired up with the woman everyone just calls Lydia. She's related to the family in a way no one has been able to explain. She's always one of the first to arrive at these things, and she is guaranteed to be the last to leave.

There are two cousins with uncannily similar names, Jason and Jaycee, playing against two other cousins whose names I can't recall.

Then there is Carson, matched up with Aunt Irene. I watch one of Carson's volleys, enjoying the way their shirt pulls up as they stretch their arm to hit the ball, revealing a glimpse of their torso, where their tattoo peeks out just a little. Just enough.

They're lithe, sneaky, as mischievous on the court as they have the reputation for being in life. With their long legs, they can cover ground quickly, making up for Aunt Irene, who is nowhere near as quick on the pickup. Carson scores a point, then looks straight at me, aware of my admiration.

"Hey, Trouble!" they call out. "Don't you have a game to play?"

Blushing, I towel off my sweat, ignoring the comment.

Dr. Ward and I hold our lead all the way to the last point. Tournaments go up to fifteen, apparently. At least this one does.

It's Dr. Ward's serve. He calls out the score, then starts the volley. We settle into a nice rhythm among the four of us. We've been beating them handily, but they're still going out with dignity.

I admire that.

Unfortunately for Ben and Laney, they've once again left open the same pocket they've been missing all game long.

Ben hits the ball toward me, and I square up my paddle, ready to close out this first match and secure our spot in the next round.

"You've been sleeping on that corner all day! Pathetic," I say as I slam the ball in the direction of the opening. *This* is how trash talk works.

Laney takes a huge lunging step, desperate to change the narrative.

At once, she falls to the ground, letting out a groan of shock that isn't quite loud enough to cover the horrific cracking sound her leg has made. Her cries of agony come next, silencing the rest of the pickleball court.

Dr. Ward springs to action without hesitation, running across the court to tend to Laney. With startling efficiency, the rest of the family reworks into a hive, assembling a plan of action before I can even process what's happened. They're hoisting Laney up, securing her injured leg, and supporting her under the arms as they carry her to the SUV that's parked closest to the nets. Jason and Jaycee follow with water and towels. The aunts start cleaning up the paddles and balls.

It unfolds as fluidly as our games on the courts. My feet are glued to the ground. I'm feeling shocked, sad. Disappointed in myself. Maybe if I hadn't mocked their weakness, Laney wouldn't be hurt.

"Are you okay?" Carson asks, startling me out of my fog.

"Your sister just broke her leg or something. Are *you* okay?"

"It wasn't your fault," they say.

"I'm not blaming myself," I lie.

"Okay then, pickleball champion. Maybe not. But just in case. That was an accident, plain as day." They put an arm around me. "Do you want to ride with me to the hospital?"

"I hate hospitals," I say, which is the first true thing I've told them all day. "I don't think I'll go. I'll head back. You should be with family anyway. Keep me posted on what happens with Laney. I hope she's okay."

"I know we haven't been able to practice again, but would you be able to drive my car to my parents' house for me? I need to ride to the hospital with them and Laney."

"Sure," I say, still dazed.

Carson hands me their keys and rushes off to catch a ride with their family. They don't even hesitate in handing over their vehicle. Not even after the atrocity that was my driving lesson, only two days ago.

Our hookup situation has evolved way too far past its original inception. Never has that been more clear to me than right now, watching the entire Ward family unite around Laney.

Family is the one thing I don't have.

One week in Trove Hills can't change that.

25

Tatum

Dawn reminds me of myself during a rush hour at the diner, in constant motion as I make sure my customers have everything they need. She's on my trail everywhere I go in her apartment, bringing me my towels for a shower, my pillows for the bed, my morning coffee hot and fresh alongside my breakfast.

We're just settling in for an afternoon movie when a series of fast, frantic knocks interrupts Dawn's attempt to make me a cheese board.

"Sorry to disturb!" June calls out. "Eleanor is on the phone for you, Tatum. She says it's urgent."

Eleanor is calling me.

Eleanor is *calling* me.

Eleanor is calling *me*. As I walk to the door, my brain keeps reworking the words, searching for the point of emphasis in the sentence that feels the most correct. The whole thing is too bizarre to understand.

June hands me her phone, and I say hello to Eleanor for the very first time.

"Laney broke her leg," she tells me, not bothering with a greeting in return.

It surprises me, her voice. She speaks in a higher register than I would have guessed. Seeing only pictures of her, I imagined her voice would be dark and smoky. But it's clear, light, almost bell-like.

"We were playing pickleball, and she and Ben were losing to me and your dad," she continues. "By a lot. It was going to be the game-winning point, so she made a hero leap for the ball, and she stepped wrong."

She's direct. Clinical. It's exactly what I need as I listen, desperate to process all the information being thrown my way. Eleanor has been going to the family reunion events. She was on a team with my dad. Laney was playing with Ben.

Laney's leg is broken.

I try again to make sense of it all, but it's a puzzle with pieces that won't connect, no matter how hard I try to fit them together.

Ben, the brother I do not know, was Laney's pickleball partner. Eleanor, the woman staying in my cottage, was playing against them. *Eleanor is calling me.*

"I'm not sure anyone else in your family has had a chance to tell you yet," Eleanor continues. "I know you're all kind of not speaking. But I just thought you'd want to know." Her voice gets quieter. "It feels like you should be here. Sorry if that's inappropriate of me to say. I just can't help but feel like I am a poor stand-in for you."

If a stranger like Eleanor can sense the gravity of my absence, what must my family feel?

And what is Laney feeling?

"I'm coming," I tell Eleanor, deciding it before I've even registered what it means.

"Good," Eleanor says. "I drove Carson's car back to the cottage for them, because they rode to the hospital with your parents. Everything happened so quickly. I figured they haven't had a chance to fill you in yet, so I went ahead and reached out. I've got to go, but I'll update you as soon as I know more."

With that, she ends our call.

The way she's brought up Carson's car snags at my curiosity. There's a familiarity in the way she's mentioned them. A protectiveness that I'm going to flag for further examination, once I've worked through everything else I have to do first. Eleanor called me. Laney broke her leg. What the hell is going on?

I relay the story to June the same way Eleanor told it to me.

"You should be with your family," June says.

Hearing it from her, I realize what it means. Since last night, we've known we're on borrowed time.

Now I've cut it even shorter.

Somehow, it's already over.

June opens the door to Eleanor's place, and I follow her, needing to gather up my stuff. She grabs her computer and begins searching, telling me who has the cheapest flight back to Illinois. She mentions a direct flight leaving in three hours, with a ticket still available.

"That sounds good," I say, needing to do so many things at once that I'm not doing anything at all. Obviously I know Laney breaking her leg isn't catastrophic. She is twenty-five and stubborn and will be determined to heal herself as well as possible.

It's that I wasn't there to help when I could've been. I wasn't the one to decide where Carson's car should go. I didn't share the news with family members who weren't around when it happened.

I was the one who wasn't around.

"I can book the flight for you, if you want," June offers.

This gives me a clear purpose. I take my wallet out of my

purse and hand it over. June gets to work, pausing only to confirm necessary details.

I begin collecting my belongings scattered across Eleanor's apartment, where I've been pretending I'm a fast-moving city girl who has dreams as big as this town. The truth is, I'm a small-town waitress who lives with her parents. I have a family who needs me, and I have been ignoring them out of a smug, mis-placed sense of pride.

I break down in tears.

June leaps up, wrapping me in her arms as we slump to the floor. Both cats start circling us, intrigued by this spectacle, walking across whatever limbs of ours they can reach.

"It's gonna be okay," June says, kissing my head.

Soon we're walking to the elevator together the same way we've done all week, exploring New York City side by side. Ex-cept now it's time for me to leave it all behind.

"Wait," I say, realizing. "Dawn."

I rush back toward her apartment one last time. I don't even have to knock before she's in the hall, hugging me.

All the tears I'd dried up resurface. We've only known each other a few days, but she's been so generous with me, so giving in a way I never could have imagined when we first met in this very hall. That's another piece of the New York magic—the way peo-ple here care for one another.

"I'm gonna miss you," I say.

"Don't you dare," she warns, sensing, correctly, that I'm gear-ing up for a bigger speech.

"Just promise me you'll act again," I tell her.

"Promise me you'll write," she responds. "All right. That's enough. I don't like to cry. Not when I'm not getting paid for it." She hurries back into her place, leaving June and me in the hallway.

I look at June, bags hung over my shoulder, and ask, "What am I doing?"

"You're doing what you always do," she says. "You're looking out for your family."

We say nothing on the elevator. Nothing on our walk through the lobby. I don't wave to the doorman. I can't even bear to let him know it's the last time I'll pass by him.

June has called me a car, and the driver is already parked out front when we make it outside.

"This is it," we both say at the same time. It's not enough to make us laugh, but it edges off the devastation.

The driver takes my bag and puts it in the trunk.

All that's left to do is say goodbye.

"I really like you, June," I say. "I have since the moment I first met you. And I've been so scared of what that meant that I waited too long to do anything about it. If I'd just gone out with you when you asked, we could have had a whole year together. But we only had these few days. Even though this was too short, it was worth it. Thank you. I'm so proud of you."

I kiss her on the cheek, ready to get in the car and go, doing what I've always done. Cutting things off before they've gotten too serious.

"Wait," June says, right as I'm ducking down to get into the back seat. "What if you moved here too? What if we lived together?"

My head hits the car ceiling, the pain of the jolt offering me a single moment to process it all.

"I know it sounds absurd, but think of how happy you've been here," she continues. "I know you have. Not just with me, but with yourself. You know? We could do this together. We could make a life here."

"June," I say softly. I'm still in the car, my driver sitting up front stone-faced. If he's listening, he's doing an impressive job of staying detached. "I can't make a decision like this right now. I'll call you once I'm settled back in Trove Hills. Okay?"

"Okay," she says, nodding.

And that's how I leave her, standing on the sidewalk in front of Eleanor's apartment, waiting for an answer I don't yet have.

26

Eleanor

Tatum arrives home around midnight. It's not unlike my own arrival a week ago. How much has changed since I took that key out from under the garden gnome? Sometimes it feels insignificant, and other times I think if I showed my old coworkers that picture Aunt Fran took at the picnic, no one would recognize me.

"Eleanor," Tatum says, scanning from my head to my shoes and back again.

"Tatum," I reply, taking her in much the same. She's shorter than I imagined, maybe because of the fact that her absence has been felt in such a large capacity I expected her to touch the ceiling. And she's scrappier too. Not tall like Carson or Ben. More similar to Laney, with a distinct energy of her own. She postures now, feet wide. A fighter's stance.

"Sorry about my apartment," I tell her. "I left it a mess."

"It was definitely a mess," she says. "I cleaned it, though. If I did too much, I'm sorry. It's just . . . There was a smell."

"Was there really?" I ask, embarrassed. "I was going through a bit of a tough time before I left. Thank you for cleaning. What do I owe you for that?" I pull out my phone. It's been a long while since I had a cleaning service, but I try to remember how much I paid then. "Is five hundred dollars enough?"

Tatum steps back, putting her hands up like she's blocking me. "I don't need your money. You let us stay there for free."

"And I stayed here," I say. "But I did not so much as wash a dish."

Tatum looks past the living room into the small glimpse of the kitchen visible from here, where the sink is in plain view. There are no dishes to be found.

"Carson washed them," I say. "What's your Venmo? I want to pay you for the cleaning." I search her name, finding a picture that looks like her—a brunette with two messy buns and a friendly smile. "This is you, right? I'm sending five hundred." Her phone pings after I deliver the money, confirming I'm right. "I should be getting out of here now that you're back. I can get a hotel in Chicago for the next few days."

"No," she says, insistent. "Stay." There's a curious pleading to her voice. "Carson wouldn't want you to leave."

This sends heat straight to my cheeks.

It never occurred to me that Carson might be talking about me when I'm not around. Maybe because I have no one to talk about them with, and I assumed that was a two-way street. Their sister knows enough to know that Carson and I are at the very least friends. That Carson might miss me.

"Are you sure?" I ask.

"You paid me five hundred dollars unprompted. Consider it payment for your stay, if that helps you. But yes, I'm very sure. The couch has a pullout bed inside it."

"How could you ever think Eleanor is the type of person who sleeps on a pullout bed?" Carson says, sauntering down the stairs to greet their sister.

The siblings don't hug. Instead Tatum wheels her suitcase inside, like Carson's presence is the permission she's needed to enter the space.

Carson leans up against the bookcase, observing her. "What's up? Have a good time in New York?"

"It was fine," Tatum says. Either she's more upset about Laney than anyone could've anticipated, or something happened while she was there. "How's the reunion stuff been?"

"Ben is like if Dad got put into a time machine and merged with, I don't know, somebody less awkward than Dad," Carson tells her.

"He's very nice," I offer, not sure what prompts me to add my assessment.

This sends Tatum's attention back my way. "How'd you get roped into the reunion stuff?"

So Carson *hasn't* told her about me. Has she deduced something based only on what I said to her on the phone? I was very cut-and-dry about the accident. What could she have gleaned from that?

"It wasn't intentional," I say. "I just ended up filling in for you."

"Got it," she says. "You're not Ben's stepsister, you're Ben's sister who stepped up."

"Exactly." I laugh. "Well, I better go get all my stuff out of your room." I walk up the stairs, leaving the siblings to catch up without me.

"You can stay with me," Carson calls out when I reach the top step.

I halt, my back still turned to them, one hand gripping tight to the stair rail. Our entire situationship has been built around me staying in this cottage. Even though Carson has slept over here more than once, going to their place feels like an admission—this is more serious than either of us planned for.

"All my stuff is here," I say weakly, unable to turn around and face them.

"You're right. Cars definitely aren't built to carry anything at that level," they respond. "Your forty-pound luggage would send my Kia Soul scraping the pavement."

"I want to get to know Eleanor better, so she should stay here," Tatum says, rescuing the moment. "She's been representing me at several family events. It's important I make sure it's been an honest depiction."

"I'd like to get to know you too," I say, sincere, taking this opportunity to finally look down the stairs.

She's smiling up at me the way I imagine a sister would, her eyes sparkling with some kind of unspoken mischief we're going to spend late-night hours unpacking. "We have much to discuss," she says.

Carson's not visible from my vantage point. So when they say, "Works for me," with their usual calm, I can't tell how much they mean it. I can only hope whatever damage I've caused by not staying with them is mild.

In Tatum's bedroom, I make quick work of stuffing my clothes and skin-care items into my bag and carrying everything downstairs.

By the time I return, Carson is gone. I do my best to keep my interest low, offering Tatum a simple, "Oh," when she tells me Carson had to go feed their gecko. Still, Tatum lets the moment linger, waiting for me to reveal what she clearly already knows to be true. She wants details. An admission. *Something*.

I can't bring myself to give it to her. Opening up to Carson was one thing. Letting in yet another Ward would be another.

We make small talk instead as Tatum helps me turn the couch into a bed. She tells me about her time staying in my building, confirming that Dawn is the woman who lives on my floor.

"In all our years of being neighbors, Dawn has never done anything but scowl at me," I say. "One time she complained to our building manager that my visitors were coming over too late and being disruptive in our hall."

"That sounds like Dawn," Tatum says, smiling fondly.

I tell her about my time at Rita's Diner, and the apple crumble versus banana cream pie debacle.

"Well," she says expectantly, "which one did you like better?"

"The crumble," I say, much to her disappointment. This is as close to any real admission as she's going to get from me. I fake a yawn, feeling like she might press anyway. "Well, I should be getting to bed."

"Me too," she says.

I expected much more resistance. Perhaps she's had an experience like mine. Something she's not yet ready to discuss.

"Good night, Eleanor."

"Good night, Tatum."

She jogs up the stairs, into the room that's no longer mine.

Alone in the quiet dark of the cottage's living room, I open my laptop up to my email drafts. The words flow fast out of my fingers. It's easy now, to be sincere. Every warm sentiment I feel for Trove Hills I pretend to feel for Broadway publicity instead.

Position Inquiry—Eleanor Chapman, I type into the subject line.

My cursor hovers over the send button. Pressing this does not guarantee the position is mine, so I don't know why I'm treating it like it does. It still has the weight of something monumental.

Get home okay? I text Carson, using it as one last test. This email is my crossroads, and I need a sign about which way I should go.

Carson sends back a thumbs-up.

Are you mad at me? I want to write. *Did I screw up?*

I'm too afraid of what the answer might be.

Instead, I send my email to Atlas Theatrical.

27

Tatum

It's been so long since I've been able to register the smell of my parents' house. I'm never gone long enough to catch the baked-in tang of our existence—laundry detergent, essential oil diffusers, and that undefinable, elusive smell of family.

Even though it smells like me, like what I've always known, I can't help but think of June, wondering what she'd label this. How would she try to bottle it up? Could she make a perfume of my life?

My mom and dad are in the kitchen, sitting at the table as I enter through the back door in the early-morning hours, much the same as our last meeting.

"I should have been here," I start, diving into the heart of it. No more tiptoeing. No more avoidance. "It was immature of me to leave without telling anyone."

"Yes, it was," my mom chimes in.

My shoulders rise into my ears. I knew this would be hard, but I thought I might get more than two sentences into the effort before running into any difficulty.

"We shouldn't have sprung the reunion on you without

warning," my dad interjects. "Carson has been sure to make that very clear to us."

Here it is, their fight blooming within my own fight. I brace myself for it, pinching the space between my eyes to help myself stay centered. I almost miss the fact that my mom's not taking a jab at Dad for cutting her off. She's talking to me.

"We thought that the less time you had to know about it, the less pressure you'd feel," she says. "You always take things so hard, and we didn't want that to be the case this time."

My thoughts scramble for purchase. Is it my need for the truth that's bucking up against this statement, or is it my pride? I want to be defensive, but doing that would only prove the point she's making.

"We hoped that you wouldn't feel like you had to plan the whole thing yourself, so we tried to do it without your input," Dad explains. "Everything was going well in that department until we lost the dang folding chairs."

"Which were in the basement," Mom says with a theatrical sigh.

"I swore I put them in the garage," Dad tells her.

"Yet there they were, in the basement," Mom adds.

"Honey, I didn't remember putting them down there. Until they invent a way for me to recover my lost thoughts, I wasn't going to magically figure out that that's where I'd put them."

"*This* is why," I say, pointing back and forth between them. Their friction has indeed arrived, just a touch later than I expected. "This is why I think I need to do it all."

Saying this might be the most effective way I've ever stopped them from bickering. For a moment, I relish the silence it's brought, the satisfaction of preventing the inevitable escalation.

"Nothing has ever been the same since we found out about the affair," I continue.

These words are so dangerous, so taboo, that my throat gets parched, like my body is physically resisting doing this. But I have to. I can't keep it in anymore.

"And you both know that's true. But you don't want it to be. You want to act like we've all gotten through it, that because it was so long ago, there's no way it's still affecting us now. None of us have gotten through it. You told me last week that I seemed unhappy. Disconnected. Maybe I am. And maybe this is why. Because when I look at what the two of you have become to each other, it terrifies me. What if that's all there is for me? Someone who resents me way more than they love me but feels obligated to see it through anyway?"

My mom's eyes go wide. I've startled her into something outside her usual composure, and she seems to know she's flailing, because she looks around the room like she's in search of something to grab. "I don't *resent* your father," she says finally. "It was just a very complicated situation. And it really was so long ago now."

I swallow back my tears so that my parents don't remember this exchange for my emotions. I want them to remember my *words*. "Yeah, which means it's been a very long time of the two of you behaving like this," I say. "You act like you're constantly annoyed to be in the same room with Dad, and he pretends not to have a negative opinion of a single person, place, or thing, so that he never appears to be the one who's making the mood sour."

If they were quiet before, they're completely muted now, not even daring to breathe.

"I'm not going to be your therapist and ask you how it is you think you're getting through it, or point out to you all the ways you could do it better, even though I have my opinions on that," I say. "But I will tell you that I've always made myself into whatever you two need me to be. I would've found those chairs in the basement and probably lied and said I was the one who put them down there, just to stop you both from politely accusing each other of it all week. I moved myself into the cottage Mom won't touch. I fix everything Dad doesn't understand so that Mom can't get frustrated at his inability to change with the times. Both of you just admitted to knowing that I feel like I have to help you all the time. Why do you let me do that?"

It's more than a question. It's a plea. A cry.

"You're right."

Hearing my mom say this feels impossible. Unbelievable. I have to blink three times to make sure it's real.

"We haven't been the same in a very long time," she continues. "But I really do love your father. I wouldn't have stayed if that wasn't true."

"I love your mother too," my dad says, tears in his eyes. "I don't . . . We don't want to make you our therapist right now, but we are aware that we still have problems. We just didn't realize how much those problems were stopping you from living your fullest life. We love having you around, but I can see how we've been selfish. We've let you do more for us than is necessary."

"It's okay," I say involuntarily.

"It's not," my mom insists. "And I'm sorry we made you think you had to do that." She's weepy now too, each word coming out a little gurgled and uncertain. "It may not seem true, but we really are trying."

"Part of why we wanted to do this week with Ben was to get better at looking the tough stuff in the face," Dad explains. "What I did to our family all those years ago was inexcusable. And I've never really known how to address it with you kids. And then to find out I have another kid. I knew I couldn't hide forever from this. So this was my way of trying to take ownership. But I can see that there's still a lot more room for improvement."

It's hard not to feel like all of this would have been different if we'd said this so much sooner. But I know now we couldn't have. That what I've been through this week in New York—and what they've been through here in Trove Hills with Ben—has made this possible.

"It's hard for me to accept that I'm not the one with the answers," I say. "That even after all this time, I can't solve this alone. That maybe I can't solve it at all."

My mom comes over to give me a hug. "I'm sorry you ever felt like you had to solve it," she says.

We're both crying now, our tears dampening each other's shirts.

"And I'm really sorry I wasn't here," I tell her.

Dad joins in, kissing my forehead as he holds us both. "It's okay," he tells me. "We just missed you. That's all."

"I missed you too," I reply, meaning it. "I'll do whatever it takes to make it up to you both. Please tell me there are some items still left on the activity list."

"Of course there are. We're doing an escape room today," Mom says.

"Consider me in," I say, laughing through my tears.

I PULL MY PHONE OUT OF MY POCKET TO TEXT THE group chat.

> TATUM: Did you know Trove Hills has an escape room?

> NYA: Where?

> TATUM: It's in the same strip mall that used to have the Dominick's. By the vet.

EMMETT: That sounds fun. We should do it when
we're home for Christmas.

TATUM: I'll let you know if it's any good.

EMMETT: Hahahaha you don't need to check it
out beforehand. Save it for us!

TATUM: I can't. I'm on the way there right now.

Every person in the chat reacts to this with question marks, emojis, GIFs.

NYA: I'm sorry. Aren't you falling in love with June
Lightbell in New York City right now?

I explain to them what happened with Laney, careful to avoid all mention of what June asked me right before I came back here. The group chat accepts my decision to return home, but it does nothing to stop their questions about June. The last they heard, June, Dawn, and I were all going to see a musical together. I've lived so many lives since then.

Right now, I want June's question to be only mine to answer. I can't have their opinions just yet. I already know what they'll want—our group chat is called WE DON'T LIVE IN TROVE HILLS, after all. Of course they'll want me to leave.

I drive Eleanor to the escape room. Seeing her in person, you would never know the state of her home. Or the sadness of her life. If I'm bursting at the seams, she's sewed herself together so tightly she appears seamless. Infinite and unbroken in her composure. But I know her secret. And seeing as she's spent the last week with my family, she knows most of mine.

It's a weird kind of intimacy. It's like she's another sibling of mine, added to the mix somehow. But it goes beyond that. She's like the inverse of me come to life, and it's hard not to feel like our life swap wasn't born out of some kind of cosmic coincidence. There is something we both need in each other, or from each other. I can never repay her for what the time spent in her place has given me.

"Did you know this escape room is going to be ghost themed?" I ask her. "We're investigators breaking into a haunted mansion."

"That should be interesting," she says. "I like ghosts."

"Do you like actors dressed as ghosts committed to scaring you no matter what it takes?"

"Guess we're about to find out," she says. "By the way, have you talked to June today? She sent me a picture of my cats a little bit ago."

"I haven't," I say, hoping to sound neutral on the subject. "But the investors bought into her company. She's still figuring out all the logistics, but it looks like she'll be joining you over in New York very soon."

"Of course they bought in. June's very good at what she does," Eleanor says.

This assessment is so direct, stated as fact, that I get second-hand flattery. Eleanor's opinions hold real weight. She doesn't say things without meaning them.

In the gap I don't mean to leave, the pause that says I have a personal stake in this, Eleanor picks up on it. "Are you guys—"

"We're friends," I say, cutting her off before she can finish that question.

"Got it."

Eleanor has developed some new secrets here too. I could tell last night that she didn't want me to ask her about Carson, so I didn't. She's offering me the same courtesy in return.

We arrive at the escape room. Carson's driven over with Laney. Her knee is wrapped up, and she's on crutches. They're waiting out front when we park.

"We better fucking dominate this," Laney says in greeting, picking up one crutch to wave at me.

"See? Now *that's* trash talk," Eleanor tells her.

I give Laney the hug she doesn't show she wants. "We'll absolutely demolish this escape room, I promise."

Our parents arrive next, offering apologies for running behind.

Then a man who really does looks like a variation of my dad put through a time machine and sprinkled with someone else's nose and chin walks up to join us.

My brother.

I stretch my hand out to shake his hand. I'm afraid if I hug him, I'll cry, and I'd like to not establish myself as the emotional sibling in any more ways than I already have. "I'm Tatum."

"The one and only," he says warmly. "I'm Ben."

"I hear you're my brother."

"That's what they're saying around here these days."

"It's nice to meet you."

What do I say to him that fills in the gaps? How can we cross the wide chasm of time that we've spent apart? Will he understand the story about the trip to Wisconsin when Laney threw up three times on the car ride over, and everyone had to wear our dad's clothes for the rest of the drive? Is it uncomfortable to share all the memories he didn't get to experience?

"I'm sorry. I don't want to be bad at this," I tell him.

"The escape room?" he questions. "I'm actually pretty good at them. It's just puzzles really."

I laugh. "No. Knowing you."

"Oh," he says, blushing. "I don't want to be bad at knowing you either. So that makes us even, I think."

"He's not as good at pickleball as he thinks he is," Eleanor informs me. It's a perfect tension breaker. Everyone laughs.

"You should see him bowl," Ben's wife offers.

"Don't bring bowling into this," Ben warns, and it's so deeply strange to see a piece of myself in the way he squeezes his lips together.

All this time, there has been more of me walking around the world than I've known about. Yet another person who shares some of the idiosyncrasies that must be embedded in our DNA.

When we get inside the escape room—or, pardon me, the haunted mansion—I find myself gravitating toward Ben as we puzzle our way through the dark, moody house. He laughs at not just my little quips and asides, but my reactions to the supernatural effects as well.

It's fun to amuse him. It reminds me of when Carson, Laney, and I are all sitting at our parents' table after Thanksgiving dinner, eating one final reheated dish. We've all decided to be on our best behavior, telling old stories and making each other laugh like we're getting paid by the joke. Ben might be treating this reunion in the same way—a special occasion where he needs to be in top form—but there's also a newness to our dynamic, coupled with some kind of common understanding that makes us get along. It's simple, really. We like each other's presence.

Near the end, surely close to solving the mystery at the center of the escape room experience, Ben and I get tasked with figuring out where the headmistress of this haunted house has hidden her prized jewel necklace. We return to her bedroom, where Ben and I search for the clue we both know must be here.

"We have to put the headmistress's portrait on top of her dresser!" I wish I could say I figured this out through the clues we've received, but really, I just notice a slight fade to the wooden surface atop the dresser, the same size as the portrait sitting crooked on the mistress's nightstand.

"You're totally right," Ben says, grabbing the portrait and putting it where I've directed him.

The locked drawer pops open, offering us a key.

"The jewelry box!" I say, charging into the closet. The key fits in the lock, and the lid opens, revealing a necklace with a giant ruby in the center and bulbous pearls along the chain. It looks straight out of a game of Pretty Pretty Princess.

Ben lets out a whoop of appreciation. "Nice job!"

It's so sincere, so openly appreciative, that I feel the same kind of regret that bowled me over in New York when I learned about Laney's leg. I should've been here for more of this.

"I'm really sorry I missed most of this week," I say to him.

He picks up the ruby necklace, and we head back to the living room, where the rest of our team has been reassembling the ghost's skeleton.

"Carson said you went to New York," Ben replies. "That must've been awesome."

"I only went because I was afraid to meet you," I admit. "Like I thought it would mess up my family somehow. It was shitty of me. I regret it. You're a great secret brother."

He laughs good-naturedly, something I'm coming to understand is part of his personality. "You know, I didn't take it well either when I found out that my dad wasn't my biological father. So I get it."

I think again of how June defended him that first night at the bar. She'd seen this somehow, had the foresight to empathize with him before she even knew him. My heart aches just remembering it. She was right. More than I even understood then. Ben went through something even deeper than what we're experiencing on our side. My dad is his birth father, but he's not the man who raised him. He's not his actual father. And for most of his life, he had no clue.

Seeing him with this new perspective, I reach out and hug him. He responds to my hug with a sweet little puff of surprise.

"Aw, Tatum," he says. "It's okay. I swear. I've made a lot of bad decisions in my life too."

"Like what?" It's hard to imagine a guy like him doing anything wrong. He's so unfailingly nice in every moment, in a way that seems truthful too. Just good to his core.

"For one, I didn't speak to my wife for ten years," he says. Hearing himself, he backpedals. "Not when she was my wife! God. Sorry. It was years ago. It's a long story."

"A story I definitely need to hear."

As if summoned by this mention of her, Ben's wife, Dee, finds us in the hallway. "Are you guys seriously having a heart-to-heart while holding Mrs. Weathermaster's special ruby necklace, which you know good and well is the key to unlocking her skeleton and bringing her back to life?" she asks, exasperated. "We're on a time crunch here!" She grabs the necklace from Ben's hand and runs into the living room.

Dee places Mrs. Weathermaster's necklace around the bones they've managed to turn into a decent-looking skeleton.

The lights begin flickering, and the room fills with smoke. It's all pretend, and I'm priming myself to crack another winning joke to Ben. I scan for him, realizing that every other person in the room is reacting to this final show with genuine awe. Unclear if this is a bit or not, I spend more time watching them than I do watching the *apparition* that now appears, also known as an actor in a costume, dressed up in gaudy clothes to play the role of Mrs. Weathermaster. She tells us what her husband did, and how we've succeeded in freeing her spirit, but we must release her from the mansion altogether so that his ghost can no longer torture her.

All the while, our group begins forming pairs. My mom stands with her back pressed into my dad's front. Ben puts his arm around Dee. And Carson, I notice, lets Eleanor peek over their shoulder. I go for Laney, of course. She and I have always enjoyed being the bratty little sisters who can mock everyone else. But seeing the room of partners, of people paired together with someone they've chosen, I wish again for June. And for that version of myself I found in New York.

In the end, it's Eleanor who figures out how to free Mrs. Weathermaster. We make it out of the escape room—ghost of Mrs. Weathermaster included—with only minutes to spare.

Overflowing with excitement, Ben and Carson hoist Eleanor up, as our whole group chants her name.

"Eleanor, you're truly one of us," my dad says proudly.

28

Eleanor

It's tough to pack without making noise. The ruby-and-pearl necklace replica the Wards made me take home from the escape room slips out of my hands, clanging against the hardwood.

I stand frozen.

Minutes pass, and I decide it's safe to keep going. Most of my belongings are already packed away. It's the little things like chargers and hair clips I might just have to lose.

With agonizing restraint, I turn the doorknob as slowly as possible, using my unending patience to battle every squeak.

I'm seconds away from being free, when Tatum appears.

"Where are you going?" she asks, startling me into opening the door all the way again. There's a crooked eye mask on her face and a sock curler around her head.

"Home," I whisper calmly.

"Okay," she says, still half asleep. Then she processes the words, and she rips the mask off. "Wait."

"I know," I say, already sensing what she will say. "It's for the best for everyone."

"Carson really likes you."

Just hearing their name makes my stomach plummet.

I don't dare respond.

"They don't bring anyone home ever," she continues. "We didn't even meet the gecko girl."

"They didn't bring me home either," I remind her, schooling my voice to stay low. "*You* brought me here."

"You know what I mean."

I do. I know I'm being difficult. I can't let her see that it matters to me what she's said. That I care what Carson thinks, or that I care that I could be different for them.

"It can't work," I say. "My life is in New York."

"What do you like about New York?" she asks, surprising me.

My defenses rear up, as if she's asking why the sun is hot or water is wet. "Everything."

"Can you name five specific things you enjoy?" The rumble in her voice is starting to iron out, which isn't a good thing. She's getting more alert.

"Of course I can." I lean against my luggage, feeling like it's ten years in the past and I've been stopped by Billy Eichner on the street, suddenly incapable of remembering anything I've ever known about myself. "I love autumn there. I'm looking forward to seeing it soon. I like that I can walk everywhere. I like . . . my cats. And I like other things too. I just can't remember when you put me on the spot."

"There's a certain way the light comes through your living room window in the morning," Tatum says. "The one between the console table and the bookshelf. It slices right through. I think I could live there, in the sliver of warmth."

"Yeah," I say, pretending I've ever noticed what she's describing. "I like that too."

"I like knowing that someone will always be there to witness me," she continues. "Even though there are so many people there, and I'm one of millions, I still feel like I could never get lost in it. I'm never really alone there."

Her words make me ache. Because it's the opposite of how I feel, I realize. When I am in New York, it doesn't matter how loud I scream or how much of a mess I make—no one can see me at all.

She's still going, listing things that are obvious to her, so easy to identify that she's able to itemize in the dead of night with no preparation. "When you walk on the street, everyone has such purpose," she tells me. "They're going somewhere. And I like that even if I'm just going to get a coffee or to meet a friend, I have a purpose too. It's like it gets injected into the air. You can't help but move like life matters."

"Yes," I say, even though I've never, not once, thought that.

Or maybe I did, when I was younger and less aware of how life could hurt me. Maybe I used to have that same kind of hope. It's been so long now it may as well have never existed.

"You could love it here," Tatum tells me. "Our fall is just as beautiful. Nobody really walks anywhere, but that's not to say you couldn't. You could probably start an entire walking club at the park district and get half the town to join you if you want. And your cats would get lots of greenery to look at out the window. Not that your views of Central Park aren't amazing. But they could enjoy seeing the woods. There are a lot of deer."

"Thanks," I say. "But I really do have to get going. I can't miss my flight."

"You don't have to run away," she says. "Carson wants you here. They want you to stay."

"I promise you I don't need you to solve my problems for me. I have been by myself for years. I can solve it all on my own." I pull my luggage across the threshold, making it official. "Thank you for letting me stay here. I really appreciate it. Let me know if you ever need a place to stay in New York. I promise I'll get a cleaner for it."

It comes out harsher than I mean, but that's for the better. If Tatum thinks poorly of me, she can tell Carson I'm the wrong person for them. That's exactly what I need.

It's time the fantasy ends for good.

"Does Carson know you're leaving?" Tatum asks.

"I have a job interview with a new press agency. I need to be back as soon as possible," I say, as if that's somehow an answer.

"Please talk to Dawn," she calls out as the door closes. "If nothing else."

29

Tatum

The grocery store had one last package of the break-and-bake cookies Carson and I love, and I'm pulling them out of the oven when Carson shows up at the cottage. These cookies have always been our comfort food. Whenever something bad happens in our life—a failed test in the school days, a bad day at work now, and on the rare occasion, like heartbreaks we can't speak about—we bake them up and pick a movie to watch. Then we rot on the couch together until we feel a bit better.

As soon as Carson sees the tray of oozing chocolate chips, they back up, startled by their presence.

"She's gone, isn't she?" they ask.

"She's just scared," I say. "I think if you explained to her how you feel, she'd come back. But until then, I figured we could couch rot."

"What did she tell you?" Carson asks, uninterested in any of my solutions.

I explain what Eleanor said about their different lives, and how she's got a whole world in New York, watching as each piece of information seems to devastate them anew. It's agony, but I force myself to say it all. It's better if they have every piece of information.

"I've seen the way she lives," I say. "And I know she's had a hard life. She doesn't think she deserves someone as good as you. It's not true, but it's what she believes."

Carson puts their head in their hands. "What am I going to do about it? Fly to New York and ask to live with her?"

"You could," I say earnestly. Pitching this is a bold move considering the question I've been sitting on, but it's always been easier for me to see someone else's answers.

Carson gives me a look of disgust that's so complete, so fully realized, it could be used to teach babies different expressions.

"That's what people do in movies," they tell me, committing to their role as the bitter cynic the same way I commit to Waitress Tatum. They need this performance, and it isn't the time for me to tell them that's all it is—an act. "I am not inside a movie. I barely have enough money to pay rent next week, because I still haven't gotten the first advance check from the park district for the mural I'm going to do for them. This isn't the time for me to be flying off and asking a woman I've known for a week to give me a real chance."

They want me to think they're unaffected by deep feelings and big gestures. But it isn't true. Longing flows through their every action. I know, because when I was a kid I used to sneak into their room and read their journals. And I also know because it's a trait we share—a desire to be loved with exclamation points.

I want so badly for them to be happy. I want them to get this chance at love, knowing full well they've never let themself get anywhere near this close to it before.

"I have to go," they say abruptly.

"To the airport?" I ask, half joking, half serious. "I can drive you."

Maybe this is the nudge I need to do the same thing. Maybe Carson and I can do it together.

"No, Tatum, I'm not going to the airport. I'm going home to stare at my wall for twelve hours. Then I'll make myself some microwavable mac and cheese. Maybe I'll get really fancy and pair it with the Two Buck Chuck from Trader Joe's that's actually, like, five dollars now. Then I will rot in my bed for the next twelve hours. Then I will get up, and I will build a fucking chair or something, and eventually, everything will go back to the same nothing it's always been."

"Come on," I say, gesturing to the living room. "You've never missed a couch session with me."

"This is different."

And in my heart, I know it is. This isn't like when Carson asked a girl to the dance senior year, and the girl pretended to misunderstand them completely instead of rejecting them. Whatever Carson had with Eleanor was brief, but it seems like it was realer than anything they've had in a very long time.

I know because I'm right there with them. We're in the same boat, side by side, much the way we've always been.

"At least take a cookie for the road," I say, handing them the plate.

"I'm not hungry. But thank you." They head for the door, leaving the same way Eleanor did, fast and wounded.

Maybe it's not love. Maybe it can't be love that fast. But the care they've built in my absence has turned into something much bigger than I've ever personally seen Carson experience.

I can rewrite this scenario for them, coming up with a hundred ways they get their happy ending. I wish Carson would be brave enough to let in the good. But wouldn't that mean I'd have to do the exact same thing?

Maybe I need to show them. Maybe I can be brave first.

I get out my phone and call June.

"Hi," she answers. Right away, her tone is wrong.

"Hey," I say, infusing every ounce of warmth into my own voice in return, hoping she's just had a bad day and I can help her through it. "Sorry it's taken me a minute to call. The family stuff has been overwhelming."

She already knows this. We've been texting, mostly updates about Laney. Pictures of Eleanor's cats. All the exchanges she's had with Dawn. We haven't discussed her question, because it wasn't a conversation for texting. I'd told her I'd call.

And here I am, calling.

She's aware this moment is the big one. The decision.

"I'm sorry," she says, tone still cool.

"How's New York?" I ask, feeling stuck in these pleasantries like we're back at Rita's, incapable of admitting our real feelings.

"It's good. I think I found an apartment."

"Really?"

"Yeah. I'll send you pictures in a bit."

It's the perfect segue into what I'm about to say, and I take a breath, composing myself. In that silence, June says, "Tatum," low and serious.

My whole body stiffens.

"I know I asked you to come live here with me," she continues. "And I meant it. I really did. I want you here, because I want to be around you all the time. But I've had some time to think about it, and I know I also want you here because I'm afraid to be here by myself. I'm doing what I always do, rushing into this, making it way too serious too soon."

"What happened to let's just try?" I ask, my head still buzzing from what I was just going to do, the answer I was moments from giving before she pulled the rug out from under me. "What happened to run toward the unknown?"

"I know."

"Don't I get a voice?" I ask her. "I don't have to live with you. You can have your own space. But what if I want to live there too?"

"Do you?" she asks. It's flat. Not excited or hopeful. But not angry either. She's not placing any expectation on it.

I am, though. I'm expecting an eager yes to fall out of my mouth. Instead all I can manage is, "I . . . might."

"Your family," she says, filling in the piece I haven't yet said.

"They'd understand." Because they would, in time. But I know that I can't go running again. Not right now. I can't leave in the middle of us figuring out how to actually be a family.

"Tatum." She says my name so carefully, the way you'd talk to a wounded child. "This is for the best. We got out before it hurt too bad, just like you wanted."

It's not true. This still hurts just as much as it would've if we'd been together a year. A lifetime.

Maybe it hurts more, because we only got a week.

"Congratulations, June," I say, meaning it. "I hope New York treats you well."

It's petty, and a bit irrational, but I hang up, unable to keep this conversation going a second longer.

All this time, I expected I would be the one to break June's heart.

I never thought that June could break mine.

September

(TWO MONTHS LATER)

30

Eleanor

In my first month at Atlas Theatrical, they've made me the lead agent for a Broadway revival of *Barefoot in the Park*, starring film actors Joseph Donovan and Sloane Ford, newlyweds in real life and onstage. They're both from Hollywood legacy families. Classic nepo babies. Lucky for me, neither of them minds talking about their famous families. It makes for a lot of great press opportunities. More actors should be this way—honest about their upbringing and the opportunities it's offered them. Being in on the joke makes them way more interesting than any of their peers who attempt to deny it.

Today we're at the Condé Nast offices, where Sloane and Joseph are getting set up for a lie detector interview. They'll ask each other playful questions about their life and relationship, hopefully sneaking in some references to their upcoming play in the process. It's always a well-received PR move, and they're a perfect pairing for this interview style. It's not hard-hitting journalism, but it can be riskier than other outlets, and Sloane and Joseph are game for anything.

Joseph gets strapped in first. Sloane begins her interview by asking Joseph if he likes her cooking. When he says yes, the lie detector reader tells him he's lying. There is laughter all around.

I get an overwhelming urge to text Carson. It's like being struck by lightning, how quickly it happens. I have no choice but to pull out my phone. I convince myself that the more impulsive this decision is, the less pressure there is around it.

> ELEANOR: Have you gotten any other reviews on your cooking since I left?

When several minutes pass without a response, the only thought that gives me peace is remembering that Carson was the one who asked me to be their hookup buddy. We had an agreed-upon situation, and the fact that I left without a word is not unusual behavior for that kind of dynamic. Before the engagement disaster, there were weeks where I didn't speak to Anthony. Some of the names on my roster I used to reach out to once a year. We never acted like it was odd to do that.

It's not strange for me to have texted Carson out of the blue right now. Not strange at all.

As the minutes continue passing, my peace turns to resignation. They aren't answering me because we shouldn't speak. I should know better than to try to change that.

Which is why I drop my phone onto Joseph Donovan's feet when Carson *does* text me back, right as the interview is wrapping up. I haven't even read the message. Just Carson's name on the screen shoots an unexpected bolt of energy through me, and my phone goes flying out of my hand.

"You all right?" Joseph asks, picking up the device. He has a lovely Irish lilt and one of those soul-piercing gazes, eyes so blue it's unnerving.

"My apologies," I tell him. The last time I spoke about my personal life in any work-related capacity resulted in my getting fired. I'm certainly not going to divulge my romantic details to an actor I'm tasked with accompanying from place to place on a press tour.

It's Joseph's wife, Sloane, who grabs the phone from Joseph and hands it over to me. "Texting someone you like?" she asks with a pleasant curiosity.

"Yeah. It's my . . . ex," I say. "Anyway, they want us to wait in the green room here. It should only be about an hour before we do the next segment. We already ordered your lunch. It'll be here any minute."

Joseph sits down on the green room couch and folds his foot across his thigh. Sloane plops down next to him, placing her head on his shoulder and tucking her feet under her as she looks at me.

"What happened with your ex?" she asks.

"They live in Illinois, and I live here," I say.

I don't know why I even indulge this conversation. Or why I'm continuing to pretend Carson was ever my ex in the first place. It's rather disingenuous of me to call them that. We only knew each other a week. I've known the bananas rotting on my kitchen counter for longer.

"Nothing bad?" Joseph confirms.

"No," I say with too much quickness. "Not at all. They're a wonderful person. Almost too wonderful . . ." I trail off, not sure where I'm going with this.

"What did your ex say to you?" Sloane prompts, pointing to my phone.

Checking this notification alone is already hard. Checking it in front of two famous actors I don't really know? A nightmare. Yet I have to indulge them. Because ultimately, my job today is to keep them happy, and keeping them happy now involves sharing the details of my personal life.

When I open the text to read it, the squeeze in my chest gets so tight that I forget how to breathe.

> CARSON: I haven't taken on any new customers since you left.

> ELEANOR: Good.

My fingers flew over the keys faster than I could think. I read it back, shocked by the possessiveness of my own words. Heart racing, I rush to correct myself.

> ELEANOR: Just don't want any softhearted liars in there. They might mislead you.

This *also* feels like a mistake. I read it again, convincing myself of a hundred interpretations, none of which are kind. Carson could read it like I think they'd only date liars. Or that I'm not softhearted. Or that they're often getting misled.

"Wow, you're really in it," Sloane comments.

My head shoots up, and I look over at her, pasting on the tight smile that's always gotten me through these kinds of interactions. "Sorry." I shove my phone into my purse. "They were just saying hello."

Sloane gives me one of those loaded gazes. Actors and their keen observations. She's probably writing mental notes in her head about what kind of character I am. "Who broke up with who?"

"I broke up with them," I say. A lump forms in my throat. I might as well be the actor here, the way I'm creating an entire world that never existed.

No one broke up with anyone. We were never even dating.

This is harmless, though. Sloane and Joseph each have their own personal publicists who are also in the room with us, pretending not to listen but hanging on every word. It's fine if I make conversation. It's keeping everyone entertained. It's my job.

And my job is all I have.

"Do you want to get back together?" Joseph asks.

He and his wife are grilling me the same way they grilled each other when they were strapped into a lie detector vest. Maybe this can be my own version of a lie detector. What would I say if I was sure someone would know I was lying? If I could only tell the truth.

"I miss them," I say. "And I wish that we were different people living different lives. That's the only way it would ever work between us."

"You could be," Joseph says, sitting up straighter.

I laugh, dismissive, thinking he's kidding. But he keeps looking at me, probing me to ask more. "Okay, I'll bite," I say. "How do I become a different person?"

Sloane nudges Joseph in the shoulder, a wordless conversation unfolding between them that must have to do with how he's close to crossing the line.

Joseph thinks for a bit before he responds, saying, "Look. If this is something you really want, there might be a way to make it work. That's all. And maybe that takes you some time, or it takes some big changes, but if there are any broken pieces of this in your control, then you should do whatever you can to fix them. We never have as much time as we think we do."

When my parents died, I hadn't seen them in a few months. I'd planned to visit them in the oncoming summer, not wanting to come home until my school year was done.

I never got the chance. I didn't see the new flowers my mom just planted in the garden, or the way my dad finally replaced the drainpipe that had been plaguing him every time it rained. Those were the tiny things that filled most of our phone calls. Mundanities that kept us bonded across state lines. They were details no one would ever think to notice without being prompted. Their house got sold with no one but me knowing any of it.

I became very aware of my place in the world. How up to that point, I'd done nothing to establish myself. That when *I* died, no one would carry a piece of me with them at all.

I thought it meant I should make a name for myself in my career. That was how I wanted to be remembered. The best way to make an impression would be to work so hard no one could possibly forget me. That my replaced drainpipes and new flower gardens might get lost, but the everlasting impact of the shows I helped promote would be remembered for decades to come. My name would be in every *Playbill*.

Now I know with certainty that my work will never keep me in anyone's memory. No matter how good I am at my job, I am replaceable. If I got up and walked out of this room, one of my coworkers would begrudgingly take my position, and Sloane and Joseph wouldn't even notice the change.

Keeping my composure, I look Joseph in the eyes as I say, "Very true." I place a firmness in my voice that lets him know there's nothing left to say on the subject. It's not harsh. I wouldn't make the talent hate me. Not on purpose, at least. It's just a boundary. No more discussing this. It's not entertainment anymore.

Our lunch arrives, providing the perfect transition. Sloane and Joseph slide into their own conversation as they eat. Their personal teams chat among themselves. I get out my phone again.

CARSON: I wouldn't trust any other person's
opinion of my food. Only yours.

It's such a relief I bite back my smile, not wanting Sloane or Joseph to notice. But I think of Joseph's words, and it prompts me to respond to Carson with something a little deeper.

ELEANOR: How have you been?

I'm sorry I left, I add, deleting it before sending. That's too far. We're not there yet.

CARSON: Bored.

ELEANOR: Wishing for yet another secret sibling to appear?

CARSON: I'm at a clinic right now, having my DNA tested. Ben can't be the only one.

ELEANOR: You're looking to build an army of Wards. The world wants more of your kind.

CARSON: You know what everyone is always saying. We need more nonbinary queers around here!

I can't help it; I smile.

ELEANOR: I overheard three old women on the train saying the same thing on my commute this morning.

CARSON: The elderly tend to be the loudest on the subject. Every day another granny falls to her

knees and prays for more trans representation in
her life.

> ELEANOR: You know what they say? Be the change
> you wish to see in the world.

They send back an emoji of the globe surrounded by little
stars.

> ELEANOR: Did you get to paint the mural for the
> park district yet?

This creates a longer pause than I'd like. Maybe the game
between us is to never mention anything too personal. Then, let
me lose it. It's not like I've been any good at playing in the first
place.

> CARSON: I'm ashamed to say they still haven't
> even let me start. I told them in our initial contract
> that they could request two adjustments to my
> initial design. So far they've requested five. Waiting
> to hear back on that last round.

> ELEANOR: I wouldn't take you for such
> a pushover.

I send it off too soon. It's careless and rude, not at all how I
want to be around Carson.

> ELEANOR: If memory serves, the townsfolk over
> there tend to think of you as trouble.

CARSON: My memory seems to tell me you were
the Trouble with a capital T.

ELEANOR: Hmm . . .

CARSON: I've been in a bit of a funk these days.

ELEANOR: Why a funk? I thought you were bored.

CARSON: Bored of my funk.

I disappoint myself by letting them get out of answering me in earnest. If they'd told me it was because of me, it would have given me permission to admit I'm in a funk too.

But I'm not. At least not professionally. This is the busiest I've ever been. Not to mention the fact that I've managed to keep my apartment relatively clean too, which might be the biggest accomplishment of all. The only place I feel different is in the core of me—the one place that can't be touched by work or living spaces or whatever other things I do to fill my time. My essence has been changed, and it's such an unfamiliar shift that to acknowledge it is to admit that I don't want to be lonely anymore. That I've never wanted to be lonely, and all the years I've let myself live this way were years I was too scared of all the ways I am capable of wanting more. The want I possess could move mountains if I let it. And I'm dangerously close to letting it do just that.

ELEANOR: Well, I hope the funk passes soon.

CARSON: I'm not too sure it will. But I do take
great stock in your hopes for me.

"Are you making it work?" Joseph asks me.

When I look up, Sloane's salad bite hovers in front of her lips as Joseph steeps a tea bag into a to-go cup.

"I don't know," I say. "But I think I want to."

"Good." Joseph looks to Sloane as if my answer has solved something for both of them.

> ELEANOR: Let's catch up on a video call soon. I
> want to see your face.

31

Tatum

Lately, whenever they don't need me at Rita's, I take the train into Chicago. The city isn't exactly like New York, but there's an energy that feels similar enough. When I walk around, I can almost convince myself I've once again become the person I discovered there.

Ben lives here, and he lets me pop into his place whenever I'm traveling through. He insists upon it, actually, because he likes getting any opportunity he can to know me better. It inspires me to be a better sibling to him in return. We may not have known each other for the first third of our lives, but we have a chance to be present for the rest of it.

He's agreed to meet me and Carson at the Art Institute. Carson wants to "get some inspiration from the art." Really I think they're restless, and they need some sibling time to rejuvenate them, but I'm more than happy to entertain their cover story. I love an activity.

"Did you get up here all right?" Ben asks when Carson and I meet him outside the museum. "No issues?"

He asks this every time, which I find funny, because I always arrive in one piece. But it's a sweet impulse, the way he worries. He falls between Carson and me in age. Carson and I have always treated each other more like equals than siblings of a different age. Ben's presence throws our years apart into sharper contrast, makes the hierarchy more apparent.

"All good, Brother Ben," Carson tells him.

As we walk inside the institute, we fill Ben in on the latest on Laney's leg. Apparently she doesn't tell him much over text, because she doesn't want him to feel bad about it as her pickleball partner. Of course Ben didn't cause the accident. No one did. But the injury was more complex than first expected, with some ligament damage to her knee in addition to the bone situation. Still, she's healing well.

"She's planning to run a 5K on Thanksgiving," I add, noticing that Ben really is still taking it hard, squinting his eyes like he's experiencing her pain secondhand. "She's doing just fine, I promise."

"Does she want me to do the 5K with her?" he asks.

"She'd probably like that," Carson says. "God knows we two queers aren't running it."

"Gay people can run," I say.

"Yeah, but we're not the gay ones who do, now, are we?"

Ben laughs his good-natured laugh, never intimidated by us in the way I expect him to be. We know his wife a little better now, having learned she hosts a very popular podcast where she talks about her personal life and experiences. Shock factor is baked into a lot of what she does. Ben must be immune to it.

As we walk through the lofty corridors of the Art Institute, Carson tells us about certain pieces we pass by. They've always been smarter than they let people know, and it's a nice treat to see them willing to flex their art knowledge around Ben instead of pretending to be ignorant so as not to seem like a know-it-all.

Ben and I both like to know the history of things, and Carson is someone who can tell us. It works out for all involved.

"By the way, how's it going with Eleanor?" Ben asks.

"Oh, we're just friends," Carson says. "Have you ever seen a Degas? They have *On the Stage* on view in Gallery 226. It's not far from here."

"Don't they think he's Jack the Ripper?" I ask. Then I turn to Ben and say, "I don't know if you're fluent in Carson-speak yet, but they're *not* just friends. Carson is obsessed with her. And she's obsessed right back."

"I am going to trip you in front of this Manet," Carson says. "And yes, obviously I've heard about that theory. Which is why we should go see the Degas."

"I'm just saying, there's obviously a lot more going on than what you're saying."

"We talk on the phone a few times a week," Carson says to Ben.

"Well, I really liked her," Ben responds. "And so did Aunt Irene. Also, people think the artist Degas is Jack the Ripper? Why?"

"Yes, Aunt Irene's obsession with Eleanor is well-known," Carson replies. "And you really need to get online more. I say that with love. Sometimes it's hard, how clinically offline you are. I'll send you some articles about it, since god knows you won't be able to open a TikTok link."

"I've always thought Aunt Irene could be queer," I say. "Who knows? She and Eleanor might be the next Sarah Paulson and Holland Taylor."

"What about Uncle Paul?" Ben asks. Then he follows it with, "And who are Sarah Paulson and Holland Taylor?"

"Uncle Paul probably won't even notice," Carson tells him.

"Now, don't you want to ask Tatum about June? Sarah and Holland are actresses and gay icons."

"There's nothing to ask me about," I announce, whispering as if I might disturb the artwork. "We haven't spoken in months. But thanks for bringing it up. Very sensitive of you."

"You're welcome," Carson says.

"Why haven't you spoken?" Ben's mature, sensitive responses sometimes make me feel like the world's most immature twenty-nine-year-old. Maybe someday we can convince him to join us in the familial teasing.

"Nothing to say," I tell him. "She ended up moving to New York after our trip. And obviously, I live here."

"Doesn't Eleanor also live in New York? And Carson's managing to talk to her, right?"

"Benjamin, I don't welcome this line of questioning from you. I'm trying to appreciate"—I read the placard in front of the painting where we stand—"Manet's *Fish (Still Life)* right now."

"I'm sorry," Ben says sincerely.

After we see the Degas, Ben expresses an interest in knowing all of Carson's favorite paintings, which sends us on a quest, moving from gallery to gallery.

I almost miss it when my phone pings with a notification to my special inbox.

It's Ben who says, "I think you got a text or something," pointing to the place where the sound has come from— my big bag slung across my right hip. Fumbling through it, I see the submission request on my lock screen.

Writing other people's messages has lost its luster since the whole debacle with June. It's like my anonymous customers can somehow feel my detachment. Where I used to get four or five requests a month thanks to my long-standing presence on Tumblr,

I now get one or two. It's nearly the end of September, and this one is the first request I've gotten all month.

APOLOGY FOR SOMEONE WHO MESSED UP IN WAYS THEY DON'T QUITE KNOW HOW TO EXPLAIN is the title.

"Hold on a sec," I tell my siblings, sitting down on a bench. "I have a new client."

Hello,

I've recently made a really big mistake. I've pushed away someone important to me. Now we no longer live in the same place, and I've left so much unsaid. I'm going to try to put it all down here. You're the writer. Maybe you can tell me the best way to say it. I hope you'll be able to understand me enough to make my point clear.

I tried to make her something once. I spent weeks on it. And I couldn't get it right, for a lot of reasons. But now I know I was missing the most important piece of the puzzle. I was missing the reason why I wanted to capture her at all. I was trying to re-create her because I always wanted her around me. I wanted to bottle the essence of her into this one compact thing, and she really couldn't be limited to that. Which was why I was trying to do entirely too many things at once. I was trying to capture every single piece of her to prove just how full she was in my mind. I wanted to create something that occupied every little bit of her.

That was before I even really knew her.

I was lucky enough to take a trip with her. And I learned her compassion. Her heart. Her generosity. I learned that she's protective of herself because she's scared to be hurt in the same way she's seen the people around her get hurt. I never wanted to be the one to do that to her. I tried so hard to make sure I didn't, even though the longer we were together, the harder it became for me to separate my feelings from my actions. In the end, I did exactly what she was afraid I would.

I've been kicking myself for two whole months, replaying that moment.

I know this letter might make you think I'm a talker. That I could be good at saying all of this. But I'm really more of a doer. I prefer to act on my feelings instead of saying them out loud. I'd rather try dating someone right away than wait to figure out if we can hold interesting conversations. What happened with her was the exact opposite. All we ever did was talk. For years. A lot of those years we spoke about little things, like how much I liked to mix sauces. Or what makes for the best sandwich bread. (She thinks sourdough, I think rye.)

I've never had the chance to know someone that way before becoming romantic. She is the first person who has ever been worth the wait. She has made me see why people wait at all. Because to know her as a person makes me want her all the more for it. I don't want to be the one who hurts her. I want to be the one who helps her heal instead. I don't think I've earned that right, though. Not in the least. But maybe, if you read this, you can see a path forward that I don't?

At the very least, I want her to know that the way I feel about her has nothing to do with anything else in my life. I don't like her because I'm lonely or because I'm vulnerable or because I need help. I've lived by myself for two months now. Really by myself. I have friends where I am. Two of them, to be specific. One who's a little older than me, and one who's a lot. But I don't see them all the time. Most days, I'm completely on my own. And I can see how strong it has made me. I'm not who I used to be even two months ago.

But I do still know what I want. And that's her.

I'm going back to where she lives next week. I'll be visiting my family for my cousin's baby shower. And I'd really like to see her, if she'd be willing to see me too. I'm just not sure how to ask.

Okay. That's everything. Or maybe it's not anywhere near enough, but it's more than I've ever said before, so it sure feels like everything to me. I hope you can make sense of the tangles of my mind.

Thank you for reading.

I shove my phone back into my purse, so flushed it's hard to keep upright. "What else is there to see?" I ask. "I love art!"

"Something's wrong with you," Carson says.

"Nothing's wrong with me." My voice goes even higher. I sound like I've swallowed helium. "I just want to see more master-pieces!"

"You're being so weird. Stop it."

"You *are* being weird," Ben confirms.

Great. Now is the time Ben tries on some comfortable ribbing.

"I think June just messaged me on my website," I tell them both.

"Dude, we're prophets," Carson tells Ben, putting their hand up for a high five. "We manifested this."

"I don't know for sure it's her," I say. Even though I do. Of course I do. There are too many details that could only be us. The sauces. The sandwich bread. Calling me the writer. The two friends.

Carson takes my purse and rummages for my phone. "Let me read it."

"Can I?" Ben asks once Carson has the device in their hands.

"Might as well," I say.

And so my two older siblings sit side by side on a bench, reading June's note to me.

"Tatum, she's completely in love with you," Carson tells me once they finish.

"Shut up," I say.

"I'm serious. This is a devotional." They look over to Ben for support, which is when we both discover that Ben has tears in his eyes. "Dude, are you crying?"

He wipes his tear. "I hope you'll give her a chance," he tells me. "Everybody deserves at least one."

32

Eleanor

After a long day at work, Dawn catches me in our hallway. My key is already inserted into my lock when she opens her door and says, "It's pizza night."

Before I can get in a question, she gestures to the inside of her apartment while tapping her foot, like it's not only a given that I will be attending, but I am somehow late for this event we have not planned.

"Give me a second, let me go change," I say, to which she sighs. Inside my place, Syrup and Salt greet me at the door, meowing with desperation. "I know, I know. You're hungry."

I feed them and change, then head over to Dawn's for our supposed pizza night, texting Carson along the way.

> ELEANOR: Dawn's invited me over again. Not sure how long it will be.

> CARSON: Don't worry about it. I'll be home all night. Have fun.

I'll miss you, I type, then delete.

ELEANOR: Talk later.

"It's just cheese," Dawn tells me, opening the box so I can take out my slice. "I don't like any toppings."

"That's perfect," I say.

"We're watching *Twilight on Clarke Street*." The movie is cued up on her TV screen, with a bucket of popcorn resting on her coffee table and two glasses of wine already poured for us.

"Also perfect," I tell her. "I've never seen it."

This gets me another look of scorn, which I take to be disappointment at my lack of knowledge of the classics. Only when we get about four minutes into the movie do I realize she's disappointed in me because she's *in* this movie.

My favorite thing about Dawn is the way she throws me into situations without context. When I got back from Trove Hills in July, she knocked on my door that very morning, handing me a bag of her old dresses.

"Tatum forced me to do this," she said.

"Do you want me to donate them for you?" I asked, confused.

"Why the hell would I want you to do that?"

Eventually, after several more questions and more than one frustrated run-in with her in our hallway where she asked me when my next fancy event was, I realized she wanted me to *wear* the dresses she'd given me. And so I do. Whenever we have a bigger press event that requires something formal, I pull out an old Dawn Flores dress for the occasion. Now she's got me at her apartment for a pizza night we never discussed, playing a movie of hers from the 1970s, and it's up to me to figure out why.

"I'm so excited to watch one of your movies with you," I say, switching between young Dawn on the screen and the Dawn that sits beside me now.

"Eh." She grabs a handful of popcorn. When I linger on her too long, she nudges my attention back to the screen. There's a young man in the scene with her. Handsome. Blond hair, blue eyes. Familiar, somehow.

"Who's that?" I ask.

Dawn stares at me, expectant.

"Do I know him?" I continue.

She continues staring. I want to get out my phone and google it, but something tells me it's the easy way out, and she wouldn't like that.

Several minutes later, when the man on-screen reaches for his neck, dipping his chin down to look at young Dawn with something like longing, it finally clicks.

"This is Joseph Donovan's dad," I say.

Dawn grins. "Thought you'd get a kick out of seeing him, since you're doing all that press for Joseph's play. I've known his dad for—shit—almost fifty years now. Had to show you this."

Pleased with myself for figuring it out, I finally settle into my seat, taking a bite of the cheese pizza. "The world's small, isn't it?"

"Sometimes," she says. "And sometimes it's big enough to get lost in."

We continue watching young Dawn, so fresh to the scene. She has an arresting presence, capable of showcasing hurt and yearning and fear all in a single glance. It's mesmerizing.

"We should get you in some new projects," I say, my PR brain spinning its wheels, already thinking of the angles. "I can think of more than a few outlets we could pitch."

Dawn shoots up from her couch and heads to her kitchen. "What would you even say?" She decides right now is a great time to do her dishes.

"Whatever you wanted me to," I tell her sincerely. "We could talk about your early career, where you've been. What you hope to do next. There's a real taste for this kind of thing right now, if you wanted it."

"I don't think so," she calls out. "I could never be who I was."

"They wouldn't want you to," I assure her. "But the door is open, if you ever want to walk through it."

After a few more minutes of clanking, she returns to join me on the couch. We say nothing else about what I've offered, but it lingers in the air. And in that loaded silence, I make a decision.

I will help Dawn Flores return to the spotlight.

IT'S LATE WHEN I FINALLY GET BACK TO MY APARTMENT. Syrup and Salt both wrap around me, meowing with desperation as I text Carson again.

"You already had your dinner," I remind my cats.

Salt backs off, embarrassed to be exposed. Syrup, however, in his infinite innocence, continues to pester me with cries, following me throughout the apartment. They both chase me to the couch, where they jump up, one on either side of me, almost gnawing off my fingers as they each enjoy a squeezable cat yogurt.

My phone rings with an incoming video call. Knowing my cats aren't quite done with their snack, I open my laptop to take the call there instead, nudging off Syrup and Salt in an attempt to click accept on my MacBook.

Since we reconnected, Carson and I video chat almost every night, unless one of us is too tired or too busy. But we never miss a Saturday, no matter what.

If I transcribed our conversations for strangers to read, they'd never know the longing that sits like a deadweight in my heart. They couldn't feel the way I hold my breath every time Carson goes quiet. Every silence scares me, because I'm afraid if we're quiet for too long, I'll forget about the pleasantries and say what I really feel, and neither of us will know what to do with it.

"Hello there," I say as I finally manage to answer. Both my cats crowd the screen, eager to get back to their yogurts.

"Are you being accosted by your cats?" Carson's on their bed in a black tank, hair wet from a shower. The pixelation of the video call paints them like my memories do, with a soft generosity, gentle in the rendering of their features.

"Yes. They'll be lodging a complaint with the Supreme Court imminently, suing me for failing to feed them enough."

"Taking it to the highest court in the land. Those are definitely your pets."

"Some might say they have firing energy."

We both laugh.

"How was Dawn?" Carson asks.

"She's so funny," I tell them. "She showed me one of her old movies, because she wanted me to know she was in it with the dad of one of the actors from the play I'm working on. But I think she just wanted the company too. And to remind me she's a good actor. Which she really is."

"That was nice of you to watch it with her," Carson says.

"Honestly, I like her company too," I admit. "She's hilarious. I'm trying to get her back into acting. I think she wants it. But she doesn't want to have to ask."

Carson nods. "I get that."

My cats finish their dessert, jumping off the couch in almost eerie unison, leaving me alone to have this conversation in private.

Carson and I get into summarizing our day. They tell me about putting their foot down with the park district, *finally* getting the mural design started on the wall. I take them through the dinner I just attended with some producers.

"We ran into my old boss near the end."

"*No*," Carson says, scandalized. "What happened?"

"He congratulated me on the position at Atlas. I thought for a second he was going to mention the Anthony email in front of the whole table, but he didn't."

"Probably because he knows he was wrong to fire you."

"Anthony and his fiancée, Kelsey, are still together, by the way," I say.

"Of course they are," Carson responds.

"Kelsey blocked me on Instagram."

"She doesn't want to accept that what you said was true, and that it will happen again." Carson stops, leaning back. "I shouldn't say that. I guess my dad changed." They move closer to the screen. "What if there really are others? A dozen Brother Bens all throughout Illinois? What if there are children from whatever doctor conferences my dad used to go on when I was a kid? What if there really is an army of Wards?"

"Then I consider you the captain. Or the sergeant. Whatever the main one is. You rule them all."

"Eleanor, I can't be their leader. I never asked for this. I'm not ready for this power."

"What is this army of Wards even fighting?"

"Our demons."

We laugh.

We always laugh.

"I thought it was getting cold in Illinois," Carson says. "But today it was eighty degrees."

"When do the leaves start to turn there?" I ask. "We're still green here in New York."

"Should be pretty soon. But right now, it looks the same as it did when you were here."

In the weeks since we've been talking again, this is the first mention of my time in Trove Hills. I squeeze myself into the opening, just tired enough to keep my defenses low.

"I miss it," I say. The conversation drops down into me, the deadweight lifting a little at this admission. "I miss *you*."

Carson doesn't say anything for a while. I watch their chest rise and fall, and I sync my breath to theirs, trying to stay brave.

"I miss you too," they say.

I pick up my laptop, walking us into my bedroom. Something about the tall windows out in my living room exposes me too much. People might be able to see. I can't let anyone have access to this moment.

There is only one light on in my bedroom. It's small and glows warm, casting a halo around my nightstand. I walk toward it, moth to flame, settling under my bedsheets. My face becomes half shadow, half light. I set my laptop down, spreading my legs so that it can rest between my knees. It shows me from the hips up, with my comforter covering the lower part of me.

"You look nice," Carson says.

"I remember a time when you'd call me beautiful," I respond.

"You're always beautiful to me," they say. "You know that."

"I wish I could hear you say that in person. I wish you were here right now."

Carson leans in, like they might see more of me if they get closer to the screen. "What would we do if I was?"

"You know what we'd do," I say, breathy.

"Do I?" they question.

"*Carson*," I say, my need cracking me open.

They turn off the overhead light in their room, hiding away the same as I am, half shadow, all longing.

"I want you to tell me what we'd do," they say. "Spell it out for me."

"You'd probably push me up against something," I start. "A

wall. A door. Your lips would be on my mouth as you'd reach for my thigh."

"You'd let out your gasp," they add.

My hand wanders down under my comforter, the movement in full view of the screen. Touching myself the same way, I do as they said—I gasp.

"That's the one," they confirm, a lazy grin spreading across their face. "I'd probably whisper in your ear next."

"What would you say?"

"*Such a good girl*," they coo, soft and low.

"You'd touch me then, right?"

"Only if you wanted me to," they say.

"I want you to," I tell them.

"Then I would."

On their command, my hand moves to my clit, re-creating the gentle way they'd tease me.

"Talk to me," I request, yearning for the sound of their voice, the one they use only for me when we're alone.

"Close your eyes," they say, full of their gentle command. When I do as I'm told, they sigh, loud enough for me to hear. "Very good. Are you wet?"

"Yes," I tell them.

"Is it for me?"

"Yes."

"Good girl."

My eyes still closed, I listen for the sound of their breath, using it as a tempo to pace my own.

"I want you to touch yourself too," I say. "I need you here with me."

"I am. I'm right here, baby. Right here."

The raw edge in their voice breaks me. Together, we become a ragged chorus, words of praise and longing mixing together with the noise of our desires. Every whimper they let out unlocks a wilder piece of my own, and I feel as close to them with this computer between us as I could if they were in the room.

Closer maybe, because this way we can be sure to fall apart together, unraveling in perfect synchronicity.

It's only when it's over, and we both come back to ourselves, that the loneliness kicks in. The stark emptiness of my bed. The hollow sound of my apartment. Carson on a video screen pales in comparison to the real thing. We have undone each other, just as we intended to. But I don't know how to piece myself back together anymore.

33

Tatum

Once a month, Sunday morning at Rita's Diner is bingo time. I pass out the cards and stampers to the elderly diners with a smile. This is me in my prime, putting on a show for an audience of seniors. It's always been my favorite event of ours, and not because it's some pillar of sweet, innocent fun. No. The seniors of Trove Hills are *lethal* in their competitiveness. There are high-dollar restaurant coupons on the line. Sometimes even electronics. When one of the prizes was a flat-screen TV, I thought Mr. Tompkins and this usually very mild-mannered old woman named Anne were going to go into our parking lot and fist-fight over it, and neither of them even won. It was just that serious.

"How come you never play with us?" my dad asks when I reach his table.

"I have to work," I tell him. "I'm not meant to be on the other side of the fence. I don't think I'm safe among your kind."

"Nonsense," Denise calls out from behind the counter. "You can join them for a game!"

She's been in unusually good spirits with me. It seems to be because generally, I'm a mope. She hasn't said that. She just keeps gassing me up for silly things like bingo, or letting me leave when it's slow instead of making me inventory our sauces or wipe down the sugar ramekins like she used to do. The cooks are the ones who've told me I've been a bad time lately, because as usual, they don't believe in subtlety.

Despite knowing they're right, I haven't been able to change my ways. It's so nice to just slump around and pity myself sometimes. It's beautiful, really. They'd do the same thing if they got a letter from June. I think I'm handling it pretty well, all things considered.

"This is great," Dad says when I sit down, kissing me on the side of my forehead.

"Don't forget to grab a stamper," Mom reminds me, peering up through her readers. She's scanning some article on her phone, and in the moment, she looks so unbelievably old that it steals my breath.

My mom and dad love bingo. They've been joining us at Rita's every Sunday for years. They used to be the youngest people in the group. Gradually, they've started to fit right in. Obviously that's how time works, but it still surprises me. In my mind, they're the same parents they've always been, but every so often, I can see them for who they've become, and it scares me a little. I can never stop the clock.

"Room for one more?"

The sound of the voice cannot belong to who I think it does. This has to be my mind playing tricks on me.

"Hello there!" my dad says in his doctor voice, overly bright and friendly. "You're more than welcome to join us at this table, so long as you don't mind my elbow. I'm left-handed."

June slides into the seat across from me, sitting next to my dad. I can see the exact moment he smells her, the cloud of heavenly scent that wafts around her every move. It puts him further at ease, and he hands her a stamper and a stack of bingo cards. He gives me an eyebrow wriggle he thinks is discrete. Luckily, June isn't paying attention to him.

She's looking at me.

All the while, I stare back in disbelief. She has managed to get more beautiful, or maybe absence has done that thing I'm always hearing about—made me grow fonder. She's got her hair in her natural curls now, pulled up into a half ponytail, framing the exquisite roundness of her face. Her lips are a dark ruby. There's that touch of highlighter she loves on each cheek, drawing forward all her best features.

She holds a single coral rose, the same as the one in the bouquet she got for our first date. I shouldn't be staring at her. I know I'm betraying my own feelings by showcasing all of my yearning in this single unbroken look. But I can't help myself.

"Excuse me," I say. "I'll be right back."

Dashing behind the counter and into the back kitchen, out of sight of all the customers, I pull out my phone to do the only thing that makes sense to me right now—text the group chat.

TATUM: She's here.

Emmett responds in seconds.

EMMETT: Shut the fuck up.

Presley joins just as fast.

PRESLEY: Who?

Before I can answer, Nya's name appears on the screen. The gang's all here for me.

NYA: Obviously June. Is she on her knees groveling?

TATUM: I don't know. I got up before we could speak.

After the website submission, I caved and told them everything. There was no way to keep it to myself anymore. They've been begging me to act on it, pressuring me to show up at the baby shower June mentioned in the letter. Nya even found the gift registry for the cousin, which led to figuring out the exact date and time of the event. It's today, I realize, putting it all together. In a few hours.

She's come to see me beforehand.

NYA: Tatum.

EMMETT: TATUM!

PRESLEY: Go back there!

TATUM: She's got the coral rose. She's definitely the one who wrote the request.

NYA: Of fucking course she wrote it. You think there's another person who wants to talk to you about how they mix ranch and mustard and barbecue sauce together or whatever it is she does?

PRESLEY: She should've mentioned soup. Then we'd have known for sure much earlier.

NYA: We've always known for sure. Tatum's just pretending we haven't because she's in shock.

PRESLEY: Did we ever find out what she thinks of it, though?

NYA: Not now.

She chooses a previous text of mine to reply to next.

NYA: What did she say before you got up?

> TATUM: She didn't say much. Just asked if we had room at our table. My dad answered, which is a whole other layer of mortification.

EMMETT: Tatum, if you don't get back out there I am going to fly to Trove Hills and shove you out there myself.

> TATUM: Excellent. I can be solidly into Michigan by that point, headed for my brand-new life.

NYA: You took a risk in New York, and she rejected you. She took a risk with the letter, and you rejected her by ignoring it. You're even. What are you so afraid of now?

> TATUM: Myself.

NYA: Well, boo, bitch, scare yourself into moving it
along and getting your girl. We're waiting. And so is
she.

I run my hand through my hair, setting the stray pieces I
didn't bother to fix before leaving. It's not what I hoped to be
wearing—no-slip shoes and raggedy black jeans that smell of
fryer grease. But this is the Tatum she's always known. And I do
have on my winged eyeliner, which means a lot. Still, I have to
take out the compact mirror I keep in my staff locker, giving myself a once-over.

When I return to the diner, June and my parents are smiling
and laughing like old friends reunited.

"There she is," my dad says, noticing me first.

June looks up. The comfortable smile on her face gets replaced
with something like worry. It's here that I notice her new pea
coat, long and plaid, and a new pair of brown heeled boots that
match one of the shades in the coat.

"Hi, June," I say shyly. "Could we talk?"

"Sure," she says. "I'd like that."

"Let's go out back."

"What about your bingo game?" my mom calls out.

"Play it for me, please. And if I win, it's yours," I tell her.

"If you say so," she mutters. "Kinda defeats the point, but
okay."

I lead us out the diner's back exit, past our dumpsters and off
to the far edge of the parking lot, which presses up against the
forest preserve. This is as private as it gets here. Only the cooks
come out to this part when they want to take a smoke break. I
resist the urge to press up against June, and I settle for leaving a
sliver of space between us.

"I tried to write to you," June tells me, confirming it was her. "I'm not sure if you got it."

"I did," I tell her.

This takes her by surprise, which surprises me in return. It's a soft kind of heartbreak that unfolds on her face. The way she bared herself in that letter is not easy for anyone to do. My defenses lower, making space for what I really want to say.

"I was so hurt by what you said to me on the phone," I tell her. "That you wouldn't even hear me out about my feelings on New York. It just totally shut me down. I should've said a real goodbye to you at least. I'm really sorry I didn't."

"I understood," she said. "I would've shut me out too."

"But you were right," I say. "I wasn't ready to leave my family. We were still figuring everything out. The timing was wrong."

"Is it still wrong?" she asks, eyes flickering down to my mouth.

"Not at all," I tell her. Cupping her chin with my hand, I pull her toward me. And I kiss her.

It's nothing like the heady moment in Eleanor's living room. If that was fire, this is water, cool and refreshing, waking me up to the wonder of this sensation. My arms wrap around her waist as her hand finds the small of my back. The kiss, first delicate, becomes deeper. Less restricted. My mind, usually racing with thoughts, turns static. For once, I am here, right where I am meant to be, no resistance left.

When June pulls back, a smile blooms on her face. She presses her nose to mine, grabbing the back of my neck to do it.

"I'm so sorry it took me so long to get this right," she says.

"June, I forgave you the moment you sent me that email. Forgive *me* for not replying."

"You didn't have any revisions? No neater way to say what I was trying to put into words?"

I kiss her again, quick. A seal of approval. "You said it better than I ever could. I would never want to edit you. I was just scared. I still am."

She puts her lips to my ear. "Me too," she whispers.

"Okay," I tell her, grabbing her hands. "Let's just be scared together."

"I can't stay long," she tells me. "But I wanted to see you. And I want to see you again."

"Go on a date with me," I blurt out. "Tomorrow night. If you're still here. I seem to recall you owing me a favor."

"Yes," she says, beaming. "Of course."

I beam right back. "I'll pick you up at seven."

34

Eleanor

Dawn and I walk arm in arm down our hallway, laughing.

"That was a shit show," I say.

"A disaster," she responds.

We settle into our third retelling of our night.

Dawn glances back over her shoulder, and she's such a good actor that I can tell she's pretending to be Anthony Teller by the way she's widened her eyes and adopted his strange, wobbly gait.

"Oh shit," she says, using his exact affectation.

"He *ran*," I say, as Dawn breaks away to do just that, zigzagging across our carpet, pretending to cut through imaginary theatergoers to avoid me. She mimes crashing into a man holding a drink. "Sorry, dude, sorry," she says as Anthony. "I'll pay you back, dude."

This really makes us lose it. Dawn saying the dude line in her bro-ey impression voice. It's so pitch-perfect I can't even be mortified that we ran into Anthony Teller after a play and he fled the scene at the sight of me.

"I really thought if I ever saw him again, I'd be a wreck," I tell her. "But this was so perfectly disastrous that it might be one of my favorite memories instead."

"Honey, you came out looking like a peach." Dawn unlocks the door to her apartment. "And I hate to say it to you, but he isn't even that attractive."

"I know."

"Carson's *much* better-looking."

"Oh, it's not even a contest."

"Not at all."

We linger in our doorways, looking at each other.

"Thanks for coming with me," I say, suddenly teary. "I'm a little buzzed from all the wine, and it's making me sentimental."

She walks across the hall and pats me on the head. "You don't have to explain it, sweetheart. I know."

"But I do," I tell her, grabbing her hand. "I need to say this thank-you. If you weren't with me, I probably would've done something sad, like cry. Not because I miss him or I wish I got to be with him. But because, I don't know, it still hurts that he embarrassed me. But now we can laugh."

"Sorry, dude, sorry," Dawn repeats again. It's just as funny on the fourth performance as it was on the previous three. "I'm glad I was with you too."

"You're my friend," I tell her. There's a little slur in my voice that even I can hear. "I might be a little drunker than I realized."

She pats my head again. "Get some sleep. I'll see you tomorrow."

"Love you," I blurt out.

"Love you too," she says with a laugh.

Inside my apartment, I yank my phone out of my purse.

ELEANOR: What if we saw each other?

Maybe it's the wine talking. That's what I tell myself. That it's the drink, not me, being this bold.

CARSON: What do you mean?

Texting is the wrong format for this conversation. I'm putting too much emphasis on their inflection. In my mind, they're stern. Defensive even.

ELEANOR: In person. What if we met up again?

Their text bubbles appear and disappear over five times before I bite the bullet and call them.

"I'm not drunk, I promise," I start, almost laughing as I say it.

"That's not a rousing endorsement," Carson responds.

"I just miss you," I say. "I can't keep going without seeing you in person."

The line goes quiet. Too quiet. Hear-into-my-own-skull quiet.

"What?" I ask.

"Nothing," they say.

"It's not nothing."

"Eleanor, you just . . . left."

We pick up this dangling conversation from July like we haven't been talking every day for almost a month, dodging this exact topic.

"I know," I say with a practiced breeziness. "I was crowding up your family time."

"No one told you that you were doing that," they respond. "You decided that without speaking to me. And then I didn't hear from you for months. And then one day, you start texting me again. And I know I haven't done the best job of showing how much you hurt me. Because I like talking to you so much. But you did. A lot."

"I wasn't trying to hurt you. Not that it changes things. I just want you to know that wasn't on purpose. I thought it would be better if I left without making a big deal of it."

"It wasn't better."

Our conversation in their middle school parking lot comes to mind. How they'd told me about their high school years. How they didn't want someone to fix what they'd done, they just wanted to be asked what was making them act out in the first place.

I slump against my door until I'm seated on the ground, kicking off my shoes and leaning back. Even though no one can hear me except my cats, I still drop my voice into a whisper. "I just, I liked you too much," I say. "It really scared me, and I didn't know what to do about it, because we don't live close enough for us to make any sense together."

"What would be different if we saw each other this time?" they whisper back.

"I would be nicer," I say. "I'd let you set the thermostat to any temperature. I'd eat every meal you made me. Maybe I'd even consider giving up walking."

"I've never needed you to be nice. I like the way you are."

"And I've never needed you to pretend to be mischievous to make you make sense in the world."

There's challenge in both of our voices. And something prideful too. Not for ourselves, but for each other. A contest of who sees the most about the other.

"You can be complicated and deep around me," I say. "You can steal my sugar packets to draw my face and tell me the stars remind you of the places you go when you sleep. I like all the ways you don't make sense to me, because I know that if I try hard enough, if I soak up every second of being around you, someday they will. And that by knowing you, I will know myself better, because somehow, you already feel like an extension of who I am. Or who I'm meant to be, maybe. You feel like the rest of me."

When I finish, I expect stunned silence. Instead, Carson whispers, in a voice so soft it almost breaks me, "Do you really mean that?"

"Of course I do. Why would I lie?"

"I don't think you would. I just didn't know you felt that way."

"Well, I do," I say, still angry, more at myself than them. For holding all of this in. "I think about you every night. I lose sleep over you, replaying what we discussed, wishing there was more. Inventing more. Needing your hands on me. Needing all of it."

"If we saw each other again, I wouldn't try so hard to make you think I was cool," they tell me. "I'd admit that the banana cream pie at Rita's is actually really good. Not as good as the apple crumble, but it's a contender."

"I'd accept your invitation to stay over at your place," I say, interjecting.

"You could even look through all my drawers if you wanted to. I wouldn't even hide my old journals." I can almost hear their smirk.

"Yes, you would," I say, smirking right back.

"Okay, I would try. But I think you'd find them anyway. And I'd probably let you read them too. If you found them interesting."

"I would," I assure them. "Everything about you is interesting to me."

We both fall quiet. Our breathing seems to synchronize. What I think are Carson's breaths become my own, calm and deep.

"It sounds perfect," I say, drifting off, the wine making my eyelids heavy.

"It does," Carson echoes.

"Maybe someday . . ."

"Maybe . . ."

That's how I fall asleep. With Carson's breath in my ear, and the promise of seeing them sometime in the future hanging on my lips.

35

Tatum

I pick June up at seven on the dot.

We've lived this before, another version of us. Those people feel far removed from who we've become. It's only been two months, but we've both done a lot of growing up.

June opens her door with one hand behind her back, wearing a lacey white crop top and the short pleather skirt I remember from New York.

"I got *you* flowers this time. Irises," I say, handing mine over right as she pulls her arms to the front and reveals a bouquet of lavender roses. It's a funny synchronicity, both of us with our purple flowers for each other.

"Why lavender this time?" I ask.

"They're supposed to mean admiration," she says bashfully. "Why irises?" She thumbs a petal, then brings it to her nose. "One of my favorite scents," she says, breathing it in.

"One website told me they could represent being proud of someone for an achievement," I say. "So I got them because I am proud of you for moving to New York. And because I knew they were one of your favorite scents, of course."

"Of course," she says, grinning so wide both of her dimples pinprick into her cheeks. We exchange our bouquets, laughing as we do it. "This feels like prom."

"I didn't go," I tell her.

"Tatum!"

"My friends and I told our families we were going. We bought the nice clothes and everything. Took all the pre-prom pictures. And then we drank in the forest preserve all night. Nobody ever knew."

"I'm trying not to pass judgment on that experience," June responds, "but that sounds miserable."

"It felt very cool to do at the time," I assure her. "But yes, I'm old enough now to admit it was a lot soggier than we anticipated. The forest is just kind of damp. And very dark."

I reach for June's hand, guiding us to my car. Grabbing on still sends a flutter of excitement through me, only now there is also contentment. I don't have to wonder what any of this means anymore.

"I still get scared of the dark," June tells me. "I know that's so immature. But I do."

It makes me think of the escape room. Everyone in their pairs, watching the actor playing Mrs. Weathermaster through the haze of special-effects fog and flickering LED candles. All I'd wanted then was someone to look out for. A person to share the experience with, having me as the first one in the room they reach for when they're scared.

"I'd let you sleep with a night-light," I tell her.

It's forward, implying a future where we share a bedroom. We haven't even left her parents' yet. But it's the truth. I could dress it up as something else, using any manner of pretty words to disguise the real meaning. But I don't want to do that anymore. I don't want to hide any of myself.

"That's only fair if you let me do something for you in return," she tells me.

We get into my car.

"Can I think on it?" I ask.

This makes her smile as I back out of her parents' driveway. "The last time I let you think something over, you asked me on a date."

"Someone had to do it," I tease.

She steals a single glance. "What did I tell you on that very first night? You're courageous."

"You also told me when you think of me, you think of trees," I say. "Yet you just scoffed at my tree-themed anti-prom!"

This gets a real laugh out of her, unguarded. It makes me feel like the funniest person alive. It makes me feel right.

"I *also* told you you're the writer," she reminds me.

"Yeah, yeah, yeah," I say. "Let's get to the good stuff."

OUR DATE TAKES US ALL ACROSS TROVE HILLS. WE GO mini golfing. We eat at the town's finest pizza place. We grab ice cream—June picks mint chip. I choose chocolate with peanut butter. It's lovely. Simple and sweet. We've never needed much fuss. Just each other.

I pull us into my driveway now, leaning over the seat to kiss June again. It's meant to be quick, a gentle thank-you, but I lose track of myself, lost in the taste of her. When we've kissed enough that my head's been emptied of all sense, I invite June into my cottage.

We uncork a bottle of wine. We sit on my couch, laughing and telling each other stories. None of this is as scary as I used to imagine it would be. It isn't as overwhelming either. I don't find myself thinking in the way I feared I would, my brain like an overheated laptop, whizzing and whirring to make sense of her every micro-movement, judging myself for my every response.

When the bottle of wine's been emptied and my record player starts to skip—Whitney no longer serenading us through our evening—June follows me up the stairs into my bedroom.

She presses me into my closed door, kissing me as she takes down the straps of my dress. The way she touches me—never forceful, but assured—keeps me right where I am, even as my nerves surface. I don't have to see this nervousness as fear. I am not afraid of her. I'm *excited*. This is our chance to know each other in a new way. It doesn't have to be a big, meaningful, earth-shifting thing. It can be exactly what it is.

By the time we have undressed each other, we are on top of my bed. I'm about to reach for my side lamp, plunging us into a private darkness, when I remember.

"Oh yes," I say. "I promised you a night-light."

This makes June laugh, tucking her head into my shoulder. "I want to be able to see you, anyway."

I want to see her too. I don't want to hide from any minute of this.

So we keep the light on as she touches me. She doesn't pull the covers over us when I go down on her.

In fact, she looks down at my head centered between her legs, my tongue stroking her as our eyes stay trained on each other. How I used to fear this, I will never know. Because her unbroken attention is like a tether, holding me right where I am. Even as she edges toward her pleasure, she never looks away. Her hands grab my hair, pressing me closer.

"Tatum," she says in that low, husky way—the way I used to dream about—dizzy with ecstasy.

And I keep my tongue pressed into her, never once relenting. She holds me after, whispering into my ear. Even though we're no longer looking at each other, my back pressed into her front, I still see her. She is in my mind's eye. She is in my ear.

She is everywhere I am. She always has been.

Maybe we don't have every answer right now. But that doesn't scare me anymore. We're choosing each other. No matter what.

October

36

Eleanor

The producers of *Barefoot in the Park* invite me and a plus-one to the black-tie opening-night party at the Plaza Hotel. It's a classic venue for a classic show, the perfect marriage of all the factors of this production. The only people I can think to take with me are June and Dawn. June can't make it, so it ends up being Dawn and me, dressed in our finest, driving to the event in a black SUV.

"You don't have to take me with you," Dawn says, pulling the seat belt across her black sparkling pantsuit.

"May I remind you we're already in the car."

"You know what I mean."

"No, I don't."

"I haven't been to something like this in decades. I might mess it up."

"There's no way to mess up a party. Unless you've been sleeping with the producer, and he proposes to his fiancée you didn't know about, and you decide to send a company-wide congratulations on the subject, and then you tell the fiancée about the affair.

That might mess things up a bit. The lucky thing is, I've been there before, so I'd understand."

When we pull up to the venue, Dawn climbs out first, then steps back, waiting. "You go in ahead of me."

"Of course," I tell her. "Think of me as your personal publicist for the night. In fact, consider me that for real. We will chat our way through the crowd and find some people to mingle with who might be interested in knowing where you've been. If any conversation turns in a direction you don't like, just ask me if I want to get another drink. I'll know that's our cue to get out of there, and I'll handle our exit from that group. There are a lot of industry people here who are going to be very excited to know you want back into the performance world."

Dawn rubs her lips together, then runs a hand under each eye. "If you say so."

"Your makeup looks great. *You* look great." It's true. She wears her age with grace, and the pantsuit she's chosen is elegant. She is still every bit a movie star.

We make our way to the Oak Room, the bar inside the hotel where the party is being held. The walls are covered in rich dark wood, with high arches and intricate paneling. It's a posh affair, splashy and opulent, bona fide celebrities everywhere I look. Having a second purpose here keeps me calm. I get to be more than just one of the agents from the show, making nice with our clients so they want to work with us again. I'm Dawn's guiding light—the person who makes sure that she is provided for in the way she needs.

We find our way into conversations with actors, casting directors, producers. People I've worked with for years. When they see Dawn, they are sincere when they ask where she's been and what she wants to do now.

"We'd love to get her out into the spotlight again to let the right people know she's looking for work," I say on her behalf. It hasn't taken long to deduce that Dawn is humble about her talents to the point of self-deprecation. She could get nominated for an Oscar and she'd tell me about it like someone made a clerical error when putting her on the ballot.

People are especially touched to learn we are neighbors. That layer keeps the conversation churning, everyone loving how we've lived across the hall from each other for almost a decade, but neither of us spoke before Tatum and June showed up. It's not an exaggeration when we say we owe everything to the power of the people around us.

"The both of us are bitches. We never would've talked if they didn't make us," Dawn says, which gets a huge laugh from our current group. She has excellent timing.

There is a morning show booking agent among us. She takes a particular shine to these details, saying, "You know, this would make a great segment on our show."

I allow myself a quick, private smile. I *do* know. It's exactly what I hoped for when I led us over to this particular group of people.

"I don't know about that," Dawn says, right as I respond with, "I completely agree."

I nudge Dawn, letting her know I've got this.

"She has so many fans who could generate publicity on her behalf if they learned she wanted to work," I continue. "All we need to do is get her face on the screen again. Let people be really touched by her story. Getting her back into the spotlight is a community matter. I know we can do right by her."

When we step away for drinks at Dawn's request, she's honest with me when she asks, "Do you really think I deserve this?"

There's something about knowing this woman is over seventy years old, still so afraid to receive help that she can't even believe she might deserve it, that makes me want to fall to my knees. I tell her everything I used to fear telling myself. All the pieces I learned from my strange summer spent house swapping with Tatum.

"Dawn, you deserve to be celebrated," I say. "You don't have to hide away from the world for the rest of your life. Just because the people in the business years ago made you feel worthless doesn't mean it's true. And as long as I'm here in your corner, I will make sure you don't forget that. No matter how many times you try to tell other people that you suck, I solemnly swear to deny your own allegations every chance I get. You are worth all the trouble and more."

Dawn pats her tears away with a powder she keeps in her purse. "Nobody makes me cry."

I hug her. "Don't worry, I won't tell a soul."

As she holds me, she leans her head against my shoulder. "What about you?"

"What about me?" I question.

"Why won't you let yourself be loved in this same way?"

Knowing she's seen me, that this is my fight as much as it is hers, I'm honest when I put my hands on her shoulders and say, "I will, Dawn. I promise."

37

Tatum

We arrive in New York very early in the morning, with our luggage intact.

"This is a good sign," I tell Carson, who carries their bag like they never expected to lose it.

"Let's not make any decisions about how good this is going until we know for sure that we're going to be well-received guests," Carson replies.

"I happen to know that the woman I'm here to see wants to see me," I say, halfway between a brag and a temperature check. It's hard to believe it's real.

Carson tosses my bag into the trunk. "What if she's changed her mind since the last time you saw her?"

"Fuck off," I reply.

"Everything okay?" our driver asks, worried by my tone.

"She's my sister," Carson tells them.

"I am," I confirm. "And I want the best for you, even if you're a shithead."

"Name one time I've been bad to you."

"Let's start with when you came into the cottage and turned the thermostat up way too high."

"You keep it freezing cold in there," Carson says.

"What does the temperature of *my* home matter to *you*?"

"It matters to me energetically, because they say younger siblings carry a piece of their older siblings' DNA in them, so a piece of me is feeling what you feel, and that piece doesn't like it."

"That's disgusting. Don't ever tell me you feel what I feel ever again."

Carson nods. "You're right. I'm erasing that from the record." They lean over the seat to bring our driver back into the conversation. "Promise you didn't hear that."

"I promise," the driver says.

GETTING DROPPED OFF IN FRONT OF ELEANOR'S BUILD-ing is even more surreal the second time. The trees are browner, the air is colder, but the lingering sense of rightness, of being where I belong, has remained. There's a way I hold myself in this place that's unlike the way I am in any other place I've ever been. I'm taller. More assured.

I like who I am when I'm here.

"Wait," Carson says, grabbing my shoulder.

"Cut it out."

"I'm serious." They're a shade paler than they were a minute ago, and a thin layer of sweat has sprouted on their face.

"Are you gonna be sick? Please don't throw up on me."

"Shut up," they say, still holding my shoulder. "I'm nervous, okay?"

The sisterly urge to say that this must be impossible rears up, but I press it down. They are genuinely nervous. I am too, but we've chosen to go to Eleanor's place first, so I get to play the role of interested bystander before it's my time to shine.

"It can only get worse from here. If it does, at least then you know," I say.

Carson's forced to breathe, letting out a hissing laugh. "I should've brought Brother Ben for this."

"What the hell would he have done? Hugged you?"

"I kind of think he would've sung a song," Carson says. "I don't know why."

"If Laney finds out you think of Ben as a vocalist before our literal Nashville-living, country-singing sister, you're going to fast-track your journey to somewhere worse."

This conversation carries us to the doorman in the lobby, who remembers me from my time here in July, greeting me with an enthusiastic wave that touches my heart.

"We're here to see Eleanor Chapman," I say.

"I bet you are." He lets us through, and we head up the elevator to Dawn and Eleanor's floor.

When the doors open, I charge ahead, down the hall toward Eleanor's door. In so many places in my life, as much as I've never wanted to admit it to them out loud, Carson really has been the one to lead. The firstborn, even with the addition of our bonus brother, Carson got to everything ahead of me. They came out as queer first. They moved out first. They have taught me how the world works through living their own life, and while I tease them all the time, I'm still holding my breath as we make our way to Eleanor's door, needing them to once again be the brave one first, showing me that it's okay to want to be loved out loud.

Carson knocks, then steps back, bouncing on their toes in anticipation. Thirty seconds pass. Nothing happens.

"Knock again," I say. "Maybe she's in her office."

Carson does.

Still nothing.

The knocking turns to pounding. Carson starts to say Eleanor's name. There's a tentativeness at first, and then a desperation. "Eleanor, it's me. I came to see you."

"Don't give too much away," I whisper. "I want to see her face when you say some of the stuff we planned."

Dawn pokes her head out. When she realizes it's us, her expression shifts into delight. She disappears back inside, then pops out again. "I'm just about to head out. But I have a key," she tells us conspiratorially. "She told me I could use it in case of an emergency. I'd say this counts."

When we open Eleanor's door, I remind everyone to be mindful of the cats. Occasionally they get delusions of grandeur and try to run outside. But it only takes one quick pass through the apartment to learn for sure what I already know—the cats aren't here.

And neither is Eleanor.

38

W ill you want the apple crumble at the end of your meal?
Let me know now so I can thaw it for you."

"That would mean a lot, thank you," I say.

When neither Carson nor Tatum answered their doors, Rita's seemed like the next logical place to go. So here I am, escaping the rain and planning my next move.

"Where's the troublemaker?" Denise asks, pouring hot coffee into the mug I've overturned.

"Wish I knew," I say. "Is Tatum here?"

"She called out. Didn't say why." She leans a bit closer. "You wouldn't happen to know a June, would you?"

"June Lightbell?"

"That's the one. She used to be a regular here. But she stopped coming in after Tatum went with her to New York. Tatum won't tell me what happened, even though June showed up here last month during one of our bingo Sundays. Do you know anything about it?"

There might be some fundamental issue with Tatum's manager gossiping with me, but hand on my heart, I am not the one who will mention it. Of course I know about it. June and I are friends. We meet up for coffee a few times a month. And Carson's filled me in on Tatum's side. I might be as close as one person could get to being an expert on this very subject.

"It's complicated," I say.

Denise smacks her hand on the table, somehow delighted. "I knew it."

"Don't tell her I told you." My eyes widen, realizing that even in saying very little, I've still admitted something is going on. Tatum is the type of person to take this as a betrayal.

Denise fakes zipping her lips and throwing away the key. It's as good an NDA as I can get from a woman like her, and I accept it with an appreciative nod. "Whatcha eating?" she asks. "It's on us."

"You guys give away a lot of food. It can't be a sustainable business model."

"This place hasn't seen a fresh coat of paint in twenty years. These floors are probably older than you are, and our cash register is still analog. The overhead on this place is less than you pay for meals in a month where you live. I promise we're okay."

"Fair enough. I'll have the veggie omelet with sourdough toast." There's a small TV perched in the upper corner of the diner, right near the door. "Can we turn that on? My friend is on a daytime talk show today."

Denise hands me a remote. It takes a few tries, working with a technology that's older than anything I've used in solidly fifteen years, but I find my way to the right channel.

Sipping my coffee, I sit back and watch, appreciating the quiet simplicity—a hot drink in a small town, with the soft patter of rain tapping against the windows. Tatum was right. The fall is beautiful here.

Dawn's segment begins, and I turn the volume up, leaning forward. She didn't take any of my calls this morning, which isn't unusual. She's probably upset at me for ditching her right before her return to the public eye. I hope one day she'll understand.

The interview starts with a lot of gushing. It's all appropriate fanfare, and Dawn takes it in stride for once, following my advice to be grateful instead of defensive. She talks about her time out of the spotlight and all the ways she convinced herself she'd never be able to come back.

"Then I met three lovely young women who changed my mind," she says. "And it just so happens one is a publicist by the name of Eleanor Chapman."

It catches Denise's attention. She's leaning over the counter, watching the TV with me from a distance. She only knows me as Eleanor, not my full name, but I've already told her my friend is on this show. She looks between me and the TV a few times, wanting me to confirm I've just been mentioned.

I keep my face composed, giving away nothing, even though inside, my heart is pounding. No one's ever mentioned my work in public like this. Not the actors. Not the crew. Not the press.

"Let me tell you, a lot of things have changed about this business since the last time I worked, but one thing has stayed the same—a good publicist is going to find a good angle," Dawn continues.

"Eleanor certainly did her job well," the interviewer says. "We're so happy to have you on today. As I understand it, one of the other women who helped get you back out there is here with you too."

"She is," Dawn confirms, smiling.

"And I understand she has someone *else* with her too," the interviewer says.

It must be June. But why are they discussing this in the first place? It's a random talking point for any interview, even a fluff piece meant to generate renewed public interest in Dawn's presence. This is what happens when I don't vet the questions beforehand.

Tatum walks out to join Dawn. Tatum *was* instrumental in getting Dawn back on this path, though no one mentioned her flying out for this interview. Not Dawn, not Tatum herself.

Denise claps. "Oh my god! Maurice! Peanut! Tatum's on TV!" she yells. I watch as two cooks come out from the kitchen, joining Denise in leaning over the counter to see the screen. "And Carson!"

Carson.

Carson is on the screen now.

Which means Carson is in New York.

And I am here, in Trove Hills.

I have to laugh at the absurdity. For months we've been connected only through a screen. And somehow, some way, we've both decided to do something about it, at the exact same time.

"It's very generous of you to want to share your moment with these two," the interviewer says.

"I had to," Dawn tells her. "This is Tatum. She's the one who showed up outside my apartment a few months ago making so much noise I thought I was going to have to activate the building security."

Tatum waves.

"Next thing I know, she's changing my life for the better. I owe her everything for that." A wave of emotion almost overwhelms Dawn, but she does her best to tamp it down, squeezing Tatum in a quick hug, then continuing, forcing the warble out of her voice. "So, when I learned that her sibling here, Carson, needs to reach someone we all know is watching, I was happy to offer up my time and platform for the cause. And your producers also agreed, after much negotiating. Thank you to them."

The interviewer smiles. "We couldn't turn you down." Then she angles herself toward Carson. "The floor is yours, Carson. Who is it you need to reach?"

"Eleanor," they say.

The whole diner turns their attention to me. Denise, the cooks, the other patrons here for a Monday morning meal.

"Oh my *god*," Denise says, placing her hand on her heart.

The cooks shush her, not wanting to miss a word.

"I came here to find you, and you're gone," Carson says, looking right at me, knowing I am looking right back, feeling my presence through the screen the same way they always do, even if this time it's like one-way glass. "I know you won't want me to say too much in a place like this, so I will only say this—anywhere you go, that's where I want to be. Tell me where you are, Eleanor, and I will come find you. Please."

Pin-drop silence doesn't even cover the quiet that follows, even as the TV keeps blaring, the interviewer closing out Dawn's segment. Everyone in Rita's Diner is waiting for what happens next.

I decide to laugh again. How can I not? Carson Ward just went on national television to say they'll find me anywhere I go.

Except actually, I'm crying.

"You better call Carson right now," Denise says.

"Sorry," I tell her, wiping my tears away. "I will. I am."

The phone rings and rings, heading to the voicemail I've spent the last month memorizing. *You've reached Carson. I'm not here right now. Leave a message if you need to.*

I'd say I need to.

"Hey." My voice is quiet, but it's in a staged way, knowing full well that everyone here believes they're owed the details of this moment. In some ways, they are. If nothing else, none of this would be possible without them. "We keep missing each other. I'm in Trove Hills. I wanted to, you know, sweep you off your feet, I guess. But it seems like you and I had the same idea. We tend to do that, don't we? Call me back when you get this. I'll be enjoying some apple crumble in the meantime. On the house."

39

Tatum

A producer escorts Dawn, Carson, and me through the labyrinthine halls, passing all manner of staff and talent on the way back to our dressing room.

"That was really brave," I tell Carson, who is walking so fast they might as well be running, especially since their legs are so much longer than mine.

"Please don't be sincere right now," they say back. "I already want to vomit."

"Wait until we're in the room," Dawn warns. "They have a trash can in there."

"I don't suppose you want me to be sincere to you either?" I ask her.

"Don't even dream of it." She does hug me again, which is just as good as accepting my praise. Maybe better.

When we get inside the dressing room, the producer lets us know we're welcome to stay as long as we need. They shut the door, leaving the three of us alone.

Dawn looks at herself in the mirrored vanity lining the wall, turning from side to side like she's trying to see what the audience just experienced. Carson sits down on the couch, staring at the wall, dazed.

"You nailed it," I say, incapable of continuing to silence my sincerity. "Both of you."

"I can't believe I just did that," Carson says, still in a trance.

Dawn, however, receives my compliment. She's been much more affectionate this trip. It's almost like she might have missed me. "I hope Eleanor saw that. I don't share my spotlight with just anyone."

The producers told us to leave our phones in the green room. Sure enough, when I press Carson's lock screen, mistaking their phone for my own, there is a voicemail notification. From Eleanor.

"She called you," I say, barely able to contain my excitement.

This breaks Carson out of their fugue state. They press the phone to their ear, their dazed intensity shifting to giddiness in a matter of seconds. "She's in Trove Hills," they tell us as they listen. "She came to find me."

Dawn throws her hands in the air. "You've got to be kidding. I thought your generation was supposed to be better about telling each other where you are."

"At least you got to see her apartment," I tell them.

"And I got to show everyone in America how hot I am," they say.

Yes, they are certainly back to normal again.

"Only thing left to do is get *your* girl," they remind me.

"Let's hope it goes smoother than this," Dawn adds. "I'm not giving up any more of my press opportunities for the cause."

JUNE LIVES IN BROOKLYN, WHICH NEARLY SENDS DAWN into a tailspin. "If she's not here, you're paying for my ride back," she tells me.

"She'll be here," I say. "I've been texting her all morning, asking her what she's doing. And she's either running a very elaborate lie that involves having several photos ready to send me as a misdirect, or she's in her kitchen making her own oat milk as we speak."

I show Dawn the step-by-step images June sent me fewer than ten minutes ago. "Okay, good. But we're not coming up with you."

"That works out well," I tell her. "Because you weren't invited."

June doesn't have a doorman at her building, but she does have a locked entrance. Lucky for me, one of her neighbors comes down, granting me immediate access so I don't have to blow my cover early. Instead I text her again.

> TATUM: You should make some soup instead.

> JUNE: Hahaha! It's almost cold enough for soup
> season here, but we're not quite there yet.

> TATUM: Damn. Wish I could feel it.

> JUNE: I wish that too.

Her text comes at the perfect time, with me finishing my trek up three flights of stairs and arriving in front of her door. I don't waste any more time contemplating how to approach or what to say. I just knock, announcing my presence by saying, "Wish delivery service here for one June Lightbell."

June opens her door wearing an apron smattered with wet oats and a protective wrap over her hair. There is no makeup on her face. No shoes on her feet.

"You're *here*," she says, no question as to how or why. Just relief.

"Oh good. I was worried you saw me during Dawn's interview."

"Shit, I totally forgot to watch."

"It's okay," I say. "We won't tell her."

She stands there, still too shocked to move. It's my perfect opportunity.

"I love you," I blurt. The first time I've ever said it. "I've loved you since that very first day at the diner. I've loved bringing you your meals of the hour. I've loved waiting long past my shift for you to close out your check. I've loved watching you work, head in your hand, thinking. I love you. Everything you do, everything you are, I love."

I thought somehow this would be hard. But as I look at her, the love I feel makes all the worries float away.

"You love me," she says, her dimples pricking into her cheeks.

"I love you," I say again. "And you love me back."

At once, she throws her arms around me, holding on so tight she wraps her legs around me too. I breathe her in, savoring this moment. This love.

"I love you," she says, clinging tight enough to make breathing difficult.

"I figured out what you can do for me," I whisper into her ear.

She unwraps herself from our tangled embrace. "Make you soup?" she jokes.

"Let me move here," I say. "I want to figure out who I can become when I am not Tatum the waitress. Maybe I *am* a writer. I don't know yet for sure. But I do know that whatever I want to be, it's not happening in Trove Hills. It's here. And hopefully, if I'm lucky, it's happening with you."

"Yes!" she exclaims, no hint of hesitation. "Yes, yes, yes." She kisses my face, my cheeks, my hands.

As she works her way across all my visible skin, I tell her, "I don't think we should live together right away. I want to find my own independence here. And I know that's important to you too. But I was hoping I could crash on your couch for a bit until I figure it all out."

She laughs. "Crash on my couch?"

"You know what I mean. Crash in your bed."

Her hand holds my face as she reads it, studying my eyes for the rest. "Of course you can. Welcome to New York, Tatum."

40

Eleanor

Carson won't let me pick them up from the airport. Our texts on the subject are formal. Businesslike.

CARSON: You will not be operating a vehicle to reach me.

ELEANOR: You let me drive your car more than once this summer.

CARSON: I will see you when I'm home.

ELEANOR: Fine. If you insist.

CARSON: I do.

Needing a place to put all my energy, I do what feels most natural—I walk. All across Trove Hills. I walk to Rita's Diner and get a cup of coffee to carry around. I walk the path of the forest preserve that lines the eastern edge of town. I walk side streets and main streets, letting the crisp chill of fall numb my skin, basking in the smell of the wet soil after all the rain.

And finally, I walk to Carson's apartment.

Tatum texted me the address. It might not be fair to go here first when Carson might want to get ready before seeing me, but I have to do it. There has been so much waiting. I can't stand a single extra moment of anticipation. For once, I need to be in the right place at the right time.

They pull into their parking spot in an open lot beside the building. They open their car door, reaching across the console to grab their bag from the foot of the passenger side.

"Hi," I whisper.

Carson startles so much their head bumps the top of their car.

Instinctively I reach for them, closing the space between us far less gracefully than I planned, with half of me outside their car and half of me in it. But we've never been very neat with each other.

"I'm sorry," I say.

"Don't be," they tell me.

Chest to chest, our hearts beat together in that feverish way, adrenaline and surprise and, fuck it, longing. So much longing. We're holding each other so close there is no space left, and still we don't feel close enough. I want to climb inside Carson and live there.

I settle for letting them out of their car instead.

The fullness of their presence—upright, real, in front of me— makes up for every last obstacle we climbed to reach this. None of that matters anymore.

"Wait a second," they say, noticing the flush in my cheeks. "Don't tell me you walked here."

"Okay, I won't tell you that."

"Where are your cats?" Carson asks. "They weren't in your apartment."

"They're currently with your parents," I say. "Are these really the questions you need to ask me first?"

"No," they admit. They shake their head, ridding themselves of the last dregs of shock, letting our truth settle into their bones. "Wait. My parents are watching your cats right now?"

I press a finger to their mouth. "*Shhh.*"

They kiss me, deep and dirty, slipping their tongue into my mouth as they grab the small of my back. They pull back long enough to say, "I've wanted to do that for so long," and then their mouth returns to mine.

It's only when my hand slips under their shirt, passing fabric to find skin, that we break apart.

"Your fingers are freezing," they say, jumping back.

"Must be from all the walking I didn't do."

Carson takes me inside to warm up, into the home I once feared entering, because coming here meant changing the rules. That's as true now as it was then.

I look around at the tarp-covered floor. There are half-finished paintings. Pieces of plywood and all manner of tools. Pictures of Carson with members of their family. There's even a picture of Ben. And framed on their bookshelf is the picture of us. The one that Aunt Fran took that day at the picnic.

"*Here*," I say, kissing Carson on the mouth.

"Here what?" they ask, confused.

"I want to live here."

July

(NINE MONTHS LATER)

41

Tatum

Welcome to the second annual Ward family reunion!" I say into the mic, standing on my parents' front lawn. "This year, I made us all shirts!"

June does the work of passing them out. They're a dark green, which we agreed was universally the best color and also made sense for the Trove Hills of it all, considering the forest preserve on the edge of town. June already wears hers, pairing it with a long-sleeved striped turtleneck underneath, tucking both into the jeans she's cuffed to show her combat boots. She swears she's not sweating, but I know she is. She'll do anything for fashion, even in July. Still, she looks as lovely as ever. Our dog, Daisy, pants at her feet, smiling happily at my family members, hoping to score some head scratches.

"Per Ben's request, this year we have a game of baseball," I announce. "That will be tomorrow. Your teams have all been emailed to you. Please see Carson if you have any issues with where you've been placed. Aunt Fran, I don't want to hear anything about how you think the teams are unfair. It was randomized. The point is this year, we're doing things that Ben likes.

And Ben, as you all know by now, is a seventh-grade science teacher. Which means today, he's going to teach us about the mitochondria!"

The crowd reacts with unguarded disappointment.

"I'm *kidding*," I say. "We're going to do trivia, actually. Family trivia. May the best Ward win!"

I leave my mic to pass out sheets to my relatives. This game took me hours to put together. The questions range from silly things like, "When was the last time a Ward ate a piece of Carson's Jell-O cake?," to obscure ones like, "What are the night dogs?," to sincere ones like, "What is the name of Ben's beloved cat?"

I give my family thirty minutes to submit answers. They return their sheets to me, and June and I begin the work of grading them.

It takes over an hour for me to read the answers aloud. Each reveal brings on a new round of grilling from my family. Laney finally learns the truth about the night dogs—that they are not real—and she gets so worked up she attempts to actually wrestle me.

"I'm sorry!" I say, fighting her off. "Blame Emmett! He was the one who didn't want us to tell you the truth!"

"C'mon," Carson says. "How could you, a full-grown adult, actually believe there are dangerous wild dogs who roam our town after midnight?"

This gets Laney's attention off me and onto them, which I appreciate.

We are messy, and we are loud, and sometimes, we're rude. But I'll give us this—we Wards are always entertaining.

When I get to the last question, I take a deep breath, enjoying the spectacle. Everyone still believes they're in the mix to win this. The truth is, the winner took the victory several answers ago. But no one in my family seems to remember what they wrote on their papers, and since they don't have the sheet in front of them to refresh their memory, this last reveal still holds real weight.

"Ward family," I say, low and serious. "For the game-winning point, the question was 'How are we related to Lydia?'"

This sends the entire family into hysterics. The sound is so jarring it startles my dog, who hops into June's lap to take cover.

"Lydia has been coming to all our family events for well over twenty years," I say. "And it's a long-running joke that no one knows her relation to us. But I finally took the time to find it out. And so, it seems, did someone else among us. Our winner."

My family members begin looking at one another, trying to identify who it is. When no one stands up to claim the title, they start to grill Lydia herself, who relishes this attention.

"It's not for me to say," she tells them, winking at me.

And so, with great theatricality, I lean into the mic. In a low voice, I say, "The winner of the first ever Ward Family Trivia Contest is . . ."

June does a drum roll with our dog's paws.

"Eleanor Chapman!"

Eleanor rises, met with raucous applause. She accepts her victory graciously, coming up to claim her prize—a glass container full of candy.

"Congratulations," I say, shaking her hand. "Anything you want to tell your fans?"

Eleanor presses a hand to her heart, treating the silliness of this moment with full gravitas. It's one of her best qualities. For as serious as she seems, she's never one to back away from a joke.

"I'd like to thank myself," she says, "for always being the best at everything I do."

Everyone laughs.

"She's a riot," Aunt Fran whispers.

"And Lydia's not related to any of you, by the way," she tells the crowd. "She was Carl's neighbor growing up. She just likes coming to this stuff."

"Wait," June says. "There's one more question."

I place a hand on her shoulder. "No, there isn't. I wrote this quiz."

"There is," she insists. She looks up at me, through me, in the way she always can. "There's one more question."

She hands me a piece of paper. One that looks much the same as all the others. Yet in the space where the participant is supposed to write their name, mine has been put there in June's long, flowy cursive.

"What's this?" I ask.

"Read the question, Tatum," she commands. "It's the last one on the paper."

My eyes fly down, past all my trivia, to find there is indeed one more thing written. But not by me.

"Don't read in your head," June warns. "Do it aloud. Into the mic."

She's so commanding that I do as I'm told, reading the question aloud before processing it in my mind. "'Bonus question,'" I start. "'It's been nine months since Tatum moved to New York City. In that time, she and her girlfriend have lived in separate apartments. Is she ready to move into her girlfriend's apartment with her?'"

My eyes water as I process the question in real time. I have wondered for weeks—months, really—if we should do this. But I've been second-guessing myself, wanting to be sure June had enough time on her own. Never wanting to rush things.

"Tatum," she says. "I'm tired of waking up in the morning without you there. I'm tired of hearing about the novel you're writing while lying in a bed we don't share. I think we've both had more than enough New York independence."

Eleanor hands me back her jar of candy. "Here," she says.

"I don't need this," I tell her. She's not usually one for interrupting a moment. If she didn't want the prize, she could have told me at literally any other time.

"You *do* need this," Eleanor insists.

Looking again at June, I search her face for a clue. She gives away nothing, instead nudging her head toward the jar. When I unscrew the lid, there is a vial of perfume sitting atop a pile of Starbursts.

"How did you . . ." I start. "Did you guys rig this?"

"A little bit," June admits. She picks up the vial. Beneath the Lightbell label, where the perfume's name is usually written, it says *TATUM* in June's handwriting. "I finally got your scent right."

She uncorks the lid, and I breathe it in. "It's a skin scent," I say, knowing perfumes for real now. Skin scents are lighter, meant to enhance the smell of your actual skin.

"Yes," she says, her smile proud.

"Maybe some amber?" I guess, smelling again. She nods.

"I know how you move through the world now," she tells me. "Who you are. How you love. The first time I made you a perfume, I was trying so hard to capture my idea of you. This," she says, spraying her creation onto me. "This *is* you."

And she's right. It is. The smell is gentle at first. Subtle. It's something you have to be up close to really understand. Then it's full, warm, and woody.

It's me.

"Thank you," I say, moving in for a kiss.

She backs away. "Hold on," she says. "You didn't answer my question. Will you live with me?"

I move in again, kissing June hard, ignoring the whoops of

appreciation from my family. While they're here for it, this moment is only for June and me, in the town where we met, agreeing to link ourselves together in the city where we fell in love.

"Of course I will," I tell her.

It's the closing of a loop, and the beginning of a new one.

It's my life.

42

Eleanor

When Carson and I walk through the front doors of Rita's Diner holding hands, everyone claps.

"What's going on?" I whisper in Carson's ear.

"You'll see," Carson says.

The entire Ward family is here for a dinner in Ben's honor. Tatum has gone to great trouble to rent the place out. She's requested that all of us wear white so we can take a coordinated family photo. It seemed like a risk to me, especially with greasy diner food as our planned meal, but her email was so stern I didn't dare challenge her.

It doesn't take long to see that everyone else has neglected this request.

Tatum herself is in green. I lean again toward Carson, ready to share my confusion. How could she miss her own directions? But Carson doesn't look confused. Carson is actually smiling that familiar, mischievous smile. The one I now know well. It's the face they make when they've put my favorite snack in the fridge for me to find, or they've repaired something around our place that they're waiting for me to notice.

There is something here I am meant to see, and I look around in pursuit of it. While everyone claps and beams at us, I don't notice anything out of the ordinary, aside from the incorrect color assignment.

Oh, and they've cleared out all the center tables in the diner, leaving a sole chair alone in the open space. I assume this is for Ben, though admittedly I don't know why he needs the seat. Maybe the family will give him birthday gifts for the years they've missed, even though his birthday is in October?

"Take a seat," Carson tells me, gesturing to the chair.

"Why would I sit there?" I ask.

"Because I'm about to ask you a question."

This is not for Ben. This is for *me*. And the closer I look, the more I realize that the booths aren't just filled with the Wards. First I see a table of my coworkers from the park district, where I've been in charge of publicity for the last few months. We're opening our first show next weekend. They wave at me, beaming and offering fist pumps.

"What's going on?" I ask again, hoping maybe they will be the ones to answer this time.

"C'mon, let it happen!" someone calls out.

Then I see her, in the back booth, sitting next to Tatum and June.

"*Dawn*," I say in disbelief. "You're supposed to be on the set of the next Guy Cicero movie!"

"Not now, sweetie," she replies. "We'll talk after."

I take my seat in the chair that's for me, where I now know what question Carson will ask. Of course I know. We have lived together for months. We have even discussed this.

But never, in all my years, did I imagine this is how they would do it.

"I know what you're thinking," they start, speaking to me and also to the room at large. "You're wondering about this choice of format. Because you and I, well, we're pretty low-key."

I laugh through tears, shaking so hard I can't settle into my seat. My mind keeps looping on my own disbelief. That Carson could love me enough to want to marry me. That the other people care enough to be here for it.

"But the thing is, Eleanor, the day you came into my life, you also came into my entire family's life. And while the love we share is ours, you are loved by so many more people than me. And I didn't want to leave any of those people out for this moment."

Laney wheels in a canvas covered with a tarp.

"I want you to know I love you out loud. I want you to remember I will love you through every season. No matter how many scuffs my car has from curbs you underestimated." This gets a big laugh from the crowd. "I want you to know I will be with you through it all. And mostly I want you to know that my love is bigger than myself. You are loved by everyone in this room, and while I'm the only sucker lucky enough to get to ask you to marry me, you're also signing up for a lifetime of pestering from the people in this room. So, Eleanor Elizabeth Chapman, what do you say? Do you want to be a Ward with me?"

They take the tarp off the painting, which is not actually a painting at all. It's a giant card, filled with handwritten messages from every family member. They're all notes of admiration, listing my best traits, my coolest features. Everything they love about me. All the reasons I should say yes.

As if there is any other answer.

I look to Carson in awe. To be loved with such steadiness is to know I can fall apart here. I can sob, snotty and shaking. I can crumple into a ball, then stand up again, smoothing down my white pants, rising to meet their question. I can accept this marriage proposal.

Because this is not a love that will ever quit on me.

This love is my home.

ACKNOWLEDGMENTS

My first thank-you goes to my editor, Kerry Donovan, for helping me mold this story into its intended shape. Kerry, your patience and care is deeply appreciated by me. I am so grateful to work with you and the entire team at Berkley—Genni Eccles, Anika Bates, Chelsea Pascoe, Megan Elmore, Eileen Chetti, Crystal Erickson, Sierra Machado, and everyone else there who makes my books possible!

Thank you to illustrator Rebecca Mock and designer Vi-An Nguyen for yet another breathtaking cover. It's dreamy and beautiful and perfect. I feel so lucky to have your art represent my stories.

My agent, Taylor Haggerty; you do so much on my behalf. Because of you, I am living my dream of writing books. My thank-yous could never be enough! To Jasmine Brown and the rest of the Root Literary team, you are the absolute best of the best.

Alex Seeley, not only are you a real-life Broadway press agent, you are also one of my very best friends in the world. Thank you for letting me grill you about your job. You answered my every question, no matter how innocuous, and this book would truly not exist without you. All mistakes in here are my own! But I hope I've done the press agents proud with this one. #WeAreATPAM.

My sister Rose, you are sitting downstairs as I write this. Thank you for letting me pester you my whole life. You're my best audience for everything, and the most supportive human I know. My sisters Liz and Raina; my brother, John; my parents; and all my nieces and nephews—coming from such a big family informs everything I do. You are never the characters in my stories, but you've made me the person I am, and I love you all.

Hollis Andrews, we love to laugh! We love to cry! We love our cats! Thanks for being on life's highway with me, four hands on the wheel. Emily Wibberley and Austin Siegemund-Broka, it's such a joy to be on this publishing ride (or perhaps *quest*) with you two. You cheer me on through every draft, and you both inspire me with your talent and your kindness. Alicia Thompson, our never-ending email chain has been the highlight of my year. I love the way you think—and the way you write!—and it's such a treat to learn the lore of your universes. Rebekah Faubion, you are a total gem. I hope the ghost we met in the laundry room on the retreat is doing well. Ryan Everett, my former roommate, new neighbor, and forever friend, you've taken a crash course in publishing over the last decade, and you're almost an expert now! Thank you for always listening to me and for being the star you are. Brittany Strale, Caeli Thoma, Vince Rossi, and Jake Morrissy—excuse me so much for loving you all as deeply as I do. Mia Serafino, you're one of my favorite people in the world to tell a story to and to hear a story from. Nina Rossi, you are the sweetest human ever. Arden Fisher, we live in the grains of sand together. Lindsay Grossman, the coffee shop writing sessions are eternal.

This is a story that strongly features group chats, so let me shout out some of my own—The Chit Chat Club, Bengal Pride,

Proof of Timeline Anomalies, Bridger-Clowns, Sandy's Coven, and the unnamed one I share with my sisters. Our ongoing conversations fuel my waking hours.

This is also a story about a diner. As a child of Illinois myself, specifically Oak Forest (once home to three different pancake houses within a half mile of one another), I hope I have captured within this book the sacred feeling of such hallowed places.

This story has two cats. When I first wrote it, I did not have two cats. But now I do! Meadow and Forest, you are the lights of my life. I can't remember who I was before I adopted you, and I don't want to. You are perfect. So perfect, in fact, that I believe you can read these words somehow. Thank you for filling my world with so much joy and love.

Finally, this is a story about queerness. I love being a queer person. I love the community it's brought me. I love writing stories for other queer people. It will never stop being a delight. Thank you for reading.

Don't miss Bridget Morrissey's

That Summer Feeling

Available now!

My honeymoon started with me sprinting barefoot through the airport holding a pair of sandals and a broken bracelet that may or may not have been magical. We'd left for LAX way later than I wanted to, but I didn't mention it, because I never said anything I thought might make a moment worse. Besides, our weekend of wedding festivities had been so draining that both of us deserved every extra minute of rest we could get. My new husband, Ethan, had a gift for sleeping in late and then arriving on time. I'd watched him do it enough that I decided the talent had been extended to me through our marriage.

Traffic on the 405 was the usual nightmare. We were keeping a five-mile-an-hour pace, inching toward the promise of relaxation that awaited in Cancún. Ethan said very little. He had the kind of perpetually mellow energy that made babies stop crying when he held them. It was another trait of his I hoped to acquire through our union. I was, by all accounts, too excitable for my own good. In her maid of honor speech, my older sister Dara described me as someone who watched a true crime documentary believing that if I rooted hard enough for the people involved, their story might not end in murder after all. Then I found myself inconsolable when the death inevitably came, crying as if I were a member of the victim's immediate family.

By the time Ethan and I got dropped off at our gate, I'd taken to making up a song to coach myself through the moment, singing *This is fine, this is great* under my breath. I was always trying to find the good in my struggles, and this was me in my full glory, humming my own tune over and over as if the repetition guaranteed a successful outcome.

In the stereotypically beachy apparel I'd insisted we wear for our flight—Ethan in a floral button-down and cargo shorts, and me in a flowing white maxi dress with gladiator sandals—we took long, purposeful strides toward security, where a snaking line awaited us. We looked like textbook newlyweds, and that meant the world to me. I wanted every person who saw us to know I'd done it. I'd picked a man to love forever.

The security line moved comically slowly. As I repeated my song to myself, catching stares from strangers in the process, I checked my phone every thirty seconds, hoping my incessant eye on the time would make it stop moving. Or better yet, our flight would be delayed.

"Garland," Ethan said as he planted a kiss on my forehead. The fresh stubble on his chin grazed my sweat-slicked skin. He hated to be barefaced, but his mother had insisted on it for the wedding, so he'd shaved off his auburn beard for the first time in years. It made him look so youthful that I gasped when I walked down the aisle. He had freckles on his jawline that I'd never seen before, and two little nicks on his chin from the razor. "We'll make it."

"Our flight leaves in fourteen minutes." I illuminated my phone screen to show him the time.

"And we will be on it," he told me.

"I hope so."

He laughed softly. "Just relax. We will."

When we finally got to take off our shoes and put our belongings into bins, panic overtook me. The moment I stepped out of the body scanner, I grabbed my stuff and started running, not even bothering to put my sandals back on my feet. Ethan kept his usual pace. To him, we may as well have been strolling the beach already.

Eventually I turned my head, trying to make sure he wasn't as far away as he felt, and I ended up crashing into someone else. A very tall someone else. I was immediately torn between apologizing for not looking where I was going or running to the gate at speeds faster than ever before reached by humankind.

I chose to attempt both at the same time. "I am *so* sorry! Incredibly sorry!" I said.

To my surprise, the stranger started running after me. "Hold on," he called out. "You dropped your . . . bracelet?"

I froze.

When Dara and I were growing up, our mom and dad fought way more than they ever got along. One late night when Dara was twelve and I was ten, whispering underneath the yells of our parents' latest argument, we promised each other that we'd never let our love lives sour like they had.

Dara always said she and I had the power to bend the world to our will. We could make impossible things happen, if only we tried hard enough. Most of the time we were too busy distracting ourselves from the constant friction in our household to put forth the kind of effort she spoke about. That night was different somehow, in the way some nights just are. An extra crackle in the air. A brighter shine to the stars. Dara and I decided to finally put our energy toward rising above the circumstances we'd been given.

Under the watchful glow of a new moon, we made bracelets out of random things we scrounged up in our shared bedroom: garden twine, beads from other jewelry, charms, and random junk like small buttons and sequins. We called the bracelets our heart promises, imbuing them with a magic we believed we created together.

As we assembled them, we came up with the rules behind the promise—we would have better lives than the ones our parents had shown us. We would find people to love with care. We'd never become bitter and stubborn as we got older. We'd be happy in our relationships.

We knew it was the kind of wish that didn't get fulfilled right away. It was something that needed to grow with us. Dara decided we had to guard each other's bracelets until we were adults. Then, whenever one of us made our promise come true, we would get our original bracelet back, as a reminder to continue living out the wish we'd made real.

Through the years, we took the job of looking after each other's bracelets very seriously. What started as a late-night childhood whim had become a very deep representation of not only our dreams but our bond. We considered ourselves the protectors of each other's contentment. We would never let the other person settle for less than they deserved.

Dara gifted mine to me on my wedding day. She called it my something old, and she tucked it into an interior pocket she'd asked the tailor to hide in my gown. I nearly cried off my makeup when she handed it over. It always felt like she knew me better than I knew myself, and it meant everything to know she approved of my marriage to Ethan. She wasn't jealous that I was younger and I'd gotten married ahead of her. She was happy for me. She believed in the love I was making legally binding.

The next day, I tied my bracelet onto my wrist for the first time ever. It looked childlike against the formfitting white dress I'd selected for my post-wedding luncheon, especially since I'd pulled my long brown hair into a sleek bun, but I didn't care. I was proud of myself for fulfilling my heart promise. Every time I looked at my arm, I saw proof that my marriage was going to be better than my parents' had been.

The man in the airport extended his hand out to pass the bracelet back to me. He was in a highlighter-green tank that showed off his muscular physique, and he had shoulder-length blond hair pulled off his face by a pair of sunglasses resting on his head. He looked to me like he surfed. Or played beach volleyball. Something sandy.

As a rule, I did not trust blond men. No real reason other than pure skepticism. But this tall, toned stranger had chased me down to return a piece of jewelry that may as well have been made during kindergarten arts and crafts. He had to be a little decent.

"Thanks," I said to him, reaching for my bracelet.

As soon as my fingers grazed his palm, I was no longer in the bright, busy airport. Instead I sat across the table from this man. We were in a large dining hall that smelled like firewood and bread. It was nighttime, and the sconces on the wall cast a buttery glow. Crickets chirped outside the logwood walls. We were surrounded by what I took to be his family—Nordic-looking blonds with beaming smiles and sun-soaked skin. There was a woman beside me, about my age. She pressed her hand against my forearm as we all laughed so hard and deep that my stomach ached. I felt the kind of soul-deep contentment I hadn't realized I'd never experienced before. I could tell I was an important part of this man's life, and everyone around me loved us both.

Quick as a blink, I returned to the crowded airport, clutching the stranger's hand. When I pulled away, startled, the man didn't seem at all disoriented.

Did he see what I saw? Does he feel like he knows me too? What just happened?

My childhood bracelet in one hand and my shoes in the other, I took off, not bothering to linger for a goodbye with the stranger I somehow *knew*. My heart pounded as hard as my bare heels did against the airport floor.

This is just your imagination trying to psych you out, I told myself as my chest heaved from the exertion. *Heart promises aren't real. They were a childhood coping mechanism, and you are on your way to your honeymoon with the man you love.*

I made it onto our flight with a few minutes to spare. Ethan arrived right before they closed the gate. It all worked out, just like he'd said it would.

We had a lovely trip together.

Bridget Morrissey lives in Los Angeles, California, but hails from Oak Forest, Illinois. When she is not writing, she can be found cradling one of her cats like a baby or headlining concerts in her living room.

VISIT BRIDGET MORRISSEY ONLINE

BridgetJMorrissey.com
🅞 BridgetJMorrissey

Ready to find
your next great read?

Let us help.

Visit prh.com/nextread